Roots and wings

a *City Limits* Novel

MJ –
I love you and
Astra.

m. mabie

M. Mabie

Roots and Wings | a City Limits Novel

pinkinkdesigns.com
Book formatting by Stacey Blake, Champagne Formats
Editing by Lori Sabin

ISBN-13: 978-1530594832

ISBN-10: 1530594839

Other Books

by m. mabie

Fade In

THE WAKE SERIES

Bait

Sail

Anchor

Coming soon:

Knot

The Very Second Time

Dedicated to my

Pike, Adams and Craighead county girls.

Tough women who take care of business and family alike.

Beautiful humans who will do anything for anyone at any time.

No questions asked—with a smile.

I'm proud to call you mine.

Chapter One

Mutt

Few things were certain around O'Fallon's Service and Tire. Kenny didn't really work there, but he was there enough. Be careful what you eat in the break room. The week before I'd found some leftover cake, and, sure enough, it was harder than a wedding night dick. And last, when we did the fifteen-minute oil changes for fifteen bucks, that garage would be asshole to elbow all day.

Dad had done that promotion once a year for twenty years, which happened to be every year he'd owned the place.

It was our family business. That was, if two people could make up a whole family. I guessed families were all different shapes and sizes, and since Grandpa passed away, it had only been Dad and me.

Oh, and Dean.

He wasn't *really* family, but he'd worked there since we

were in high school. And, honestly, who the hell wasn't family somewhere down the line around Wynne?

Dad and Dean worked the shop and I ran the desk—unless they needed the help, but most of the time it was pretty slow and easy to manage.

Not that day.

There was a line out the door and cars parked along the road, waiting. All there to get their oil changed for fifteen bucks.

I wadded my thick, long brown hair up into a knot on the top of my head as I heard my dad exclaim from the garage.

"Twenty, Mutt! We're on a roll today, kid. Make sure they all keep pulling in."

Oh, yeah. My name's Mutt. Not my given name, but, ask anyone who Darrell O'Fallon's daughter is—ten to one—they'll say Mutt. My grandpa—God rest his bastard soul—called me that from the day I was born.

Sometimes it drove me nuts growing up. I'm used to it now; I don't think my mom liked that very much, but she didn't stick around long enough to do anything about it either. She left when I was two months old.

No Dear John letter.

No phone calls.

Just gone.

My grandpa called me Mutt because apparently my mom was the town bike. Every town had one, and she was theirs.

Among everyone else who had a go at her, my dad ended up getting the longest ride.

He loved her. To tell you the truth, I thought he still

did.

This one time I asked my grandpa about my name and he told me flat-out: "Your mom was a whore, Mutt. You could be anybody's kid. You could be made up with anybody." I never forgot that, and thought about it a lot more whenever I'd consider dating someone.

First, what if we were related? *Ew.* No.

Second, who would want to bring a *Mutt* home to Sunday dinner? Not many.

So most of the time, I decided, better not.

That was the only time I saw my dad raise a fist. He knocked out three of Grandpa's teeth that morning. Then he made me scrambled eggs and told me to not pay him any attention.

Don't worry. They were false anyway, so I guess there was no real harm done.

It wasn't like Grandpa had a lot of room to talk. His last wife had run off with some guy she met at a casino. That's why he was stuck there living with us.

Most people would say I was kind of a tomboy, growing up with only a dad and an asshole grandpa to show me the ropes. I didn't really give a shit. In my experience, people said whatever the hell they wanted to anyway. My name was the perfect example of that.

Anyway, *I'm not done yet*, despite how hungry I was on fifteen-minute oil change day, I *was* having a pretty damn good Saturday.

Wynne was a small town on the river and we had a great lake nearby, too. Sure there was no mall or movie theaters, but if you wanted to catch wall-mount worthy trout or a largemouth bass, you were in the right spot.

Dad's oil change promo was going great, but what was shocking me was how many spinners and lures I'd sold.

I'd made them all myself and was about to sell my last one.

"Mutt, honey, those sumbitches bit on every cast. I'm taking the rest you've got here," said Mr. Walton to me from the other side of the counter, slapping a twenty down on the linoleum top.

I should have been charging more.

A few days back, I'd set up the little display with the fifty or so I had on hand, and at five bucks each, I sold out too easily.

I wasn't complaining. I loved making them.

But Mr. Walton was right.

Those *sumbitches* did work.

The past Thursday evening, I'd caught a two-pound bass off my dock in only about ten minutes. That's called *working* right there.

"I'm glad you liked them. Which one did you use?"

"The blue and yellow one. You got any more of those?"

"No, but I can make a few up for you."

"I'll take 'em, by God. Make me ten of 'em."

"All right, I'll call you when I have them ready. Is that all you need?" I asked. He'd just been in a few days before getting new brakes and tires put on.

"Oh I'm fine, I just thought I'd come settle up from last week. Your dad's probably just been busy, but we never got our ticket in the mail like we usually do."

That was odd. My dad was always meticulous about his billing. Although primitive, his system was foolproof.

In Wynne, everyone knew everyone. They'd drop their

vehicles off, and then come pick them up whenever. Keys in the visor.

Dad always sent out invoice tickets on Mondays, and Mr. Walton had been in the past Friday.

"Sorry about that. Let me look real quick." I left him at the counter and ran into the small office. In the old wooden chair, I sat down and spun around to the cabinet where he kept all the past week's tickets and found it full. I pulled the folder out and opened it, seeing Mr. Walton's ticket about a third of the way down.

Had none of these been sent out?

I knew he was waiting for me, so I didn't want to spend too much time going through it all, but shit, there was a lot. I quickly looked at the ticket on the bottom and it was from almost a month ago.

"Hey, Mutt," Dean said from the doorway, the office was only big enough for one person. "Can you call and check on the parts order? Your dad says we should have more filters, but I can't find them. I hope he's got more coming in."

Shit.

"Yeah, I'll call, but I doubt they're open now. Do you have enough for today?"

"I don't know. We still have about ten cars out there."

Shit. Shit. Shit.

"Call down to Dub's and see if they have any to get us by."

Dub's was the other automotive repair place in town. There wasn't really any competition though, since there was enough work to go around. Always had been.

Dad and Dub even worked here together for a while, but they didn't have enough space. Dub opened his own shop about three years after Dad bought his. They'd been best friends all my life. He even came by earlier to get a free hot dog and Pepsi.

"Thanks, he probably forgot. I tell ya, the old man's mind is *not* what it used to be."

It was true. My dad would never hit the Guinness book for highest IQ, but that had been just another thing he'd slacked on.

"Mr. Walton, here's your invoice. He didn't get it out yet. Sorry for the trouble. Do you want to pay it now? It's $745.00."

"Sure, honey, let me go get my rubber checks out of the truck," he said, winking at me. I think I'd heard that recycled joke told once a week for the past ten years.

I peeked into the garage and caught Dean hanging up the shop phone. He gave me a thumbs up, then motioned for the next car to pull in.

What would we do without Dean?

He was like the brother I never had, and Dad was like the father Dean never had. You could say Dean's story and mine were similar. Me with no mom. Him with no dad. Since his mom had passed a few years back, he had no mom either. We were pretty much his only family.

I walked over to my old man, his head grease streaked and his hands moving as fast as they ever did.

"Twenty-two, Mutt. I think we're going to beat last year's twenty-eight." Pride was shining in his aging brown eyes. He loved what he did.

Then he teased Dean, "If that slacker would pick up the pace we could damn near hit forty, I bet."

"Yeah, well, you're going to owe Dub a case of beer. You

forgot to get oil filters this week. He's on his way up. This is the last one on the shelf," Dead fired back.

My dad stopped and looked at him like a coonhound with three dicks, but it wasn't Dean who was wrong. Judging by the stack of unpaid invoices, I had to start taking on a little bit more of the responsibilities around there.

"Didn't we order those?" Then he scratched his face and went on about his business.

"I'll call them on Monday and see. Maybe they left them off the truck or something? Don't worry about it," I said and kicked his work boot. "You've got a line out there. Get your old ass in gear."

He rolled his eyes at me and went back to work.

Dean and my dad beat their record. Thirty-three oil changes in less than fifteen minutes, start to finish. They drank a few beers as they cleaned up the shop for the evening and called in some tenderloins for us at Diana's, the local diner across the street. We were all hungry and one of her tenderloins could practically feed a whole family. They were plate-sized and you needed three buns.

"Hey, we're walking across the street to eat, you coming?" my dad finally asked a little later.

I looked at the clock. It was seven and I knew she'd be closing up the kitchen soon, but I needed to take a better look at those tickets. I had my work cut out for me. It was either going to take all night or all the next day, and paperwork was the last thing I wanted to do on Sunday.

It was supposed to rain a little, but that was fine. I needed to get a jump-start on making more lures. The extra money was going to be nice, and they were selling better than I ever dreamed.

"Nah, you guys go eat while they're hot. Tell Diana I'll be over there before she takes off. I'm going to settle this register and clean up. You two go." My dad ran a hand over my back and kissed the top of my head.

"Hey, how many did you sell today?"

I smiled, knowing he'd be just as excited as I was.

"All of them."

"No shit, Mutt? Hell, you'll be setting up a tackle shop next. Just you watch. Good job, kid." It was nice having someone notice how well they were doing, but, then again, he was my dad.

"Your old man's gonna go eat, then I'm hitting the sack. These old bones are tired." He winked at me as he slapped off the lights to the shop. "Love you, Mutt."

"Love you, too, Dad. See you in the morning."

It didn't take me five minutes to get the register in order, and then I went through the pile of invoices in the folder. There was almost ten thousand dollars' worth of billing in there. I sorted them and decided I'd come back the next morning to finish up.

I was starving and didn't want Diana waiting on me so she could go home. She would, too, if she saw the light in the shop. Hell, if it weren't for her, I would have starved by age three.

I closed up the building for the night and walked across the street. Teenagers were cruising, people were filing into Sally's—one of the two bars in town—and it was a normal, small-town Saturday night.

I stepped up to the brick front of Diana's, and just as I was opening the door I heard a man say, "Shit," from the vehicle parked nearby. I guess I wasn't the only one having a long day. Minding my own business, I stepped into the diner.

"Hey there, sweetie. I've got your sandwich in the oven keeping it warm for you. Want anything else with it?" asked Diana. She wiped her hands on her apron as she dropped the rag she'd been wiping tables off with when I came in.

"No, I probably won't even be able to finish the sandwich."

"Your daddy said you had a long day. Those big hazel eyes of yours look a little tiresome." She was kindhearted, so I knew it wasn't an insult.

I nodded, which turned into stretching my neck. Diana was right. Thirteen hours is a long day for anyone, especially this twenty-six-year-old chick.

She smiled sympathetically, the ever growing laugh lines on her face appearing, then she walked in back to get my food. Her grey hair was swept up in a ponytail, and as she walked away she rubbed the back of her neck, too.

She was a hard worker. There were a few high school kids who helped her out here and there, but other than that, it was just her and one other waitress running the place.

I took a seat in the booth closest to the door, and when the bell rang above it I reflexively looked up. There stood a tall man who I didn't know.

Wynne wasn't big and I knew everyone who lived there. It wasn't likely for a passerby to stop in, especially at quarter to eight on a Saturday night.

He looked at his watch, taking stock of how empty the place was.

"Hi," he said as he regarded me with the most striking cornflower blue eyes I'd ever seen. "Are they still open?"

I blinked a few times. His words had hit my ears, but not yet my brain. I sat there staring. Either I was delusional, or he was one of the finest men I'd ever seen.

What in the hell would bring him here?

"Excuse me," he added, looking for an answer. "Do you know if they are still open?"

I shook the stupid from my head and replied, "Hell, I'm sorry. Lost my thought there. Yeah, they're open, but I think the kitchen is already closed down for the night."

He took a frustrated breath, raising his arm and placing his palm to his forehead. "Perfect," he huffed as he squeezed his eyes shut, looking defeated.

I instantly felt bad for him. I always had a bleeding heart for someone down on their luck. If he was the same guy who was swearing in his SUV, which I knew he was, then this just added to whatever he was already dealing with.

I could commiserate.

"If you're hungry," I started to say when he interrupted.

"Of course I'm hungry, why else would I be here?"

I didn't take offense. I was no stranger to a hungry man with a short temper, but I also wasn't one to take their shit.

"Hey! You didn't *let me finish*. All I was saying was, she has pie up there under the counter. Chill out." I didn't shout, but my tone was a clear message that assholes were never alone in a room with me. If you want to be a jerk, bring your A game.

He froze and hung his not-from-around-here head.

"Sorry. I'm just starving and tired," he apologized. Then he pointed a finger in the direction of the pie case and raised his contrite eyebrows like he was saying, "In there?"

I nodded sarcastically.

He started it.

The guy walked over to the case just as Diana walked out with my overflowing plate. She'd even added lattice fries, because she knew they were my favorite. It smelled like heaven. An embarrassment of riches in the form of meat and potatoes.

When he saw what I was getting, his eyes grew to the size of saucers. They followed her all the way across the room until she placed the plate down in front of me. If it had been a cartoon, he would have had one of those thought bubbles above his head with my plate in it.

"Hi there, honey. You want some pie? I've got the kitchen shut down, but you can have whatever you like under there."

Diana danced around grabbing a bottle of ketchup and mustard off of the table behind where I sat and handed them to me.

"You want some tea, Mutt?"

"Yeah. Extra ice, please."

"Okay," she said, handing me a knife and fork rolled in a napkin.

"See anything in there that looks good to you?" she asked the guy.

He tapped the glass as he studied the pies. My eyes were drawn to him, trying to figure out who he might be and what he was doing in Wynne.

"All of them are good, but her apple is the best," I offered as I stared at the heaping pile of fries. Then, just before I spread out my napkin to begin hacking at the colossal sandwich, which was impossible for me to eat in one sitting, I caved.

"Do you like tenderloins?" I asked, knowing there was no way I could eat all of it anyway. It was almost humiliating having that much on one plate when this guy was clearly as hungry as a bitch wolf with nine pups.

"I do," he answered, looking at me over his shoulder.

"I've got a little over half of this that I can't eat. I'll split it with you, if you're that hungry."

Diana crooked her head to the side and opened her mouth, about to make a bigger deal out of my gesture than necessary. Then she snapped it shut just as quick. She knew better.

I rolled my eyes at her and asked, "Can we get an extra plate, please?"

"Sure, honey. And what do *you* want to drink?" she asked the guy as she set my tea down.

"I'll take a glass of milk," he answered and walked over to my table. Then with the same pointing thing he'd done a minute ago, he silently asked if he could sit on the empty side of the booth.

What was it with this guy and finger pointing questions at me?

Dramatically, I nodded again, trying to hide my smile. Even if he was grouchy, he'd be nice to look at while I ate.

Diana came back with his milk, silverware, and the extra plate with a bun on it, setting all of it in front of the guy.

"I'll be in back. Holler if you need me," she said as she winked and walked off. When she got to the kitchen door, I glanced her way and she wafted her hand in front of her face and mouthed, "He's hot."

It was almost comical how he was looking at my sandwich. With my knife and fork, not knowing his stance on strangers touching his food, I cut the tenderloin in half and forked it over to his plate. Then I lifted my plate and spilled half of the fries over to his.

"So what's your name? I don't know you," I said.

"Vaughn Renfro," he answered, but he was more concerned with his food. He smiled up at me, but quickly went back to his full plate, popping a lattice fry in his mouth as he reached for the ketchup.

I squirted mustard on my bun and placed the pickles on it just how I liked. By the time I was applying ketchup to my fries, he was already digging in to his half. I doused my plate in ketchup, not missing a single bite.

Observing my overuse of ketchup, he looked at me questioningly with his mouth full. His face had changed from the hungry, frustrated one that walked in to a friendly, more likeable one. Now I could see what Diana was saying.

He was *seriously* hot.

Blue eyes. Short, dirty-blond hair. I watched the muscles in his jaw work as he hauled ass on the sandwich. I also took note of his forearms and big hands.

We ate in almost silence, except for the moaning and grunting coming from the other side of the booth. And I'm not proud to admit it, but the sounds he made were kind of hot, too.

"Pretty good stuff, huh?" I asked, capturing a piece of ice and giving it a loud crunch.

He cringed immediately at the sound, then swallowed. "Oh my God, I thought I was going to die."

"Yeah, I could tell. You had that hungry man thing going on."

He chuckled. "Yeah, sorry about that. It's been a hell of a day."

"I hear you."

"So how is it that *you* can get served food when the kitchen is closed? I need to learn your trick." He sat back and took a long drink of his milk. It left a little white ring on his lip before he licked it off. Under normal circumstances, it would have looked dumb. But him doing it? Well, it was hot. I'm not going to lie.

"I've known Diana my whole life. I work across the street. No trick. I just called her a while ago and had her keep it warm for me."

He looked thought the window at our building across the street. "You work at that garage over there?"

"Yep," I answered as I kept eating. I was hungry too, but, unlike this guy, I liked to enjoy my food.

"Did she call you … Mutt?" he asked, his facial expression confessing he thought he'd heard wrong.

"Yep."

"Why would she call you that?"

I hated that question, but I gave him my stock response anyway.

"It's a family name."

Which was true. If my mom hadn't been such a *friendly* lady, I'm sure it never would have stuck. Before he could say anything more about it, I asked him a question to change the subject.

"What were you shitting about in your vehicle when I walked in?"

He leaned forward, propping his elbow on the table and ran his fingers over his head. Something he'd done a few times already. Must have been a nervous tick.

"Well, I'm the new dentist in Dr. Carver's office, and I've been moving all day."

That was all he needed to say. I hated moving. Not that I'd ever moved, but I'd helped friends move plenty of times, and it was total bullshit. He could have stopped there and I would have called that justification, but he continued.

"I had a flat on the U-Haul about two hours into the drive. Then when I got here I realized I'd packed the *new* house keys in the trailer. I had to unload some of the boxes on the driveway until I found the one they were in. I don't have any food in the house and I was starving. So I drove here, remembering there was a restaurant on this corner, and just as I pulled in, my check engine light came on."

Shit. That was a bad day.

"Damn."

"Yeah, but, honestly, it doesn't seem near as bad now." His eyes locked on mine and a flutter of something came to life in my stomach when he smiled at me again. "Everything looks a little better on a full stomach. You know?"

He sure as hell looked better to me on a full stomach.

Just before I let those exact words slip from my mouth, Diana called from the kitchen.

"You two doing all right out there?"

"Yes, that was amazing," Vaughn answered.

"Diana, this is Vaughn. He's the new dentist, and he's moving into the old Robinson place, right?" I knew that was right because I'd seen the *for sale* sign was gone from the yard the other day and hadn't heard of anyone else buying it. It was the last house in town on the road out to our place. I loved that house, but it was going to need a lot of work.

"I guess. It's the house just south of town on this street."

Diana came over to shake his hand and clean up our plates. "Well, it's nice to meet 'cha. Welcome to Wynne. I'm Diana. I'm always open 'til eight, but I usually shut the kitchen down at seven, seven thirty. We're closed on Mondays and only open from eleven to five on Sunday. You can always call something in if you're running behind."

"I appreciate it, thank you. I'll remember that," he said, his voice calmer than it had been before. "By the way, that was incredible. I'm sure you'll see a lot of me." He was much more charming once he ate a meal and stopped to catch his breath—even after his shitty day.

Diana blushed and waved a hand at him.

"You have my ticket, Di? I'll settle up with you," I said, knowing she wanted to get the hell out of there. She had a new grandbaby at home, and since her daughter, Faith, was now living with her, she probably had a ton of things to do before she even sat down herself.

"No. Honey, your daddy got yours earlier when he and Dean were in. Dean said he was probably gonna clean up and head down to Sally's or The Tap. You ought to go down. I think there's a band somewhere tonight."

Although that sounded fun—or as much fun as was possible on a Saturday night in a small town, population 3,400—I was ready to take my shoes off and just have a beer in the garage at my workbench.

"Not tonight, I'm licked." For those of you not from Wynne, that means tired, but in that moment I knew what I'd said and who I'd said it in front of. I quickly glanced to the man I'd only known for about thirty minutes and fire burned under my embarrassed cheeks. "I'm tired," I corrected in case he thought I'd meant something else.

He failed at hiding his amusement, but didn't laugh at me, which I appreciated.

In case you haven't figured it out yet, I was rough around the edges for a chick. I always had been. I was raised by my grandpa and dad, in a town where kids didn't go to the arcade, they went to a creek. Where we didn't go to the beach and get a tan, we bailed hay for the neighbor and got burned. I barely wore makeup, and most days my hair air-dried from my rolled down truck window on the way to the shop.

I only dated one guy in high school, and he turned out to be a real ass, which was okay because the poor dope was as bald as a knob and his wife slept around on him with the bartender at The Tap. Other than him, I'd had my share of hits and misses, but nothing major. The dating pool in Wynne was shallow, a lot like the gene pool.

I could out-fish any man in our county. Clean my catch twice as fast.

It was known that I could change a tire faster than Dean, when push came to shove.

I even killed all my own spiders, and I wasn't afraid of the dark.

Yet, there in Diana's diner, I was blushing like a Barbie doll because I said the word *licked* in front of a man whose face I couldn't quit staring at. I'd be lying if I said saying it hadn't brought up certain explicit images in my mind.

Simply put, I was a bit hard up and it had been awhile. A *long* while. I needed to get out of there before I really made an ass of myself.

In my reverie, I'd missed what Vaughn and Diana were saying. My thoughts had drowned out their words. I got up and headed for the door.

"I'll see you Tuesday, Diana. Nice to meet you, Vaughn," I said as I stepped out into the warm spring night about to cross the street to my old pickup truck.

Before I knew it Vaughn was outside, too, saying, "Hey, you said you worked over there. You think they'd be able to take a look at my Escalade next week? Like I said, the check engine light just came on. Hopefully it isn't anything major, it's not that old, but I need to get it checked."

I turned around and walked backwards, not wanting to stop in the middle of the street, but not wanting to be rude.

"Sure, bring it up on Monday. I'll see if my dad or Dean can hook it up to the diagnostic thing. Shouldn't take too long." I spun back around, jumped up on the curb and opened my truck door. It creaked—which I thought of as an anti-theft feature, even if I never locked it—then I hopped in. I chanced a look back at Vaughn, who was still standing there by the door of the restaurant.

I cranked my grey beast to life and rolled down the window.

He shouted, "Thanks for the sandwich."

"See you Monday. I hope tomorrow runs a little smoother for ya," I shouted back as I pulled out and headed for home. He lifted a hand and gave me a little wave as I drove off.

I slowed a little as I rode past the old Robinson house. We lived on the same road, but we were out of town about a mile and a half and they were the first house on the edge of the city limits. I drove past it nothing short of twice each day.

I saw the boxes he'd unloaded to get his house keys on the driveway, stacked neatly against the garage door. The whole bungalow needed a new coat of paint, and maybe even a new porch. As far back as I could remember, it had always been that color and it had never been remodeled, only maintained—if you could call it that. There were dowels missing from the railing on the porch and the screen door on the side was never shut and latched all the way. Sometimes it would swing in the wind if the weather was bad. It needed a new roof, too.

I'd been in it a few times as a child, and I was sure the inside was just as dated and neglected. It was nice that someone was going to fix it up.

I smiled to myself and my boot pushed down on the gas pedal, speeding up on my way out of town.

I didn't know Vaughn, but anyone who would move to Wynne—from anywhere—and fix up one of its oldest houses, and take over for a dentist who'd been a lifelong resident … well, he had to be pretty ambitious. And sadly, that's one thing our little town lacked.

Ambition.

I pulled into our shed, where I normally parked, and killed the engine. It was only a little after eight, but I knew if I started on the lures I'd be up all night. And I had to get those invoices straightened out in the morning.

So instead, I grabbed a beer from the old fridge next to my workbench, let the tailgate down on my truck, and sat there in the dark, thinking about the new guy and watching the stars.

Chapter Two

Vaughn

I'd had the day from hell. I take that back, I'd had the month from hell.

My ex-girlfriend Rachelle, the woman I'd been with for nearly two years, left me about a month before we were moving to Wynne to start our life together. Or what I thought was going to be our life together.

Turned out the old saying, *easy come, easy go,* rang true for us.

Therefore, all of the paperwork for the closing of the house had to be re-filed, which caused the closing date to be pushed back and only left me with about a week to work on the house before I was supposed to begin at the office.

I didn't mind going back to work. I loved what I did.

What I hated was the upheaval of it all. Having my things in boxes. Having a mile-long list of things that needed completing.

Mostly, I hated the new idea of doing it all alone. Of course I was capable, a thirty-one-year-old man who'd accomplished many goals.

What it boiled down to was I was one of those guys who *was* ready for a partner. I wanted a family, and I wanted a community like the one I'd visited when I was younger.

Besides, I liked the idea of taking a leap of faith with someone. To me, it was an adventure.

I'd always lived in bigger cities, but I never actually *knew* anyone. Never had a real connection, or a sense of belonging to a community. In Cleveland, Rachelle and I got along fine, but I looked at the move as an opportunity to get closer.

To build something *together*.

To finally put down some roots somewhere where children grew up the way I'd always wanted to.

It wasn't like I was destitute. Things would work out. I knew that. I just had to think of it as part of the ride, and if the people in Wynne were anything like the woman I'd met at the diner, offering half her meal to me without expecting anything in return, I was in the right place.

Some days I thought I missed Rachelle, then I'd think maybe it was just the idea of her. Other days, the harder days like today, I was angry I'd tricked myself into believing someone else might actually want what I did.

When I pulled up at the house, and saw the mess I'd left, out in the open for anyone to take, I wanted to give up for the night and just go to bed.

Then I remembered the furniture we'd picked out and paid for wasn't there yet. I'd had to reschedule the delivery, and it still wouldn't be there for a few more days.

I opened the garage and unloaded the rest of the trailer, sorting boxes by room. After I had every piece out and organized to move into the house as I'd need them, I opened the back hatch to my SUV, pulled out my sleeping bag and the duffel I'd packed for myself, and went inside.

Tomorrow would be a better day. It had to be.

I woke up early after dreaming about the wavy haired girl from the restaurant. It was one of those dreams I couldn't really remember, but I was sure I'd looked at her face all night. Remarkably, I woke up feeling pretty good about the day.

I'd moved all of my things across part of the country by myself.

I had a new house.

A new job.

And it was a new day.

I wasn't going to start my new life in Wynne with a chip on my shoulder. It didn't feel right unpacking all of the last month's baggage from Cleveland here. So I chose to let it go the best I could.

I showered in my empty upstairs bathroom, put on the clothes I'd packed, and headed to the garage in search of my coffee maker.

All I needed was water and power, and even if I didn't have much more than that in the house, I did have those.

I could drink it black.

My coffee mug, a few coffee pods, and the maker found, I made my first cup of coffee in my new home and listened to a light rain shower pass over through the screen door.

As I waited for the rain to stop, I took out my phone and made a list of things I had to accomplish in the next few days.

It was a long list.

It would have been much easier if I'd had more time, like the original plan. And it would have been easier if I'd had a partner to help, but nonetheless, it was my list and the only way to work my way down it was to start.

I found my radio in the garage, plugged it into an outlet in the living room, and opened all of the windows.

At only nine in the morning, I decided painting the laundry room was my first task. It was the smallest room to tackle, and if I could accomplish at least one whole room, it would be the momentum I needed to confidently attack the rest.

As I hauled out the old washer and dryer—which wouldn't ever go back inside—and cleaned the floors and walls, I listened to the country music that filled my house.

Little by little, I saw progress, and little by little, I got excited.

If Wynne was anything like the people and places in the music on the radio, I had a lot to look forward to. No more looking back.

Chapter Three

Mutt

I was right. The books at the shop were even more screwed than I'd thought.

Why had he let it get so bad?

That morning Dad went to a farm sale with Dub, not to buy anything, but because they were both nosy like that. They'd poke around through the tools and parts, and stick around to see what someone's old shit went for—all just to see what their crap at home was worth. I'd left right after he did, so I wasn't worried about him asking me why I was working on a Sunday.

He hadn't mailed anything out, or deposited anything for weeks. I was sure the account was messed up at the bank, but I'd deal with that on Monday. At the moment, my biggest concern was getting all of the invoices out and sorting through the payments we'd received that he hadn't marked as paid. After I dug in, though, it wasn't too confusing. It was like he just stopped doing it one day, so I started from there.

When I finished with the invoices, I went through all of the open purchase orders and noted some of them weren't marked as received, but I knew that Dean could help me with that next week. I'd get those paid and we'd be fine.

It wasn't a talk I wanted to have with my dad, but it was time he let me handle the billing. Also, it was a good time to get Dean into the habit of doing the ordering. We could use a new computer or two, and that would be an easy way to make my dad walk away from it.

Dad's mechanical work was still great. Maybe he just needed a break from the other stuff. And let's be honest, I had plenty of spare time at work to help him with bookkeeping. It just wasn't until then I'd noticed he'd *needed* it.

He'd always taken care of everything. Looking back, I was thankful I had a dad who cared so much about me and always wanted me around.

It was only noon when I got out of there. I was relieved everything was straight, and even though we could always do better, the shop was doing great.

Before I headed home, I ran into the store to get what we needed for the week. I wasn't sure what made me think of him, but Vaughn came to mind as I walked the aisles. That morning when I drove into town, I'd seen him carrying things into the house by himself. I wondered if he was alone, or if maybe his family was following him there. Though I didn't think that was the case because I hadn't seen a wedding ring on his hand when we were eating the night before.

I decided the neighborly thing to do was bring him a

few things as I passed by on my way home.

It wasn't much. Chips, some apples, bread, cheese, lunch meat, and water—just because it was the right thing to do. I didn't have a clue if he'd eat any of it, so I grabbed a gallon of milk; at least I was sure he liked that. Then I added a candy bar for good measure. Who didn't like chocolate?

I tossed the items in the cart with my things and made my way to the counter to check out.

I'm sure it's the same in every small town. If you want to know celebrity gossip, then find a checkout line at your nearest grocery store. If you want to know the local gossip, you can usually find it in the same place.

Mindlessly, I looked at the cold drinks by the register and waited my turn. So it was totally coincidental and innocent when I overheard BethAnne and Rhonda, the cashier, discussing our new dentist. I didn't gossip, but in Wynne, there was no way to avoid hearing it.

"I heard his fiancée left him right before they were supposed to move. Isn't that sad?" BethAnne asked Rhonda with all the sincerity of a used car salesman. "And have you *seen* him yet?"

"That's awful. I haven't met him," Rhonda said and continued to move things across the scanner.

"Well, my sister showed him the old Robinson house a few months back, when he was in town working everything out with Dr. Carver. She said he was *fine*, girl. I don't know how old he is, but if he's single and looking, I'm ready to be found."

The two laughed and cackled, like I'd seen them do before, but when they noticed me they toned it down.

"Oh, hey, Mutt. How's it going?" BethAnne inquired,

her lipstick and teased hair still all a fluff from Sunday church.

"Goin' good, and you?" I answered as I reached for the separator that silently said *this shit is my shit and that shit is your shit* and placed it in between my things and hers.

"Can't complain. I saw Dean last night at The Tap. He was having a good time." The wink that Rhonda and know-it-all BethAnne shared wasn't missed.

"That's good. The shop was busy yesterday. He deserved a little fun."

"Are you ever going to date that boy? You know he's been waiting around *years* for you, Mutt?"

Rhonda finished bagging up BethAnne's things and gave her the total.

"He's like my brother. It would be a little strange," I said. All the while remembering that BethAnne married a guy who *was* her stepbrother for a time. Paul's dad was BethAnne's mom's second husband. "Sorry, you know what I mean."

Rhonda's eyes lit up. I'd hit a nerve. I meant no offense, but it was too easy and I knew it would shut BethAnne up. I found the ones who gossiped the most had the most skeletons in their closet. And BethAnne had a walk-in's worth of bones. Literally.

Judging by the cherry red cheeks and the scowl, she *had* taken offense. She quickly loaded a cart with her bags, not saying another word until she was walking out.

"Have a good day, Rhonda. Mutt." In her fluster to leave, she banged the corner of the cart off the side of the brand new automatic doors they'd just installed. Those things were never going to last.

"Well, you sure got her all worked up," Rhonda warned. "You know she's sensitive about Paul."

"Sensitive? If she doesn't like the taste of her own medicine, that's her problem. I heard her making fun of Lesley the other day when she was at Diana's for lunch. You tell me how *sensitive* it is to make fun of a person with disabilities, through no fault of their own. BethAnne can just deal with whatever she has coming to her."

Lesley was Coach Fry's daughter. At games, she'd cheer alongside the cheerleaders and everyone in town loved her. She had Down syndrome, but don't underestimate her; she was smart as a whip, remembering every move of every game she'd ever been to. Plus, she adored everyone. And if my dad hadn't told BethAnne to shut her pie-hole that day in the restaurant, I would have.

My grandpa always used to say, "God don't like ugly, Mutt."

Sometimes I thought he was ugly, but if I ever got too far out of line, I was quickly reeled back in. Thinking back on it, my grandfather was kind of a hypocrite. He *was* the first one to call me Mutt after all.

I wonder if God half likes half ugly? Because I think that's what Grandpa was.

"Oh, that's just BethAnne. You can't let her get to you. So how'd the hot dogs go over yesterday? Did you have enough? Your dad was worried when he ordered them."

"We ran out about three. So it was just enough."

"Good. I'll make a note of it for next year."

As she bagged up my things, I had her keep separate the items I was dropping off at Vaughn's. Then I got lost thinking about how handsome he was. BethAnne was a busybody, but she was right. He was fine.

That train of thought skidded to a halt as Rhonda said, "Earth to Mutt. Fifty-nine, seventy-two." I blinked a few times to regain my focus and handed her my debit card.

"You feel okay, honey?" Rhonda asked.

"Oh, yeah. Sorry, I was just thinking. I'm fine. Thanks, Rhonda."

"You're welcome. See you later," she said. Seeing I could manage all of the bags myself, she stepped away from the register and started restocking the movie wall.

There weren't too many bags, so I hauled everything without a cart to the truck, then ran back in for the milk and case of water.

Lewis, the owner of the boat dealership, honked and waved at me as he drove by.

That's what Wynne was like.

Everyone knew everyone.

For the most part—except for election years, which were brutal in a small town—everyone was friendly and welcoming. People waved, or at the very least, lifted their index finger off the wheel, as they drove by.

If someone needed help, the town had a benefit.

If someone was sick, we'd rally around them until they were feeling better.

It was a great place to grow up, but at times it was smothering. You literally couldn't take a shit without someone knowing it and three others smelling it.

Forget Facebook or Twitter, social networking in Wynne was actually social. The men—or the local Liar's Club, as I liked to call them—met every morning at Diana's to talk over town happenings. Who hadn't mowed their yard.

Who bought a new truck. High school sports, crops and the weather.

The women had the grocery store and the hair salon where they'd solve all the world's problems, and still have time to set up all of the singles within a twenty-mile radius.

However, small town living was a double-edged sword, and oftentimes you had to take the good with the bad, keep your chin down, and take care of business. I'd like to think I did all of those things.

My truck roared to life, and I silently made a note to have Dad look at my exhaust. It was normally on the loud side, but it was getting obnoxious. I could barely hear the radio, so I turned it up.

I didn't know if I was a country music fan or if I simply didn't know much of anything else, but that's what I listened to. I mean, I didn't have a choice, there was only one station in town and that's all Sunny played.

If I had to exclude Dean and my dad, Sunny was probably my best friend. Her mom was my babysitter when we were little and we always got along. Of course, we were as different as night and day, but that's what made her fun.

She's bubbly and charming. I'm … not really.

Sunny Wilbanks had the blondest of blond hair to match her name, which was thanks to the salon downtown. She always looked put together. Laughter and good times followed her around, just like her dog Andy Two did. If you're curious, Andy One was hit by the school bus a few years ago. Andy Two wasn't even the same breed as Andy One, but Sunny liked the name. She was a huge Shawshank fan.

She didn't work on Sundays, but she would pre-record

segments to play when she was out.

"All right, Wynne-ers, it's Sunday afternoon and the sun is shining. How about a feel good song from a few summers back? It certainly brings back a few memories for me. Now put on your boots and go cause a little trouble. It's good for you." The recording broadcasted over my radio as I drove through town.

The music filled the truck, and before I knew it, I was approaching the old Robinson house, or Vaughn Renfro's house, I supposed.

I came to a stop on the shoulder of the road in front of the old home and killed my beast. Before I got out I sat there for a moment and thought about how nice it would be if he actually renovated the whole house. Most of the neglect was cosmetic, but it would be a tough project to tackle alone.

His vehicle sat in the driveway and the garage door was open, showing boxes and furniture piled inside.

All of the windows were open in the house and I heard the same song I was listening to filter through them.

I was a little nervous.

Wynne didn't get many *new* people. Sure, people moved away, and sometimes they came back, but it was an entirely new thing to have a total outsider with no ties to our small town.

It was exciting.

I grabbed the bag of things I'd bought for him and started up the long, uneven sidewalk that led to the front porch. Each step I took, the swell of anxiety grew and that was a new feeling for me. It wasn't exactly shyness, because I wasn't particularly anxious around people. I just wanted him to like me.

We were neighbors after all. Besides, it was probably hard not knowing anyone in a new place, but what the hell did I know about any of that? *I was a lifer.*

I'd thought about him quite a bit the night before when I was having a beer in the back of my truck. I didn't know what it was like to be the new girl, but I knew plenty about being a little on the lonely side.

If being alone was our only thing in common, then so be it.

I was curious about him, and why he'd chosen to move to Wynne.

On top of it all, what Diana had mouthed to me in the diner the night before hadn't been at all wrong.

He was attractive—in a clean-cut kind of way—and refreshing. Most of the men around here were doing pretty damn good if they were wearing a shirt *half* the time. Maybe that's why he was so alluring to me? Because he wasn't like anyone I knew.

The door was open, but the screen door was closed and latched. I peeked in to find a completely empty room, save for a lamp in the corner, but I didn't see him. I knocked my boot against the bottom of the door, since my hands were full, and waited to hear any movement.

Nothing.

I kicked my foot against it a little harder and called, "Hello, Vaughn?" Then waited again.

There was a nice breeze and the warm spring weather was welcome; it had been a long cold winter. I noticed there were tulips popping up by the stairs on the side of his front porch, which led to the other side of the house. The grass was getting greener, and soon the dogwood tree in the yard would be blooming.

"Hi," I heard from outside as I saw him peek around the corner to see me standing at his front door.

He was less put together than he had been the night before. His sandy blond hair was a little messier on the top, and he had an older looking pair of faded jeans and a white T-shirt on. He wore a pair of brown leather gloves and the sight of him made me forget what the hell I was even doing there.

"What's all that?" he said with a friendly grin.

I looked at the bag and I lifted the milk in my hand, realizing I needed to say something but struggling to find the words.

"You … you like milk," I stammered. Why is it as soon as you say the wrong thing, the right thing suddenly becomes so clear?

"I do." He laughed and climbed the three stairs leading up to where I was. All three of them creaked, and then every board he stepped on followed suit.

"I was at the store, and since we're neighbors now, I thought I'd bring you a few things you might need."

He pulled off his left glove and stuck his right hand under his arm, pulling off the other and holding them there as he reached out for me to hand him the milk.

"Thank you. I appreciate that." His face didn't seem as tense as it had the night before, and when he smiled his eyes did this thing where they glistened like the sun dancing on the lake.

Had I really just thought that?

I handed him the milk and shifted the bag of things to

get a better grip.

"Come on in, we'll put this in the kitchen." He walked past and I trailed in, breathing in the scent of sweat and soap. "It's still really empty in here. Sorry about that."

"Oh, it's fine, you just got into town. I saw you put a lot of stuff in the garage. Maybe you should think about bringing some stuff in," I teased.

He opened the old refrigerator and set the milk on the top shelf. I placed the bag on the counter and handed him the meat and cheese. Vaughn looked at the food I was handing him, and judging by his expression, you'd think I brought him a damn steak and crème brûleé.

"It's not much. I just know from experience how time gets away from you when you're working hard and you probably don't have much here. By the way, the store downtown is open on Sundays but only until about five. I wouldn't want you to starve."

"Well, it's really nice of you. I think it's going to take me a little while to learn all of the business' hours around here. In Cleveland, I could get food around the clock. I suppose I took that for granted."

Why someone would chose to move here—the actual Middle of Nowhere—was fucking nuts.

"Cleveland is where you're from then? That's a big move all by yourself." Then I immediately regretted saying it, remembering what BethAnne had said about his girlfriend or whatever.

His eyebrows shot up and he nodded his head in agreement. "Yeah, it is. That wasn't exactly the plan, but it'll be okay."

The twinkle I'd seen dimmed and knowing it had been

my fault—at least today—I felt bad. How could anyone leave a man like this? He had to have some crazy flaw that I hadn't come across yet. Or maybe she was plain stupid.

Sometimes, people are just dumb, and she was president of the Idiot Club.

Before I knew it, I said, "Well, I don't have much going on. I can run my groceries home and come back."

"You'd do that?" He looked as if no one had ever offered to help him with anything. Ever.

What the hell was going on up in Cleveland?

"Sure. What do you need help with?" Expecting him to turn down my offer, and half hoping he would, I emptied the rest of the bag and wadded it up, not knowing what to do with it.

"Here," he said and took it from me. "Normally, I'd say not to worry about it, but I only have a week to get this place..." He looked around and I followed his gaze throughout the kitchen and into the front room. "It's not that it isn't livable or anything. I'm sure there's far worse. I just had plans for paint and sanding the floors. I have carpet people coming Tuesday, and our new appliances and a lot of our—*my*—furniture coming at the end of the week. I want to stain these cabinets before the new countertops come in. And, you know, just give the place a good scrub."

He stuffed the empty sacks into a trash bag hanging on a door leading out to the back deck. "I start working in the office with Dr. Carver next Monday. If I can get some of that done, I'll be happy for now." He leaned against the counter and ran both of his hands over his head. It was clear he was a little overwhelmed.

However, he was right. It was an old house, but it was

built well and it wouldn't take much more than what he'd mentioned to get it looking great.

"Well, put me to work then. Come grab this water out of my truck, we're gonna need it. And I'll run home really fast and come right back."

There was something about him that caught my interest. The way he talked to me was different than the other people I knew. Maybe I wanted to get to know him more because he *didn't* know me. There was something kind of refreshing about learning about someone new, and I enjoyed that I kind of had a clean slate when it came to his knowledge of me.

He seemed easygoing enough, and an attractive man around my age moving to town was just about the most excitement I was going to get anytime soon.

Besides, as soon as anyone else in town noticed him, he wouldn't need *me* bringing him groceries.

New, cute doctors don't socialize with the town Mutt. That was purely a guess, though. We hadn't had a new doctor … ever really.

"Are you sure? You really don't have to. Hell, you don't even know me."

"Well, I guess we'll get that sorted out today then, won't we?" I offered him a friendly smile and he followed me outside, lifting the case of water out of the back.

It only took about two minutes to get to my house from his, and it didn't take me any time to throw my hair up in a ponytail, grab my toolbox—yes, I have my own and it's not pink—and I was driving back down the road.

Back to Vaughn's.

I tucked my phone in one of my back pockets, got my

gloves out of the toolbox, and stuffed them in the other. As I walked back in the front door to find out where he wanted me to start, he appeared at the top of the old staircase.

"Do you really want me to call you Mutt?"

Thanks, Grandpa.

I took a deep breath and sucked it up like I always did. "Might as well. Everyone else does. Mutt O'Fallon at your assistance," I said as I made myself at home walking through his house.

"O'Fallon." I heard him say a few times on his way to the kitchen, like he was trying that on for size. "I like O'Fallon better."

"Suit yourself. Where do I start? The day's getting shorter by the minute."

At that he hopped to, and headed for the back of the house.

"I was sorting the paint we bought—I bought—on the back patio. Like to paint?" he asked, looking hopeful. The way he kept correcting himself spoke a lot about what had happened.

It wasn't my business, though. I was just there to help.

"Sure."

"Good. I've already got the laundry room taped and trimmed."

I followed him into the laundry room off the kitchen and saw that he had, in fact, taped around all of the doorways and windows. He'd removed all of the cover plates from the outlets and he'd even moved the machines to the backyard. That must have been a chore by himself.

"No problem. Where's my brush, boss?" I said, trying to make it seem like I did this kind of thing for people all of the time. Although, I definitely would have, it simply wasn't often when I found myself volunteering my time to people I'd known for less than twenty-four hours.

Okay. It was never.

I'd never just shown up at a stranger's house, brought them food, and offered to do some light remodeling, but something about it was so right. Felt so good.

Plus, I liked his smile.

Chapter Four

Vaughn

She was a damn hard worker and fun to talk with. You can get to know someone pretty fast that way, I guess, because she'd only been there for a few hours and already we'd painted the laundry room, the upstairs bathroom, and at the moment we were trimming the master bedroom.

She didn't have any trouble saying what came to her, and telling me things she'd do if the place were hers.

Like not painting the original wood trim, which actually looked pretty great after a good scrub. And, how if she lived there, she'd keep the towels in the small closet across from the bathroom instead of putting shelves up. She said it would seem bigger without the extra "shit on the walls."

"You're telling me you think the grey color would look better in the front room?" I asked, after considering if I even had enough paint to do what she'd suggested.

"Yeah, you're not going to see much of it in the kitchen

with all the cabinets up anyway. It's your house, but I like it better for the living room."

It was straying from the plan, but fuck the plan. Half of the people who came up with the plan didn't even live here after all. It was another moment where it hit me that I was starting all over and this was my house—and only *my* house.

"You know what? I actually liked the color we put in the laundry room for the kitchen, too." I'd voiced my opinion about it when wall colors were being chosen, but it was an argument I didn't really care to have when it all was said and done.

"Yeah, see I like that better, too!" she exclaimed, slapping my arm. "Sorry. You're staining those cabinets, right?" she asked, surprisingly into the whole thing.

"Yeah, it's like a dark walnut color."

"And you've got new counters coming this week?"

I thought about the granite that I wasn't able to cancel because it had already been custom cut. Granite I didn't like.

"Yes," I said, but I wasn't really that enthusiastic about it.

"Yes, but..." She urged me on, hearing how underwhelmed I was.

"Yes, but it wasn't what I would have picked."

"You have samples?"

I did actually. I'd seen them that morning.

"They're outside in the garage," I said and started walking that way.

"Wait, I wanna go," I heard her say as she dropped her trimming brush into the paint pan then followed me. I liked it, but hated the thought of spoiling her day.

"Are you sure you don't have stuff you'd rather be doing?" I asked, still a little skeptical of someone volunteering to help like she did.

"Yeah, because there's *so* much happening in Wynne on Sunday afternoons."

"You don't have to be sarcastic, I was just asking." I shot back on the way out the back door, then I held it for her as she came right behind me.

"Thanks," she said and kept walking. "Really, I didn't have much to do, and it would suck doing all of this by yourself. I like helping. You never know, I might need help sometime, and I hope someone would do the same for me."

Remember learning about the golden rule when you were a child? This woman actually lived by those words and it made me pause. This was the kind of person I was looking for when moving to a small town. Not that I'd planned on coming here to find a woman. Not in the least, but there she was.

O'Fallon was pretty and sincere, easy to talk to, and even though I'd only been there a day, I knew she was someone I was going to get to know better.

Not because it was a small town and I had to, but because I was truly interested. Curious. Intrigued.

How could I not be?

It didn't hurt that she danced a little as she painted. It didn't hurt that she sang along to songs she knew, but still admitted when she "fucked up" the words. And, I was single, so it didn't hurt that I thought she was sexy. I took stock that I didn't feel guilty thinking it either.

It was simply unexpected.

But we'd just met, and we were alone, not that she couldn't handle herself, but I didn't want to flirt with her and make her uncomfortable when she was being so kind to help me and everything.

I didn't even know if she was single, though she didn't wear a ring and no one had called to see where she was, as far as I knew.

I'd get around to asking her about it, but it wasn't the right time to do it.

"Damn, it's getting hot out today," she said and pulled the T-shirt over her head, leaving her standing in my garage in a white tank top, her jeans, and boots.

And then it *was* the right time.

"Are you seeing anyone?"

"No, why?" she asked, almost like she was accusing me of something. "Do I need to be? I happen to be single *by* choice. I do not *need* a man to be happy. You got that?" It was obviously a sensitive subject. She walked out into the driveway, paced a few times, and kicked a rock. "You know what? You're going to fit right in here in town. Seems you think like everyone else."

She'd completely misunderstood me, but it was kind of amusing seeing her get fired up. I'd have to remember how I was saying things from now on with her.

Which was fine. I liked being direct much more.

I dug around for the bag I'd seen earlier, and I found it right where I thought it was. Knowing I wouldn't have Internet access for a while, I had all of the receipts and delivery slips inside it, too.

When I turned around, she wasn't talking, but animated, like she was having some sort of argument in her head.

"Are you okay?"

"Yeah, I'm okay. I'm great, in fact." She was being a smartass.

"Great. Me, too. Let me explain what I meant, because you took my question the wrong way. I asked if you had a boyfriend, *not* because I thought you needed one, but because I hoped you did *not* have one. And, once more, I was hoping you were single."

Her face looked like I'd just told her I was Batman.

"You did not just say that."

"Yes, I did. And I meant it," I said and walked back into my house.

She followed.

For it only being the first day, I'd say we killed it. Three rooms painted and ready to move into.

When we finished what we could for the night, and after she helped me clean all of the paintbrushes and put stuff away, I asked if she wanted to hang out and eat a sandwich with me. I hadn't eaten anything except an apple all day.

She said *no, thank you* and quietly slipped out the door without even saying much of a goodbye. I'd just heard her truck start, and when I looked out the front door, she waved as she pulled off.

I thought about her the whole night as I found more things to do. As surprising as it had been when she walked into my house, it was just as unexpected when she occupied my thoughts after she left.

The check engine light was on in my Escalade, just like it

had been on Saturday night when I rolled into town, and I dreaded taking it in.

I had to return the U-Haul to the trailer place up by the highway first thing in the morning. Afterwards, I stopped at O'Fallon's garage to see if they could tell me what was wrong with it.

Hopefully it was just something minor or a sensor gone bad.

I pulled into the lot and stopped just short of the double garage doors that were wide open, then walked into the door on the side that had the hours of operation stenciled on it. It was a small waiting room with a counter.

"Hey there, how's it going?" an older gentleman said from a chair in the corner, looking quite at home. "Whatcha needin'?"

Maybe the guy was on a break.

"Well, I drove in from Cleveland over the weekend and the check engine light came on in my Escalade," I answered, pointing outside to where it sat.

He stood and looked out at the lot.

"Don't say. Was she doin' anything funny? Actin' up?"

"Well, it was shifting a little hard on the way in, but I thought it was just because of the trailer I was pulling."

"Don't say," he said again and sat down in his seat and slapped his paper open again.

"Well, can you take a look at it?" Did I need a password or something?

"Hell, kid. I don't work here. Mutt walked down to the post office and Tweedle Dee and Tweedle Dum are in the shop."

I looked out the window and saw O'Fallon walking up

the street. I stepped outside to meet her. When she saw me, she smiled brightly and sped up.

"Good morning," I said as she got near. "Think your dad can check this out for me?"

"Oh yeah, I forgot. He's in here, come on."

I followed her into the garage area and saw two guys near a smaller dock door in the back.

"Dad, can you hook his..." she paused, looking for the make of my vehicle.

"Escalade."

"Look at his Escalade?" The older of the two handed the younger guy a clipboard and headed for us.

"Well, shit, who are you?" her dad asked me.

I held out my hand and answered, "Vaughn Renfro."

"Nice to meet you, Van," he said, but I didn't correct him. I didn't have to.

"He said Vaugh-n, not Van, Dad," O'Fallon clarified. It was clear that they were close and enjoyed one another by the animated faces they were giving each other and the way they bantered back and forth.

"That's what I said. *Van*." And he gave her a *take that* look, sticking his tongue out.

"I told the guy in there, I drove it from Cleveland this weekend pulling a trailer and it didn't really act too bad or anything. It shifted weird a few times, but other than that, it was okay. Then when I pulled into town the check engine light came on. It's still on."

"You told all that to Kenny?" he asked.

"Well, I thought he worked here."

He looked around me into the waiting area and saw what Kenny was doing. "Do you call that working?"

O'Fallon shoved her dad's arm and said, "Knock it off. You don't have anyone coming in this afternoon or anything. Want him to pull it in?" Her tone wasn't one to play with.

"Yeah, yeah, yeah," he said and waved over his head, motioning for me to bring it inside as he walked back over to the other guy.

"Just pull it in on this side and they'll hook it up," she instructed.

It was nice knowing someone, and the fact that she looked even better after a night's rest and a shower, was a wonderful bonus.

"So did you get anything else done last night?" Her voice was a little softer, laxer than it had been.

"Yeah, after you left I took all of the doors off the cabinets, carried some boxes with clothes and stuff upstairs."

She smiled, but didn't say anything else and we stood there looking at each other for a minute.

"Hey, Van, we close at four," her dad shouted from the back of the garage where he and the other guy were watching us.

I looked at my watch; it was still morning.

"He means hurry the hell up," she said, laughing at me. "He's giving you shit."

I didn't want any shit from her dad, and I had a lot to do. So I nodded and went outside to pull in my Escalade.

When I walked into the waiting area, O'Fallon was telling Kenny he needed to quit bothering the customers. I could tell by the way she was tilting her head at him that she was only mostly joking.

"You tell your customers," he fired back, giving me a

glare, "that I've been reading my morning paper in here—in beautiful silence—since before the turn of the century."

"Kenny," she warned.

"What? You know what my wife is like. If I wanted to hear someone yappin' and a hollerin' at me, I'd go home and read it."

She laughed and I took a seat by the vending machine, captivated by their conversation. I liked the way she looked just as ornery as he did, and there was a facetious glimmer in her pretty hazel eyes.

"Your wife needs to bring me some more strawberry jam, I'm almost out again."

"She isn't giving you any more. She said you were an ungrateful brat."

O'Fallon's mouth hung open, shocked at what he'd said.

"Kenny! She did not."

"She did so. She said you could shove her jam right up your ass for all she cared." He pretended what he was saying wasn't too interesting to him as he licked his finger and turned the page.

"Well, why'd she say that?" she asked, actually looking a little worried. "I didn't do anything."

"She's just mad because I told her you said the last strawberry batch she made tasted like shit." From behind his paper I could see his face, and he shook his head, letting me know he was pulling her leg.

"Kenneth Bennet, I didn't say that!" Her tone was the same as when she'd gotten angry about me asking if she had a boyfriend.

I liked her fiery temper.

He was winding her up on purpose, I could only assume it was because he liked it, too.

"You didn't?" He played innocent. "I coulda swore…"

"You know good goddamn well I didn't say that. Why did you tell her that? I love her strawberry jam. It's my favorite. I eat it for lunch." Then she stomped her foot and cocked her head to the side.

"I had to."

"Had to? Why?"

"It was an emergency, she was about to make more strawberry … but I like *peach*."

"You rotten bastard."

He snickered and snorted at his own joke, then declared, "All is fair in love and war … and Momma's peach jam."

"I think I'm sick of your shit for the day," she said, sighing and straightening the flyers and pamphlets on the counter.

I had to concentrate on not laughing. What a pair.

About that time, he folded the paper, tossed back the last of the coffee he was drinking, and stood.

"I was just leaving anyway," he said as he opened the door. Then he spun and said, "See you tomorrow, Mutt."

To which she replied, "See you tomorrow, Kenny. Bring me some jam."

"Okay, okay," he said as he walked away.

"He's a character."

"Yeah, he's something all right," she agreed without missing a beat.

I didn't want to bother her while she was working, so I sat there quietly and waited.

Soon enough, her dad came back in and I stood to talk

to him.

"So I called down to the Cad-o-lac dealership, Van, because I didn't know what that code meant. Turns out, your timing is off. That ain't good. I can tear into her tomorrow if you want, but you probably shouldn't be driving it around."

Just what I needed.

"Okay, is there anywhere I can rent something to drive until it's fixed?"

"Well, as long as I can get the parts and you didn't completely tear it up, I should be able to have it back to you in a few days. I might be able to find something for you to drive."

I looked behind me to O'Fallon, who was listening to the prognosis. She gave me a phony smile full of teeth.

Really nice teeth, to be honest.

I'd love to get a closer look at them.

"How about you walk around back and I'll show you my rental. You're going to love it."

I had a suspicion that he was *still* giving me shit.

"Now, Van, this is no Cadillac, but she does turn heads," he said as I walked around back with him. O'Fallon, hot on our heels. "There she is."

I couldn't help myself that time. I laughed. And then I laughed a little more. There sat a red and orange, nineteen eighty-something piece of suburban history.

"The Astro Van?" I asked.

He answered, "The Astro *Vaughn*."

Perfect. It was too funny, too ugly, and too awesome to say no to. What choice did I have anyway?

"You'll rent me that?"

"Well, Astro, you're going to have a big bill from me.

I don't need you out blowing your money on rentals. You know what I mean? I'm practical."

"And generous, too. And did you just call me Astro?" As much as this guy liked giving me a hard time, I kind of liked him. I saw easily where O'Fallon got her spunk.

"I like Astro better than Van. It suits you. Mutt, go get the keys and show him the *Vaughn*. Would you?" he said and then took the steps up the side of the loading dock back into the garage.

Clearly, the van hadn't been driven in a while, but it was well taken care of, as far as thirty-year-old Astro vans went.

I walked over to it and tried the handle, but it was locked. Cupping my hands around my face, I pressed my head against the glass to look inside.

It was clean and the back seats were pulled out. It would actually work out pretty good for hauling things from the hardware store, which was the next place on my list.

"It's not that bad. I drove it," O'Fallon said, walking up beside me.

"It'll work. I can't really be too picky, can I?"

"Nope," she answered as she dropped the keys in my hand. "Sometimes you have to pump it a few times for it to start, but be careful or you'll flood it. The air conditioner doesn't work, but it's not that hot yet, and…"

"I think I can manage," I said, focused on trying to get the door open. The key wouldn't turn. The handle stayed stuck up when I lifted it.

"*I wasn't done yet*," she rattled off then pushed me out of the way. She shoved her shoulder against the door and the handle fell back into the normal position. "Sometimes you have to give the door a shove. It gets stuck."

So I noticed, and I noticed the other guy who worked there watching the whole thing play out as well.

I gave him a little wave, but he turned and walked in.

"There you go," she said with an eyebrow cocked. "Drive safely."

She was feisty.

As many shitty things as the universe had thrown into my life over the past month, that hot, smartass look on her face made everything okay with me.

I was so glad I was there.

Chapter Five

Mutt

I couldn't believe he drove off in that thing. I hated the van. I only drove it for a summer in high school before I couldn't do it anymore and dipped into my savings for my truck.

It didn't seem to faze him at all.

Vaughn had shitty luck. I was almost scared to spend any more time with him, but, still, I couldn't stay away.

I went to the house that night and helped him after work, and the next night, and the one after that.

I didn't finish a single lure that I'd promised Mr. Walton, and I knew he'd be up my ass if I didn't get them done, but I liked going to Vaughn's place.

It was really coming together, too.

The flooring people came. Appliances were delivered. The new countertop arrived, and even though he hated it, I kind of liked it. I thought it was different.

Soon, we were moving furniture around, and I helped him unpack some of the kitchen things, putting silverware and pots and pans where they needed to go.

He asked about local sports and what it was like growing up in a small town, and I tried to only hit the highlights.

I didn't need him running off, or looking for somewhere else to go. Not after all of the hard work we'd—*he'd*—put into his house.

So I was surprised when I showed up and he wasn't in his normal go-getter mode. He was unpacking some stuff in the living room. When I came in the front door, he roughly shoved something back in a box and shut it. It looked like a picture.

I wondered if it was a picture of them before they broke up. Or before whatever happened, *happened*.

"Sorry, was I interrupting?" I said. It was Saturday morning, and the night before we'd finished painting the two extra bedrooms upstairs. We'd been up late, and I don't even think I made it home until about midnight.

He sighed. "Why do you keep showing up here?" His voice wasn't angry or rude, mostly solemn. Maybe a little curious.

It made me think, who wouldn't want to be there with him?

"Why don't you tell me to go away?"

We stood there, me in his doorway, him on the other side of the room, and stared at each other.

Neither of us answered, and after a while, I didn't know what I should do. I considered going home or going fishing, since it was nice, or just leaving.

But I didn't.

Instead, I went into his laundry room, like I had every right to, picked up the basket of clean towels I'd folded and left there the night before. Then, I marched past him, up the stairs and put them in the closet in the hall.

After that, I went into one of the extra bedrooms, unpacked the new bedding he'd brought with him and made the bed. When I was threading the curtain rod through one of the sheer linen panels for the windows in that room, he came in and helped me.

He didn't say anything else about it, but when we were done with that room, he said, "Thank you."

Then we went to the next.

It was odd. I didn't belong there. But you know what? I wanted to be there and I knew he wanted me there, too.

That day was pretty quiet. I decided to go home that afternoon and work on the new spinners I had to make and get Mr. Walton's finished before he got upset.

Not since that day, almost a week before, had he asked me again about a boyfriend or anything like that. Maybe after spending some time with me, hearing how I talked and seeing how I behaved, he wasn't interested in me at all.

That would be fine.

Not awesome, because I was really beginning to like him, but I'd understand, and if anything, we might be friends.

He must have realized I wasn't the dating type.

Still, my daddy didn't raise a sissy, and I didn't hide from stuff like that. Vaughn was a good guy, and I wanted him to know that if he needed or wanted a friend, now that his house was completely livable, I'd like to be his.

"Did you know the Cozy Cone opened up today,

Mutt?" Dad asked from the living room. "Me and Dub stopped in there. Saw Dean. He wanted to know what you did last night. I told him if you weren't at Astro's you were probably just out in the garage."

"Yeah, I was out there working," I said as I rinsed off my plate from dinner.

"Figures. Anyway, they have your favorite lemon ice cream right now. Thought you'd like to know that."

I loved lemon ice cream.

After I cleaned up the kitchen and finished a few more lures, I hopped in my truck and drove to town. Slowly, trying to decide if I wanted to stop at Vaughn's or not.

I stopped. I had something to get off my chest. I hated that feeling.

I'm sure he heard me coming. He met me at the door wearing shorts and a T-shirt.

"Hey there," he said.

"Hey. Want to go for a walk? The ice cream place is open for the summer now."

"I'll buy," he offered and smiled brightly, and I was one hundred percent better. Funny how someone else's smiles could make me happy.

"Okay, but I'm getting a large."

"That's fine, get whatever you want. Let me grab some shoes and my wallet."

I waited outside and sat on the concrete cap that ran along the front wall of the porch.

He came out and I stood, then for some reason I wanted to hug him. I didn't though. I didn't need to be any weirder than I already was.

We walked to the Cozy Cone, which was only about

five blocks from his house, and were back by the time it got dark.

We sat on his steps and finished our large lemon ice creams. Turned out he liked it too. That's not a totally honest depiction of how it happened, though. I basically told him it was the best thing on the planet and that he was a fucking idiot if he didn't want some.

So he got a large like me.

If he didn't like it, my plan was to eat his, too.

"You know what, I think I'm going to replace a few of the boards on this porch and paint it," he said as we sat there watching the fireflies flicker and glow against the night.

"What color?"

"I was thinking maybe a dark brown or black, maybe a dark grey color. I'm not sure yet. Then get a few porch swings for either side of the door. What do you think?" His bare knee nudged mine, and I nudged him back.

"Sounds good." I didn't want to impose on him anymore. Yesterday didn't feel good, and I knew I needed to take a few steps back. Give him some room to breathe.

"Maybe you could help me sometime?" he asked, his voice nonchalant.

"You don't *need* me to help you with that."

He turned toward me, so I mirrored what he did and faced him. "I know I don't *need* you to, but you didn't come by all day and I found myself looking for projects to start so that you'd come back."

Then his large hand glided across my leg and I wasn't sure what was happening. He didn't like me. Not like that anyway.

I looked down at it and then back up at him, then swatted a June bug that had been flying around on the porch attracted to the light.

"You wanted me to come back?"

"Yeah," he said, relaxed and cool. "You're fun to be around. I like looking at you."

I swallowed hard. "You do?"

How was that even remotely possible?

"I know I just moved here and we've only known each other for a few days, but I like spending time with you."

He leaned in. Then I leaned in, feeling like my heart was about to jump out of my mouth.

"I don't know how to do this, Vaughn," I admitted.

"Do what?" he asked quietly, so close I could smell lemon on his sexy lips. His eyes never left mine and I felt like I was blinking every second.

"I'm not the kind of girl many guys want to … do remodeling projects with," I admitted, knowing that it wasn't cool or smooth, but that he'd understand what I was trying to say.

"We don't have to do any remodeling projects until you want to. Then—when you're sure—we'll paint the porch together. We'll paint the hell out of it." I liked the way he humored me. I liked the way his hand was still on my leg. And I really liked that, instead of kissing me, he just put his forehead against mine. It was sweet.

"No projects tonight," he added. "Just come back."

The sound of a car going by startled me out of the moment.

"I've got some stuff to do the next few nights, but I'll come back," I said, standing up and walking backwards toward my truck. I needed time to process what he'd said. I'd never felt like that. I'd never expected someone like him to ever be interested in someone like me.

But, even though I couldn't explain it, I really liked that he did.

"Okay, stop by when you want to," he said and stood.

I got in my pickup and went home, my mind racing with thoughts and feelings I'd never experienced.

I didn't know what to do with them, but I knew I needed to think.

What if I was reading too much into what he said?

What if I let myself like him and then he changed his mind?

What if he only liked me because I was the only girl he'd met in Wynne so far?

What if he was serious?

Chapter Six

Vaughn

Yeah, I wanted to see her. Ever since the other night—when we almost kissed—I hadn't been able to stop thinking about the way she was looking at me. Like she wanted me too. Like if I didn't kiss her she'd be disappointed.

It was almost too much.

I'd only been in Wynne for little over a week. Regardless of how much progress I'd—*we'd*—made on the house, I hadn't been there long.

Still, I sensed I knew her. From the first night, when she shared her dinner with me—sure, that was probably pity, but I took it—to the next day when she brought me things from the store, knowing I probably hadn't been there. To her help and fast friendship when, all joking aside, I'd really needed one. All of this.

How did she know?

Why did she think to do all of those kind things for me?

And why did it strike something so deep down inside my gut that I wasn't sure what to do with it?

It was just about sunset when I walked out of the office. Despite it only having been my second one, it was another great day. I didn't know if it was the beat-up, old Astro van or me, but as I pulled out of the parking lot, we were looking for her.

I drove slowly around town, seeing if I could find her truck. I rolled the stubborn window down in the off chance I could hear her loud pickup tearing down one of the side roads I wasn't on.

When that failed, I decided I'd just ride down the road. She'd said her house was the first one you got to and that we were neighbors.

I passed my house, and no more than a mile or so down the road, the pavement turned to clay dirt gravel. As I looked in the rearview mirror, there was just enough light to see I was kicking up dust.

It was like I was in one of those country songs I'd heard over and over, and I smiled. I'd never really driven out on an old dirt road, and I can't lie. I enjoyed it. All two hundred feet of it.

I'd enjoy it a little more if she were with me, I thought.

Wasn't it too soon to be thinking things like that? Wasn't it too soon to be at the beginning of a relationship when I was only a month or so out of my last?

I needed a dude friend. I'd be on the lookout for one.

Since she wasn't in town, her house was the next best guess, as far as I knew.

The road turned into a wye and her house was around the bend to the right. Two large trees flanked a sidewalk leading to a small front porch that looked like it wasn't used for much. The Astro and I pulled into the drive and I looked around.

Her truck wasn't there. Outside at least.

Not seeing anybody around, I wondered if I should go up to the door and at least say hello. It was a little odd for me to just pull in. It wasn't like there was any reason I should be out this way.

Except there was.

I wanted to see her. Find out what she was up to. Be with her.

Most of all, I wanted to figure out why I couldn't get her off my mind.

The house sat on a large green lot. There was a garage and an old barn that had open doors on both ends. If anyone was there I didn't want to look like a creep poking around, but I still found myself getting out of the van. The door creaked loud enough for anyone within a mile to hear.

I walked up the drive further, so I could peek into the shed. No one was in there either.

Then, around the house I saw another door, which looked much more used. There were boots lined up next to it and a faded, old rug that said, "Come on in."

I wasn't about to do that, but as I stood on it, I knocked.

And I waited.

And nobody came.

I honestly hadn't planned on using it, but I was at a loss.

Earlier, going through patient files and getting familiar with how the women in the office did the paperwork, I may or may not have found a file—notably, it too said Mutt O'Fallon—and wrote her phone number down. I wasn't familiar enough with the phone numbers around here to tell if it was a cell number, one to the shop, where she usually was during the day, or if it was to their house.

But, as I stared at it in my hand, I prayed it was her cell phone number I'd unceremoniously stolen.

Then, while I sent arbitrary prayers to a God who was too busy to listen to my silliness, I added that I'd also like it if she answered.

I took a deep breath and touched the green spot on the screen that said send.

Again, I waited.

It rang. Once. Twice. Then three times.

It clicked over and I thought she'd answered, but then realized it was her voicemail.

"Hi. You got me. Leave a message. I'll call you back. If it's an emergency, and you need my dad, call our after hours number. Three one five. Six three three. Nine one. Nine two. Talk to you later."

Beep.

Hesitation hit me, but after a few seconds, I began to speak.

"Hi, O'Fallon. It's Vaughn. I was just seeing what you were doing. I thought maybe I could buy you a beer for all of your help. I mean, I owe you more than a beer. I owe you a lot actually. Well, anyway, I was just thinking if you weren't busy we could see each other. I guess I'll just talk to you later. Now you have my number. Give me a call."

I hung up absolutely sure I sounded like an ass. Chicks always dig guys who ramble and leave thirty-second voicemails that don't really say shit except, *hey, maybe you want to get a drink with me.*

I didn't want to get drunk. It was a Tuesday. We both had to work the next day, but it was still pretty early. And who knew, if she was like me, maybe she liked having a few cold ones after a long workday.

Yet, another thing I wanted to know about her and didn't know *why*.

I hopped inside the Astro, gave it a pump, and turned it over, the smell of exhaust heavy inside. That couldn't be a good sign, but it always smelled like that right after I started it up.

I threw my phone in the handy cup holder in the middle console, fastened my seatbelt, and looked behind me as I moved the gearshift into reverse. A feeling of disappointment crept into the passenger seat and left with me.

Oh well. You know what, if she was busy? No big deal. Now she had my number, and if she didn't call, or stop by anymore, I'd get the hint.

I turned onto the lane and slowed at the yield, and then my phone rang.

The number was unknown, but having looked at it only a few minutes ago, I recognized it.

She called me back. *Quickly.*

I stopped the van and put it in park.

"Hello?"

"Hi, Vaughn. It's … me. I got your message. Sorry I didn't answer, I had a big bastard on my line and couldn't pick up. I got him though."

A big bastard? I wasn't sure what she was talking about, but I also didn't give a fuck.

She called me back.

"Yeah, I didn't need anything really. I was just going to see if you wanted to get a beer or something."

"I'm already having a few, but I could always use a few more." Her voice was playful and she sounded happy to hear from me.

I wasn't sure if it was her or the whole town, but the people here were so friendly. So accommodating. So kind. They were often pains in the ass, but it was all in jest.

All of it was very nice, but when you were trying to figure out a woman and, more importantly, if she was interested in you or not, it was a little confusing.

Was she into me or was she just nice to everyone?

"Want some company?" I asked, knowing it was possible she already had some.

Say yes.

Say *yes*.

"Sure. I have about four beers left, if you want to grab a few more, I have room in my cooler."

My thoughts drove off into the gutter where "room in her cooler" sounded like an innuendo, but I fought the urge to flirt like that.

"Ha. Room in my cooler," she said, laughing. "That sounded pretty bad, didn't it?"

"Actually, it sounded good to me." Okay, I *was* going to flirt like that. She did it first. Maybe it was being around her so much, but my filter wasn't catching much these days.

"So where are you? Home?"

Yes, I knew she wasn't at home. Clearly. I was at her home, but she didn't need to know that.

"I'm down at Johnston's Chute, fishing. Do you know

where that is?"

No.

"Yeah, I think so." I laid my head on the steering wheel. Why couldn't I just say no?

"Oh, well. Okay then," she said and paused for a second. I'm sure trying to figure out how the hell I knew about Johnston's Chute. I looked at the phone to see if the call had dropped.

Then she went on. "Okay, it's only six. You can still buy beer at the truck stop or Willard's. That's the grocery store. I'll tell you, though, it's colder at the truck stop."

Fun, trivial facts like that were exactly some of the reasons I always wanted to live in a small town. *The beer is colder at the gas station.* Always good to know.

"All right. Do you need anything else?"

"Yeah, I need the radio station to play something new. I'm sick of the same fifteen songs on repeat. Sunny must be napping on the job."

That was a lot of information. And how in the hell could I get the radio station to play anything else? I'd need to work on that.

"Really? What would you want to hear? What do you listen to?" I said as I pulled onto the road and headed back to town.

"Hell, I don't know. I like all of the songs, I'm just sick of these. Just something new, I guess."

I'll be honest, I wasn't really that versed in country music. I'd always been more of a rock or alternative person.

"I have an iPod dock at home," I offered.

"Nah, that's okay. Just get out here."

That sounded better to me, too.

We hung up as I passed my house, and for a fleeting moment I thought about all of the things I could be doing instead of grabbing beer and going to Johnston's Chute, which I was only guessing was a fishing place? But none of the things I was putting off couldn't keep until tomorrow.

I wanted to see her tonight. To talk to her, get to know *her* more.

I was sure she'd already heard—at least in part—some of what had happened between Rachelle and me.

If she was interested—and I was hoping she was since she'd not only called me back, but seemed to want to hang out—then I'd want to tell her what actually happened.

I wasn't naive. It was a small town, and I was the new guy. A new guy, who'd come to town with a girlfriend looking at a house, and then moved there single.

I hadn't talked about it much with anyone, except Dr. Carver, but I didn't really think it was anyone else's business.

However, when it came to O'Fallon, I wanted her to know I wasn't pining away waiting for a woman, hoping she'd just show up.

She wasn't going to show up, and I was fine with that.

Had I been shocked? Yes.

Hurt? Yes.

Pissed? Definitely.

Who doesn't feel those kinds of things when they find out their girlfriend, who they were planning on proposing to at *their* new house, had been sleeping with a guy they called a friend?

Shit. I'd even introduced Rachelle to Brad and his wife. Yeah, that's right. His wife, who Rachelle had explained the last time we spoke, he was leaving.

What a mess.

I was hurt and pissed and all of those things. But, after a few days with my thoughts in a new place, I realized I'd dodged a huge bullet.

True, that was only a month ago, and hell if I didn't think that this was a little soon to feel interested in another woman, but when someone you thought you loved cheats on you, for as long as she did, if you're anything like me, you're done. Like done-done. All of the love you thought you had for them dies.

Then after that, you feel lonely.

And, being in a new town, it was only amplified.

So fucking sue me. O'Fallon was fun and kind. A little on the tomboy side, but I found that endearing. She was so different than any other woman I'd encountered. She could take care of herself. She didn't wait around for someone to make plans. She lived her life every day how she wanted to. She was smart. And *damn* was she beautiful.

Even though she put off this kind of tough exterior, I had to wonder, if deep down, she wasn't lonely too?

I wasn't sure how old she was—I guessed maybe twenty-five or twenty-six. Most people our age, especially in Wynne, were already paired off.

Married.

Had kids.

Not her.

O'Fallon was sweet and thoughtful, which was a giant contrast to Rachelle. Would Rachelle ever have just stopped to help a stranger on her day off? Fuck no. That's the answer to that. A big, conclusive fuck no.

She would have thought, "Not my problem," if I knew her at all. And in hindsight, maybe I didn't.

I pulled into the truck stop, hoping whoever was working was just as friendly as everyone else, because I had a few questions.

"Hey there. How ya doin'?" asked the older man from behind the counter as I walked in.

"Pretty good, thanks," I answered as I strolled toward the cooler in the back. "How are you?"

"Oh, I can't complain. Wouldn't help if I did, would it?"

I chuckled, everyone here had some quip or anecdote for everything. "Probably not."

"Whatcha huntin' for?"

"I need a few beers. I'm headed down to Johnston's Chute. You know where that is?"

He seemed nice enough to ask. I didn't have many options.

"Yeah, I know where it is. What kind of beer do you want?"

"I was thinking about grabbing a twenty of Bud Light." I figured he was just making small talk, but when I looked at his face as I reached into the cooler for the beer, there was something off about it. "Why? Is there something wrong with the Bud Light?"

"No. Hell no. There's nothing wrong with it. I was just thinking, if you're headed down to the Chute, I think you might enjoy Newcastle."

I liked Newcastle. Hell, I liked most beers, so I took his suggestion and exchanged the blue box for the tan and red one. It didn't sound too bad, to be honest.

As I approached the counter, I looked for a nametag.

Usually, attendants wore them, but I was learning that kind of thing wasn't necessary in Wynne, and he didn't wear one.

"Thanks for the suggestion. I'm Vaughn Renfro. I'll be taking over for Dr. Carver at the end of the year. I just bought a house in town."

"Yeah, I figured that's who you were. You stick out about like a turd in a punchbowl. My name's Donnie. So ya fish, huh?"

His expression wasn't hiding that he was trying not to laugh about something.

"I guess. I haven't been since I was a kid."

"Oh, I'm sure you'll catch on fast. Everyone around here fishes. Hell, my dog fishes."

I chuckled and his big belly bobbed as he rang me up. Then I thought it might be a good time to find out how the hell to get to Johnston's Chute.

"So, I'm a little turned around here. Which way should I go to get out to Johnston's Chute?"

A knowing smile spread across his face and I began to think he was on to me. Did he know she was out there? She might have stopped here first.

"Yeah, just take the highway north out of here and you'll see a sign," he answered. "But, you know, some people don't fish right there at the Chute, some go just south of it."

He winked.

He knew exactly what I was doing.

"Just south, huh?" I lifted my chin, feeling a little foolish, but also like he was trying to help.

"Yup, when you see the lot for the Chute, pull in, then take the little side road on the left and just keep following that." He coughed and grinned. "Needin' anything else?"

I took my card out of my wallet and ran it through the machine on the counter. "No, thanks. I think you've got me all set."

He ripped the receipt off the machine after it printed and handed it to me.

"You have a good night then."

"You too, Donnie. Thanks."

I put the beer in the back of the Astro and headed out of town, following his directions.

He was right, there was a sign on the highway. I took the road for a few miles, it turned into gravel, and sure enough, there was the lot he was talking about and I saw the road off to the left.

The lane was rough and I wondered if the old van would make it. I took it slow, but it seemed to go on and on. Soon I was driving past little cabins that were up on stilts, but I still hadn't seen her truck. The road led into the woods, but I just kept going on blind faith that he had told me where she'd be. Donnie never came out and said it, but it was too coincidental not to hear what he *wasn't* saying.

The van drove along the terribly battered road, parallel to the river, and I hoped I was close. Sure enough, about a mile past the other cabins there was one more, right where the road ended.

Her truck was there.

Thank you, Donnie, my new best friend.

Chapter Seven

Mutt

I saw the headlights on the van pulling down the lane and wondered how in the hell he knew how to find me. I was expecting him to call back so that I'd know when he was close … and so I could run in and check my hair.

That's right. Check my hair.

I'd never in my life been a girl who wanted to *check her hair*. I'd never bothered with trying to impress anyone. It just wasn't in my character. I knew he'd seen me looking less than my best on many occasions. Okay, on every occasion, but this time I—at very least—wanted to make sure I looked halfway feminine.

I'd spent most of the past two days out there, at my cabin, thinking about things. What I came up with was, I really, really wanted him to like me.

Good thing it was dark. I could find some excuse to go inside the cabin and freshen up.

"I can't believe you found me all the way out here."

He smiled as he stepped out of the Astro. It still made me laugh seeing him drive that thing. And when he didn't laugh and turn down the offer for the rental, it did something else to me. He was genuinely relieved to have a ride while Dean and Dad fixed his SUV, even if it was taking longer than they'd originally thought.

He was still wearing nice clothes. Dress pants and a white button up shirt. Had he even been home after work? The thought of him looking for me first caused a buzz inside me, like there was a spinner in my body zipping around, bumping into the walls of my chest.

"I didn't see your truck in the Johnston's Chute lot, so I took a chance." He reached into the back and pulled out a twelve pack of Newcastle.

My favorite.

"You drink Newcastle?"

"Yeah, it's good," he said, walking my way.

I was sitting in a fold out chair next to the bank of the river, and I began reeling in my line so I could give him my attention.

The sun wasn't gone, but it was fading fast. I'd already had four beers and certainly feeling the effects of them—not drunk, but on my way. In the summertime, that was what I usually did on Tuesdays. So, *what you see is what you get* rang very true for me at that moment.

"You can put those in my cooler. There should be plenty of room."

He came to my side and knelt to open it. Then, one by one, restocked me. What a sight.

"I must confess I thought you'd bring cheerleader beer,"

I teased. Not that I didn't drink Bud Light or Coors or whatever was handy, but if given a choice, I always went for something a little darker.

"Cheerleader beer?"

"Yeah, you know lightweight stuff. Bud Light. Light beer, in general. I just thought you'd bring something more mainstream."

"I like variety. I drink that stuff, too. I guess I was just in the mood for something different."

I hoped to myself he felt the same way about women. I wasn't mainstream. I wasn't typical. I was rough around the edges and even *I* knew it. Maybe that was why I was still single, but I didn't really care. If there was someone out there for me, they'd like *me* for who I was, not what trends I did or didn't follow.

"Well, it's my favorite," I admitted as he packed the cooler. "That's what I usually drink."

"This place is great, you own it?"

I might have lived with my dad in town, but that little cabin by the river was all mine. Dad came out every now and again, but on many weekends when the weather was nice and the water was low, I was out here.

Dad played cards with some of the guys in town on Tuesdays. Sometimes they were at our place, but they moved around. That's why I started coming out on card nights, just to get out of their hair. It was quiet and the fishing was good.

"Yep, it's all mine. Want to see inside? It isn't much. Kitchen, living room, bathroom, and a room. With a bed." I set my pole next to my chair and pulled my beer from the cup holder, downing the little that was left.

“Sure, I’ve never been in a cabin with legs.”

“All right, I’ll give you the nickel tour. Grab us a beer,” I said as I headed for the stairs that led up to the wraparound porch at the top. It was an A-framed cabin with sliding doors on the front and back.

It really wasn’t much, but it was great in the summer. Coming out here. Swimming off my small dock, fishing and boating around with the other river people.

He followed behind me as we took the stairs up. The cabin sat about twenty feet off the ground on stilts, and those steps were tricky bastards the more I drank.

“The view is great in the morning. That’s my favorite time out here.”

He walked straight to the front edge of the deck and looked out, handing me the extra beer he’d brought up and grabbing my bottle opener off the small table so he could open his.

“It’s awesome up here. Crazy how much more you can see.” That was true. From up here you could see down the river a little more, and looking down at it somehow made it seem bigger, wider than when you were standing on the bank.

The sun was setting and the sky turned pink, orange, and purple, causing the water to look like it was on fire.

“It’s beautiful out here,” he said quietly, almost like it was only for him to hear.

“I think so, too. It’s peaceful and I can think.”

We silently leaned on the rail, having put off the tour for the minute. We drank our beers, not saying a word, but it was also comfortable. It was nice letting someone appreciate something I cherished so much.

After a little while, he turned to face me, and flashes of our almost kiss raced through my mind. We weren't nearly as close at the moment, but we were leaps and bounds closer than the last time I'd thought about it—which was about every five minutes all day long.

I wasn't sure what was happening. I wasn't sure if it was the same for him. For all I knew, I was growing a crush on the town's new shiny toy and he was trying to score off a rebound. I was so different around him, not knowing how to behave—like a fish out of water.

Surely I wasn't the only one who'd noticed how handsome he was. How he walked with a rhythmic gait, or how when he smiled it was devastating and contagious at the same time.

Nevertheless, he hadn't kissed me. And I didn't kiss him. So there we were. Standing in front of each other, beers in hand, watching the sun play tricks with the way the brilliant colors lit up his eyes and made the short whisker stubble on his cheeks almost look red.

I was staring, but, if I was right, he was staring, too. Then I remembered I looked like hell warmed over.

"Do you want to look around inside? I'm going to the bathroom." I tipped my head for him to follow me. "Or you can stay out here. Whatever you like."

"No, I want to see this place."

As we followed the deck to the far side of the cabin, where the other door was unlocked, his hand touched the small of my back, and I swear I almost tripped over my clumsy feet.

I had to find a way to say, "Hi, I'm available, if you're interested," without actually saying it.

He was just out of a relationship, from what I knew, and he probably wasn't ready to jump into another this fast. But, hopefully, while I was being patient, he'd pick up what I was putting down.

As I took pleasure in the feeling of his hand on me, I knew I could be patient. I'd let him take the lead.

Or I'd attack him and look like a wanton whore, but I was going to do my best to avoid that and pray he jumped me between now and then.

I opened the screen door, and then the inside one, and I propped it open with the door stopper.

"So this is the living room and the kitchen is right over there." I pointed to the opposite side. There was the other large sliding door, the one that faced the water where we'd just been.

"I like it." He grinned as he passed me, taking it upon himself to look around. Which really shouldn't have surprised me since I knew my way around his house from helping him the past week.

"Did you catch all of these?" He was looking at my fish mounted on the wall.

Nobody had ever asked me about my fish. *Ever.* And there had been some guys inside that cabin. I supposed they didn't give a shit.

Did that mean he did?

"Most of them. Some are my dad's; some were my grandpa's. That largemouth bass is mine, though. You said you fished a little when you were younger, what did you guys fish for?"

He chuckled before answering, looking embarrassed. "Whatever my Snoopy pole would catch. I think they were sunfish, but I did pretty well and I remember catching quite a few."

"I had one of those too. That didn't last me very long, though. I think I broke it after a week and Dad got me a real pole."

"You fish a lot then, huh?"

"When I can. I do a lot in the summer when I'm out here by myself. It's calming. I like the game of it. What can I do to make them want my line? You know? I think that's why I make lures and flies. They're both relaxing."

"I think I need a relaxing hobby."

"I saw some clubs in your garage. You golf?" I asked as I turned on a lamp in the living room and walked over to one of the windows on the far side to get a breeze moving through the cabin. Since I used mine a little more than most it never got that musty smell, but it always smelled better with fresh air in it.

"I did. I mean, I do. Dr. Carver said there was a small course here?"

"Yeah, it's actually pretty nice, I think. We get a lot of people from around the area for tournaments and stuff. There's a nice clubhouse and restaurant out there. I don't go out very often. Special occasions. Weddings. Stuff like that."

I walked over to the bathroom and flipped the switch. "Excuse me. Make yourself at home. Poke around."

When I saw myself in the mirror, I was pleasantly surprised I didn't look as bad as I'd imagined. I opened a drawer where I had a few things and ran a comb through my hair. I'd had it up in a ponytail, so it was going back up because I had that lovely ring that the holder left, but at least it would look nicer. I rummaged a little more and found a tube of mascara and threw a coat on my lashes, pinched my cheeks. Then I debated brushing my teeth, but I hated the way toothpaste made beer taste, so instead I swished a little mouthwash and water in there. I applied some Chapstick, and although I wasn't a supermodel, and I never would be, I decided it was a significant improvement.

I quickly peed and washed my hands, then rubbed some sweet smelling lotion on my arms, noting that I wouldn't be catching anything if I touched my line after that, but I didn't really give a shit either—if he liked it.

I didn't want to smell fishy. And even though I hadn't been keeping any of my catches, I had in fact touched a few. Fish and romance weren't really a match made in heaven.

I rubbed the jasmine lotion in. Then added a little smear to my neck, and, even though I knew nobody would ever reap the benefit of it, I rubbed some through my cleavage.

I had to be prepared for anything. You know, like me forgetting my patience and throwing myself at him like a wanton whore.

Although what I'd changed was subtle, the look he gave me when I came out of the bathroom was not.

"O'Fallon, you look pretty tonight," he said, almost like he hadn't even thought about the words. Like they just fell out. And I had to admit he looked pretty damn good too, standing there in my cabin.

I hadn't been looking for compliments, but there I was smack dab in the middle of one—and I wasn't used to it at all. Nobody called me pretty except my dad, but he was my dad.

Hearing I looked pretty from Vaughn's mouth was

something completely different.

Different in how I reacted, which was to nervously look around and pretend like he hadn't knocked the wind out of me.

Different in how I felt. I almost believed him, and I would have, had I not just seen myself.

But, mostly, different in how I didn't know how to respond. I had no sassy comeback.

I'd been told I was hot before, in a bar, by drunk guys who were looking for a little companionship. And, to be honest, when I actually went to the bar, I was also looking for companionship.

Girls get horny, too.

Girls want intimacy and closeness, too.

And sometimes the quickest relief for that longing was a roll in the sheets with someone just passing through, or someone from out of town.

I made sure to never get with anyone in town because I knew it would spread like wildfire, and I didn't want my dad hearing about it over coffee with the town's men.

I didn't sleep around a lot, but every now and again over the years, I found myself over or under one in a bed. Usually, the bed in this cabin.

I nervously tucked my head; the feeling of his appraisal was unlike other men giving me attention.

"Thanks," I think I mumbled.

He took a few steps closer to me, and my body was screaming *get out of here* and *jump him* at the same time.

Not knowing what to do with myself, I just froze—which was totally not like me.

I'm Mutt, for fuck's sake.

He stepped up to me and I could smell his cologne, or deodorant—hell, I wasn't sure—but whatever it was, it added volume to my lungs and I wished I could inhale it forever.

"The other night," he began softly, and then he tenderly took ahold of the hand I had by my side, "I had a lot of fun."

"I did, too." I couldn't help myself from staring right into his eyes. They looked back and forth in mine, like he was testing the waters.

"The water is fine. Come on in," I heard some wanton whore say in the back of my head.

"The ice cream was good," I added.

"Yeah, it was, but more than that I'd like to get to know you more. Spend time with you. And not just because you helped me with my house, and have been so nice, but because I'm attracted to you."

And there went my stomach.

Who says things like that? Do men really say that kind of thing outside of Wynne? Because how do women walk around with clean underwear knowing there are real live men wandering around out there talking like that?

A rush of air left my chest and it collapsed like it was going to cave in.

"You are?"

I couldn't misunderstand that, right? Attracted to you means the same thing everywhere, right?

"I am. Since the moment we met, I've wanted to talk to you. Know about you. There's something about you that stays with me when you're not around. I think about you a lot."

His thumb was circling mine and it was nice, comforting. I was nervous as hell, and, in this small way, he was soothing me.

"I think I like you a little, too," I admitted.

His eyebrow teased me, rising on the end. "A little?"

"I said, *I think*."

Why was I so embarrassed? We were adults. He was attracted to me, by the grace of God himself. And I was attracted to him, a lot. We weren't the first humans to encounter such a thing, but, for the life of me, I didn't know what the hell to do about it. I didn't want to make a wrong move and have him realize he'd just been lonely or sad or on the mend.

"Well, it's a good start. I hope you'll be a little more certain after tonight. How about I start a fire? I saw you have a pit. That's actually something I'm pretty good at. Then we'll see if there's anything I can do to help you officially like me."

If he only knew that he'd already done it. I just needed to figure out if I was purely attracted to him, or if this was something else.

Chapter Eight

Vaughn

I have no clue where any of that came from, but I didn't regret saying it. It was all true. I am attracted to her and I'm so damn curious about her.

When she came out of the bathroom, I could tell she'd fussed with her hair. Her lips were shiny. Then when I got closer I smelled something sweet that hadn't been around her before. I knew it was all right to tell her, in plain words, no pretenses, no expectations, what I was thinking.

That was one of the things about her that was growing on me. She was easy to talk to, easy to be honest with, because *she* was. She was authentically her and I was drawn to it.

What came with that honesty was this fleeting flash of vulnerability she had around me. I'd seen her with other people, but with me she was quite different. A little more calm. A little softer. A little less on guard. A little less protected.

If she was willing to do that for me, then so could I.

O'Fallon had wood piled in neat rows under the cabin, only a few steps away from a really great fire pit. I wondered if she chopped all the wood herself. I didn't think I knew a single woman who did stuff like that. The fire pit looked a little worn, but I wondered if she built that too.

She was so capable. And something about that challenged me. Made me think about what I could do to impress her. What I could do for her that she couldn't do for herself. What she would need me for.

I knew one thing—I was going to do my best to find out what that might be tonight.

I built a fire, remembering I'd seen a lighter in the console of the Astro. When she came down, a few minutes after the flames really took off, she pulled her chair over to the fire and then found another in the back of her truck. She set them close to each other near the flames and placed the cooler in between them.

There wasn't a single aspect to the situation that I was familiar with. All of it was new to me. The cabin. The river. It was a Tuesday. I was with a fascinating woman.

She was even more beautiful in her element. That fact alone was exhilarating.

We both sat, opened new beers, and then she asked me, "So how do you like Wynne so far?"

I was glad she asked me a question, because then it opened up an opportunity for me to ask a few of my own.

"I like it. It's always a little strange in a new place, but so far I'm glad I took a chance on it." It was my turn. I decided to start small. "Have you dated anyone in town?"

Subtle, Vaughn. Real subtle. But I had to know what I was strolling into. I'd, obviously, had a recent relationship. It was only natural to wonder if she'd had one, too.

She laughed and said, "Back to this?" Then she kicked my foot on purpose as she crossed her legs.

"No. Not really. I mean in high school I dated a few town guys, but nothing serious. I've never been a real relationship kind of person." She took a drink, and I watched her face in the firelight, the sun having completely disappeared. "Not that I wouldn't, I've just never been in one. You know? It's just kind of worked out that way."

"I get that."

"At first, I thought all of the guys in town were scared of my dad. Then I thought maybe I was just too much of a tomboy to hit anybody's radar. But eventually, I realized I really didn't see anything I couldn't live without walking around here either. Then I got used to it."

However, she looked uncomfortable talking about it, not looking me in the face as she spoke, and that wasn't my intention, so I changed the subject. "Do you have a boat?"

Immediately, she lit up.

"I do. I have a nice jon boat I troll around in—it's at home in my shed—but last summer I bought a Rinker and I'm excited for it to warm up and take it out. It's fun down here on the weekends. There are a few sandbars just south of here and people congregate there. Cook out. Socialize. Have a few drinks. It's a good time. You'll have to come out with me."

"I think I'll take you up on that."

The conversation with her was great all night. She talked about how she'd always dreamed of opening her own bait and tackle shop with her own lures, which I thought was cool. In turn, I told her about how I got into dentistry because of my crazy awful childhood overbite.

The beers tasted good, but I wasn't concerned with drinking much. I needed to remember what she was telling me and to say things the right way.

I wanted to kiss her, without any doubt in her mind it was because I'd had too much to drink. She'd slowed down too and the conversation, up until then, had been pretty light.

"So what does the town really think about what happened with Rachelle and me? I know they're all talking because the ladies in the office keep looking at me like I'm some sad, lost puppy dog or something."

"You'll get used to that. Small towns are good for lots of things, but the flip side of that is having everyone know—or think they know—*all* of your business. Sometimes before you do."

"So what do they think?"

She looked at me hesitantly, like she didn't want to admit what they were saying. Like she wanted to spare my feelings, not knowing what was true and what was false.

I didn't care what everyone else thought. I only cared that she knew the truth. I didn't want her hearing something and thinking it was true, if it wasn't.

"Out with it. How bad is it?"

"Okay," she said and sat up to face me head on. "There are lots of people speculating, but what it boils down to is, you had a girlfriend who was planning on coming, and then she didn't. But I'm not sure I'm buying all of that. I think something else happened. You don't seem like you're terribly heartbroken, or like you're missing her or you know ... upset. Sorry if that sounds bad. It's not my business, but I've been around you, in your house. I just figured that when—or if—you wanted to talk to me—or anyone—you would."

"Well, some of that is close." Vague, but close. I think she was sparing my feelings not telling me all of the juiciest gossip.

"We don't have to talk about it," she admitted.

Only we did.

I wanted her to know that she was right about a lot of what she said and I wanted her to know why.

"No. It's fine. You're right. I'm not that broken up about it. Not now. I was when everything first happened, but after some thinking, it was all for the best.

"Rachelle and I started dating about two years ago. It was fun because we hung out in the same circle. We got along great. About a year after we were dating, we went golfing with another couple, Brad and Cami. And as things sometimes go, Rachelle and Brad got along well. Too well."

I ran a hand down the back of my neck and squeezed it, catching my breath and giving her time to let it all sink in before I went on.

"He left Cami about a month before I was moving, and that's when Rachelle came clean and told me she had been seeing him.

"At first, I was pissed about being lied to, cheated on. Then I was frustrated because I felt like a fool, having been friends with Brad and introducing them. Then I realized, if she really loved *him*, and he really loved *her*, it was best for Cami and me that they came clean before they got caught—or worse. Cami and Brad were already married."

"You weren't engaged?" she asked. "I mean, moving to the middle of nowhere with a guy is a big step."

"We weren't. Yet."

I took a deep breath, ran my hands over my head, and reminded myself that I'd dodged a bullet. I didn't want a woman who didn't want me. I didn't want someone I couldn't trust. I didn't want to be someone she'd resent later if she hated it there. And, in hindsight, she would have.

"Oh," she said quietly. "You were going to?"

"Yeah, I planned on packing the ring in one of her boxes, the box you saw me with on Sunday, and then let her find it when we were moving in. She probably would have hated it. Not dramatic enough." I hadn't told anyone that. "But things didn't work out anyway."

"Well, for the record, it was a really sweet idea, but I think guys over think it. If you want my two cents, it shouldn't be have to be staged or planned out so much." She kicked my leg gently, pulling me out of my daze. Honestly, she was right.

The fire was starting to get low, so I got up to add a few more pieces of wood.

"Okay, now tell me something," I said. And this little thing had been on my mind a lot. "Mutt?"

She shook her head, and I couldn't be sure because it was dark, but I think she blushed. Her leg began to bounce slightly as I chucked logs into the pit.

"What?" she asked.

"Why? What's with the nickname?" I knew she wasn't embarrassed about the name. I'd heard everyone call her that. In fact, I didn't even know what her real name was. Her damn file, in the small town dentist's office, even said

Mutt O'Fallon.

Of course, things were a little different than they were in the city. The files were all accurate, but not necessarily done in the most efficient way. I could change all of that, little by little, as needed when I took over. At the moment, I was focused on getting to know the patients, learning how things ran. Then I'd focus on improvements.

At that moment, what needed improvement most was my understanding of why the whole town called this gorgeous woman Mutt.

"I don't think my grandpa thought it would stick like it did, to tell you the truth. I think he was just calling me that to dig at my mom, who then left my dad and me. I was a kid and didn't know what a mutt was at first. I remember him saying, 'You're the sweetest Mutt I know.' I don't think he was trying to be mean to *me*. Then everyone else started calling me Mutt, and the meaning of it kind of wore off. I don't think anyone even thinks about it anymore. It's just my name."

I didn't like it. It wasn't a thoughtful or flattering nickname; it was cruel, even if it wasn't meant to be. I had to respect the way she dealt with it, though. Even if her grandfather hadn't meant for it to be mean, I thought it was sad. Here she'd been abandoned by her mother and then everyone called her a dog.

Admittedly, I hated it.

I'd never call her that.

"What's your real name?"

O'Fallon looked at me like I was nuts, like she didn't want to tell me. She sat back and crossed her arms over her chest, looking at me defiantly.

"Tell me," I urged, then nudged her leg.

"No."

"Want me to guess?"

She rolled her eyes and then opened the cooler to get another beer, silently offering it to me first. I took it and she retrieved another for herself.

"You can try, but I doubt you'll guess."

"Will you tell me if I'm right?" I'd be able to tell by her face, I thought. She didn't seem like a very good liar. Then again, I was just getting to know her. I didn't even know her real name. Yet.

"Suzanne?"

She laughed. I committed the sound to memory as it echoed off the nearby water.

"Do I look like a Suzie?" Then she laughed some more but leaned in, enjoying the game.

"No. I'm just warming up. Samantha?" I asked and leaned in a little myself.

"No."

"Vivian?"

She shook her head, forehead scrunched.

"Natalie? Ashley? Danielle?"

"No. No. No." Each no punctuated with a flip of her wrist and her finger checking them off.

I stretched my legs out in front of me, and admitted, "This might take a while."

"That's okay. I've nothing better going on. Besides you look cute when you guess."

"Cute?"

"Yeah, after you say a name your face does this *I'm waiting* thing, like you actually might be right. You're nowhere close, though."

"Men don't like to be called cute, O'Fallon."

"Oh, sorry. What do you prefer? Handsome?"

"Do you think I'm handsome?"

She shrugged noncommittally.

"Come on. You think I'm handsome. That's fine. I'll keep guessing. Lydia?"

She giggled, actually giggled. "No."

"Judy?"

"I'm twenty-six, not eighty! No."

"Carmen?"

"No."

"Can you tell me what it starts with?"

"I can," she said with a shit-eating grin on her pretty lips. "But not yet. This is entertaining."

I needed leverage.

"I'll keep guessing, but I'll just say this, I don't kiss women if I don't know their name." It was a stretch, but it might get me a little clue.

Her eyes flared wide, like I'd challenged her.

"Oh, Vaughn, Vaughn, Vaughn," she tsked.

"Oh, you, you, you," I mocked.

"You're flirting with me."

By then we were both leaning over the cooler that separated our chairs.

"Maybe."

"No, you are. I like it, but sweet-talking me isn't going to get it out of me. I've been months and months without a kiss. I can hold out. I'm patient." She leaned forward and licked her bottom lip.

Shit. She fought dirty.

"You better get to guessing."

I guessed every name under the sun. She never relented and gave me a clue, and even though the conversation would veer off when I'd mention a name that struck a memory with one of us, we laughed and enjoyed each other until it started getting late.

I didn't want to leave.

Correction. I didn't want to leave without a kiss. Something. Anything.

The more time I spent with her the more I wanted to touch her, and all night I found myself fighting the urge to reach out and put my arm on the back of her chair. Or put my hand on her leg. Anything. I was starving for her.

For the most part she kept her cool, but there were these amazing little moments when I'd catch her with this dreamy look on her face as I spoke to her. And I kept catching her looking at my hands, so I played that to my advantage and used them animatedly when I spoke.

"I hate to say this, because I could sit out here all night, but I need to get home." My watch read a quarter to eleven. I wanted to be in the office at seven.

"I know. I actually think I'm just going to sleep here tonight. I'll just drive home in the morning."

Was that a hint?

Was there something in the way she said that? The way she leaned her head to the side and the amber from the fast burning coals colored her hair, cheek, and neck might have played a trick on me.

I had to adjust a little in my seat.

Knowing I couldn't, for it would be breaking some rule of the little game we'd created, made me want to kiss her all the more. I wanted to please her with my lips. I wanted my mouth on hers. I wanted to taste her warm skin, get in there and get a lungful of her scent—the same one I'd been teased with all night. I wanted her to moan a little and part her mouth open, and then I wanted her to sneak her tongue to meet mine when I took too long, just so I could see how long it would take *her* to want more. Then I'd give her more.

Still, I didn't know her name. And even though I'd made up that stupid rule about not kissing a woman when I didn't know her name, I was going to stand by it.

As much as I wanted her in that moment, I needed her to know where I stood when it came to giving my word.

I wanted her to trust what I said, to know my words and actions had more value than my touch. Than my kiss.

I'd believed in that kind of thing once.

This time I was going to know the person I was with, and there was something so damn seductive about prying out all of the pieces that made her … *her*.

"Can I help you with anything before I head back to town?" I asked, totally disappointed that I hadn't guessed her name.

"Nope, I'm good." She sighed, looking disappointed too. I liked that.

"So," I began as we stood at the same time, "do you think you'll let me guess your name again? Maybe Friday night?"

She bit her lip and failed at hiding a smile. I couldn't resist any longer, and my hand reached out and touched her arm as she was looking down, making up her mind.

She sucked in a breath and said, "Sure."

"Good."

I moved my fingers over her arm and fought the urge to lean in, but failed. Near her ear I said, "And, Friday, if I guess, I'll kiss you good night."

Her head leaned into mine and our cheeks touched. O'Fallon's skin was warm and I wanted more, I'd wait. Then she'd know for sure if she liked me or not. No more, she *thinks* she likes me *a little*.

Two could play her sexy little game.

Chapter Nine

Mutt

Where did he come up with that stuff? Who in their right mind says those things? I was literally hanging on his every word all night. Something about that voice. Something about the way he spoke. It was so sexy. The words he chose. The intention behind it when he told me he wasn't going to kiss a girl until he knew her name.

I liked it more than a little.

I liked him.

A lot.

He was funny and sincere, which made me comfortable enough around him that I could be myself, the real me. Not just Mutt, Darrell O'Fallon's daughter. He was easy to talk to and interesting to listen to.

That was just skimming the top of his appeal.

The way he walked. The way he sat, long legs out in front of him. I'm a pretty tall girl at five-nine, but he stood taller, even over me. His broad shoulders, slim waist.

I wondered what he looked like naked.

I wondered what he looked like during sex.

Shit.

I needed to fall asleep, but I was finding it rather difficult with all of these new thoughts swimming around in my head. Never before had a man had this effect on me.

When he was around I was relaxed, yet I felt a pulsing tension. I told him things that I'd never told anyone. Not that they were secrets, but no one had ever bothered to ask. We'd talked about my dream of having a tackle shop. I'd *never* told anyone about that. Ever.

I lay on my bed in the cabin, glad I'd washed the sheets and blankets a few weeks back. It was the first night I'd stayed there that spring and already I knew I'd be spending a lot of time there that year.

How in the hell did he know where my cabin was? And Newcastle?

Must have been Donnie at the gas station, I figured.

Who better to tell him how to get out here? I'd bought the cabin from him. I should have known. I could have teased Vaughn about poaching information at the gas station.

I rolled over to look at the time on my phone. One-thirty.

I was going to be tired the next day.

Wednesday dragged by slowly.

Thursday did the same.

I didn't go back out to the cabin, and I didn't stop at Vaughn's house every night as I passed, even though I really wanted to.

I was waiting for him to call. Then again, he'd asked me out. I didn't know what the rules for dating were. Should I have called him? Was the ball in my court? Was I already messing this up? Maybe it wasn't even a date-date. He didn't have many friends in town yet, and it's possible all city guys flirted like that.

How in the fuck was I to know any of this shit? It was Thursday night, and all I could think about while I was in my shop working on a lures I'd promised to finish before the weekend.

My earbuds were in and I was lost in my thoughts, the pieces I was working on, and the music.

Then my phone rang—not that I'd been waiting for it to the past few days or anything.

Vaughn.

I took a deep breath and squeezed my hands tight with excitement before answering the call.

"Hi, Vaughn," I said, using the mic on my earbuds, not bothering to pull them out.

"Hi, you." Was it weird that I liked that he wouldn't call me Mutt? And that him calling me "you" was really kind of hot. It *was* weird, but I was weird and I liked it. A shitload.

"What's up?" I asked, trying to be casual and praying he wasn't calling to cancel.

"Not a lot. It's been a busy week at the office and I haven't seen you, even though I heard you drive by every night. So I thought I'd call and make sure we were still on for tomorrow."

Relief. I was alone and my balled up hands shot up in the air like I'd just scored a touchdown.

"Yeah, I'm still good for tomorrow. I hope you made a list of names to go through."

I hope you'll finally kiss me.

"I have done nothing else but think of names to try."

I laughed because he actually sounded a little desperate. Desperate for me? For my name? For a kiss? I was getting a little desperate myself.

I played with the lure I'd been working on and held it up to inspect. Things were looking up. Lots of things were looking up.

"Good for you. I hope you crack the code. You know, I suppose you could always ask Donnie."

The line was silent.

"The gas station guy?"

"You know who I'm talking about."

He chuckled, having been caught. "I've never asked him anything. In fact, I was a little nervous that the hints he was dropping were leading me to some sort of community hazing thing or something. It was strange."

"Yeah, right." Although, Donnie was strange as hell.

"I wouldn't lie to you. I went in, and we talked a little bit. He suggested Newcastle. Then I asked him how to get to Johnston's Chute, and he gave me directions to your place."

I shook my head, all along picturing Donnie doing it.

"What a shithead. I knew you didn't know where my cabin was." I laughed despite myself. It totally sounded like something that old fart would do. He was always telling me I needed a man, but I thought he was just teasing me since I never had one.

"He might have a thing for you. If you want to see what he's doing tomorrow I think you've got a good shot."

"Nope, I've got plans." I sat up a little straighter, proud.

"Plans, huh? Anyone I know?"

"Just some guy. I'm not sure it's a date, but I *do* have plans."

His voice grew lower and the sound of it gave me goose bumps on my arms. "O'Fallon, it's definitely a date."

I smiled to myself.

"So tell me what we're doing."

"Well, I have a few things in mind. I thought I'd pick you up and maybe make you dinner, and then I was going to see if you could show me around town a little. I can get from work to the store, but I'd like to see the back roads. You know, get the scenic Wynne tour."

I loved the sound of that.

Often I'd drive around for hours by myself. I could get lost for hours on end on those old roads, but they always led me home. I had to admit, it sounded so much better having someone with me.

"That sounds great, but you don't have to pick me up. We can take my truck."

Then I felt a tap on my shoulder and it startled me. I spun around to see Vaughn, in a black V-neck T-shirt and jeans, standing right there.

In my shed.

At my workbench.

I swallowed the holler that almost flew out of my mouth and pulled the earbuds out of my head.

"You scared the shit out of me." I quickly tucked my hair behind my ear and cringed thinking about what I looked like. Was he ever going to catch me on a good day? Did I have good days?

"Sorry about that. Well, kind of. You looked happy it was me on the phone." His wicked grin earned him forgiveness, but I didn't want him to know I'd been swayed so easily in his favor.

"I was. But you should be sorry—if I had screamed bloody murder, my dad probably would have shot you and asked questions later."

His eyes grew wide when the realization hit him.

"I didn't think about that." He turned around and looked toward the house, then back, satisfied we were alone.

"I'm surprised he didn't come out when you pulled in anyway. He must have fallen asleep in the chair."

"So back to tomorrow. I'd like to pick you up. Dean called and said my SUV will finally be ready tomorrow. I'll take you home whenever you want, but I want to drive."

I didn't see what the big deal was. I knew the roads, and, if given the choice, I'd rather be the driver. He might be a maniac, but, then again, his eyes were so trusting. Big, blue, and honest.

"I don't know," I answered hesitantly. "I know the roads; you don't."

"I'll have to learn sometime—besides, who better to be my first road trip co-pilot?"

He had a point. His co-pilot had a ring to it. Plus, I knew the roads like the back of my hand.

"Does your fancy ride have an input jack for music? I love the radio and Sunny does a great job, but I can't listen to that station all night."

"It does. And I have lots of CDs."

This date was sounding better and better all the time.

"What are you going to cook?" I asked.

"That's kind of what I wanted to talk to you about. Any allergies I need to know about? Any dislikes?"

Had I ever had dinner with a guy? Then again, had I ever been out on an actual date?

This was a little disconcerting. I was almost twenty-seven, and up until that moment, I hadn't realized I'd been missing *anything*. Aside from a few adolescent group dates, I'd never actually been out with a guy.

All of a sudden, I felt inadequate. I didn't know how to act.

Was I supposed to tell him I hated pizza?

Would he try to make pizza?

Should I tell him I hated broccoli?

Was it too soon for that?

Shit. What was I thinking? Too soon for broccoli?

There were too many things I was trying to work through at the same time. Best-case scenario, he was strangely attracted to me and we'd mess around. I was undeniably attracted to him. He was gorgeous and fun, sincere and flirty.

What the hell did he see in me?

I was the daughter of a grease monkey who liked to fish. My hair was always a mess. I barely wore makeup, mostly because I wasn't sure how to use half of the shit. I wore boots, not heels. Jeans, not skirts. I drove a beat-up old Dodge truck.

I wouldn't even fuck me.

Messing around wasn't the best-case scenario; it would have been a miracle.

I bet he's a damn good kisser.

"I don't like pizza," I blurted.

He'd been looking around, but when I spoke, his attention returned to me. "What? Who doesn't like pizza?"

"Me. And I don't like broccoli either."

"So, no broccoli pizza? Got it." Then he winked. A full-on, movie star wink. I think I heard a little bell ding off in the distance somewhere. You know, the sound a wink makes in a Disney movie.

He was the beauty; I was the beast.

"Well, I'm a guy and I can make about seven different things. So it's burgers, spaghetti, tacos, stir-fry, sloppy joes ... I can grill just about anything, or I can make breakfast."

My heart was still thumping to the beat of the *William Tell* Overture after being startled, but the mention of breakfast made the beating twice as fast. And a little more south.

"Breakfast sounds good." Where had that come from? My mouth was working much faster than my brain. A beaming smile broke across his face and his eyes lit up. I clarified, "I mean, I love eating breakfast for supper."

He didn't take the easy path, which led to teasing me for practically saying I'd love to be around for breakfast—or at least that's what I'd secretly meant, but I didn't actually want to say it.

Vaughn tried to hide his amusement, but the gleam in his eyes told me he was enjoying the whole situation.

"I do, too."

"Okay, what time are you picking me up then?"

"What time will you be done with work?"

"Four-thirty or five, maybe a little after. Just depends."

"And how long will it take you to be ready?"

"I don't know—half hour or so?" I looked up into the rafters as if the correct answer was hiding up there. Whatever time I had, surely it wouldn't ever be enough to make myself look like someone he would be with. Then my anxiety bloomed, but it was overpowered by anticipation and excitement.

"All right, I'll be here at six."

Crap. I should have said I needed more time, but who was I kidding? I couldn't wait. And let's face it, he knew what I looked like.

Unless, maybe he wanted the date to start early so it could end early? I hated feeling so insecure. It was completely new to me. I never had a reason to feel like this.

It was scary.

"Well, I interrupted you, so I'll let you get back to it." He glanced at my bench where I was working on a new spinner.

"You'll have to show me how you do that sometime. I don't know much about them, but that looks tricky."

"They are tricky," I said, following his eyes to the shaggy skirt I was attaching to the head of the one I was working on, thinking about how, at the moment, everything felt that way. *Tricky*.

I held it up for him to inspect.

"They're pretty, but they can get 'cha if you're not watching it. Gotta take your time with them."

His face sobered. "That sounds like good advice for lots of things. Take your time and be careful."

He picked it up out of my hand, spun it around, and then placed it back on the workbench. I swallowed a lump of anxiousness, still a little insecure when he was that close.

All of my flaws, or plainness in plain sight.

Our eyes locked, and something in his gaze reminded me that he'd just been through a breakup. And even though he said he was fine with the way things ended with him and Rachelle, it still had to hurt.

I might have been green when it came to relationships, but maybe that was better than experiencing such a terrible one. He didn't seem sad, but my heart still thought of his in that moment.

I cleared my throat and tried to finish what we were talking about. Better yet, I tried to chase away my crazy thoughts, but it was difficult when his blue eyes looked like they were asking so many questions.

"I'm always careful and I have plenty of time."

I stood up, and the space between us shrunk even further. Vaughn didn't move, and in that moment I considered telling him my name and then grabbing his face and kissing him mad.

Then again, I *had* just told him I was fine with taking my time. That may have been a lie.

"Kimberly?" he asked quietly.

God, how I wished that was my name.

I shook my head, feeling my ponytail swing behind me. "Want me to tell you?"

He shook his head, then he squinted and some of his playfulness came back. "You know I don't kiss women when I don't know their name, but I didn't explain myself. I just don't kiss them on the mouth."

I swallowed and my damn legs about failed me. I sat back down on the bar stool so I wouldn't hit the dirt floor.

He stepped closer like he was going to catch me, but I

only fell an inch or two back to the stool.

His hand came up to brace me, but when he realized I'd only sat, it gently touched my face. It was tender and maybe the first time anyone had ever touched me like that.

My eyes fluttered, feeling his hand on my skin, and my lips parted to let out the air that had warmed and expanded in my lungs.

Vaughn leaned in and, like before, his face was so close to mine that I could feel his breath lick across my flesh.

"I want to kiss your lips—so bad—but I want more than that is to know who you are. It's important to me." His fingers moved behind my neck as his nose ran along my ear. "So maybe I'll just kiss you somewhere else."

As I watched him lean in, not daring to stop him or even move, I fixated on his chest moving in and out before me. My eyes closed and my head rolled ever so slightly to the side, inviting him to place his lips wherever the hell he wanted. He moved closer still, until our legs were touching, and his other arm wrapped possessively around my waist.

I didn't know what to do with my hands and I was having a hard time focusing, so they just hung limply at my sides. I was in a trance.

His lips moved against my neck as he spoke slowly, "Maybe I should kiss you here? On your sweet neck?"

He moved unhurriedly to my jaw, still not kissing really, but touching me nonetheless, and I thought I was going to combust. The sensation of him in my space, in my shed. The smell of his clean shirt. How his voice deepened and vibrated against my skin.

"Or your jaw here? But that's so close to your pretty lips. It's too tempting."

I think I whimpered, or whined, or groaned. I can't be sure. I'd never heard that sound come from me. I'm not sure my ears were even working correctly, because the things he was saying sounded like some sort of script from a movie. I didn't know how to process any of it and I sure as hell didn't know how to react.

He must have thought I was mentally deficient, and he wouldn't have been too wrong at the moment.

Then his nearness left and my eyes blinked open to find him looking into me. Like all the way into me.

"I'll figure out your name, O'Fallon. Then I'm going to kiss your pretty little face off. So be ready for it." After he spoke, he pressed his lips against my forehead and lifted my chin so that our eyes met again.

His pupils were dilated, only a fraction of that watery blue visible.

"I'll be here at six tomorrow. Good night," he said, and then he quickly kissed the top of my head and left.

I was frozen to my seat.

Any words I may have tried to say wedged in my throat.

I'd never been an emotional person. I'd always prided myself on handling things with a level head.

Vaughn had, in a few short weeks, changed all that. I was feeling things, emotional things. Massive, unfamiliar things.

I sat out there by myself for a while longer and thought.

I wasn't sure if he'd still be interested in me after he got to know me better. I knew I wasn't likely going to change much, but maybe changing a little wasn't the worst thing in the world.

For the first time, I wanted to impress a man. Not because I wanted his business, or simply to warm my bed, but I wanted a man to desire me, and even if I hated to admit it, I wanted to be treated like I was special. Like I was beautiful.

And, there in that garage, he'd done just that.

I felt, more than anything, that he desired me—all of me—and I craved more of it.

Chapter Ten

Vaughn

I could have just called. Really, all I wanted to know was what she wanted for dinner.

Who was I kidding?

I wanted to see her. After only knowing her for a few short weeks, I missed her.

I was with Rachelle for almost two years and I didn't miss her, at least not like I did O'Fallon, and she was just down the street.

But you know what?

Life is short.

Did I feel strange starting a relationship so soon after Rachelle, moving, and everything that happened? Yes.

But, on the other hand, I didn't.

I wanted O'Fallon.

I wanted to touch her.

I wanted *her* to touch *me.*

I wanted to kiss her and tell her how beautiful I thought she was, and that the time we spent together was never enough.

Something told me she was just as surprised by it as I was. From what she'd told me, she had never been in a relationship. At least not like the one I wanted with her.

I had to figure out her name. Between the look on her face each time we'd almost kissed and the way she reacted to me, it was all I thought about.

I could ask someone in town what her name was, but that would be cheating. Like going behind her back. If she wanted me to know, she'd tell me. I think she liked the game. And, in a way, I did, too.

It was a paradox. I wanted to know, but only on our terms.

As I drove back to my house, after showing up in her barn that night, I imagined what it would be like when it finally happened.

Two things were possible.

One. It would be just as good, if not better, than I imagined.

Two. It was possible that when we kissed she wouldn't feel it like I did.

Something happens to your ego when a woman you love, or think you love, leaves you for someone else. Someone with whom she had already started a relationship with.

It made me think about how she must have compared us. And, the fact was, she hadn't chosen me. There was a little voice inside my head that hinted maybe I wasn't good enough. Maybe I didn't make her happy enough. Maybe I pushed too hard, or came on too strong.

Even though Rachelle said none of those things were the case and that it *just happened,* a man's head would play tricks on him. What if these feelings I was having for O'Fallon were just my way of regaining some of the pride I lost?

I was uncertain. Or maybe I was just nervous. All of this was so different. Thrilling and fun. Learning about her and telling her about myself was gratifying. I didn't feel like there was anything I couldn't tell her.

She was amusing and spirited. Outgoing and one of the most authentic women—hell, people—I'd ever had the pleasure of meeting.

Sometimes when you meet people you wonder: *how are they going to change my life*?

And sometimes when you meet the right person, all you can think is what a privilege it would be to change theirs.

I didn't want to change her, per se. I wouldn't change anything about her, but, rather, how I could make her life better. How I could make her happy.

I pulled in my drive and, unlike when I lived in Cleveland, I didn't second-guess the need to lock my SUV. I honestly didn't need to. No one there even locked their houses when they went out of town. It was the strangest thing.

We didn't really nail down what I'd make for dinner, the only logical reason I'd gone to her house, but at least I had a handle on what she wouldn't like.

As I looked through my refrigerator, I made a mental list of the things I'd need, choosing to not go with breakfast. Maybe another night … or morning.

I also decided that I'd go in a little early, and leave a little early, the next day from work. I was only taking a few patients in the mornings, and then helping with overflow in the afternoons if there was an emergency, so it wouldn't be a problem.

The staff in Dr. Carver's office was great. The receptionist, Julie, was a mom of three and married to her high school sweetheart. There were also a few dental assistants, Cindy and Valerie, who were best friends and kept the atmosphere in the office energetic and full of laughter.

I was a good fit for the practice. Not to brag, but I was kind of a hot commodity in the small town dentistry community. When I began looking for a practice to either join or buy into, like I had with Dr. Carver's, I found that someone with my skills wasn't all that easy to come by.

I was top of my class at the University of Michigan, and extended my education into orthodontics and oral surgery. The kicker was I had experience working with implants, prosthetics, and things of that nature, which made me stand out from your typical general dentist.

I'm not usually cocky, but I kind of had a lot working for me, with respect to my profession.

Finding a place that would feel like home was a more difficult task.

I'd received many great offers, but it had come down to finding the right house in the right town. As it turned out, I loved the bungalow, and the town was turning out to be a great place to live.

The people were friendly and, regardless of their motives, genuinely interested in what was going on in your life. There weren't many, but Wynne had just enough businesses that you really didn't have to leave for much. People waved as you drove by and called you by name when you passed them on the street.

And O'Fallon was there.

Funny how things worked out.

The next morning flew by and I found myself checking the clock almost constantly. I was glad time was on my side and the minutes peeled off at record pace.

"I told Dr. Carver and Julie I'm heading out a little early this afternoon," I said to Cindy and Valerie in the break room, where I found them taking their lunch break together. "I hope that doesn't cause any issue for you guys."

They looked at each other and laughed a little. I wondered what it was like to have a friendship that had lasted as long as theirs.

I had one good friend growing up, a friend or two from high school that I used to run into every now and then, and a few more from college, but other than that, I was solo.

"Whatcha got going on tonight, Dr. Renfro? Hot date?" teased Cindy.

I wasn't sure what to say.

Yes, I did have a hot date, but it felt too personal telling them. It was practically our first official date and I didn't want things getting all over town before O'Fallon was comfortable with it.

Shit, especially until I knew her first fucking name.

Then I realized they probably knew what it was. It was my chance. I could find out and then pretend to guess it sooner than later tonight.

But I couldn't do it.

"I have plans," I said, not going into detail. "I just wanted to make sure you knew and that someone would be here to lock up." I'd been locking up on most nights, since I was trying to get into the groove of the office procedures.

They shared a conspiratorial look and a unison, "mmm-hmm," and then went back to their lunches and conversation.

Just like the morning, the afternoon flew by much the same. Before long, it was three thirty and I was driving to the store.

For as small as Willard's was, surprisingly, they had most everything. The produce was fresh and the meat counter had a great selection. It was just funny that there were only about a dozen parking spots. I smiled to myself as I watched one of the guys who worked there carrying out an elderly lady's bags, just like a Norman Rockwell postcard.

This was a good place to live.

I grabbed a few vegetables, a nice—for Wynne—bottle of red, though I wasn't sure if O'Fallon liked wine. I also picked up Newcastle, which I was sure was a good alternative, just in case.

I found two really nice New York Strips, and was walking down a few of the aisles, checking things out since I had the time. I was glad to find they had deodorant and shaving stuff, and just about anything a man would need. They had general medicines and I was shocked to see they actually carried condoms.

Good to know, but who wanted to buy a box of condoms there?

Plus, I doubted I'd need them. At least not that night. I

wasn't in any hurry to get that physical with O'Fallon, but it did remind me when—and if—things *did* progress that way, I'd need to think about it.

I checked out at one of the two registers they had and grabbed a cold drink out of the cooler nearby.

"So you think you'll be sticking around then?" asked the lady who was ringing me up.

We'd talked briefly last time I was in and she tried to convince me to move back to Cleveland, that Wynne had nothing to offer a handsome, young doctor like myself. I most certainly was staying, but she was completely wrong. Wynne had a lot to offer.

"Of course I'm staying. I like it here."

"Doing some grilling tonight? Weather is right for it." She changed the subject and kept her eyes on what she was doing.

"Yeah, sounded good."

"You got *two* steaks in here?"

These people and their fishing for gossip. They knew just how to dig for information without coming right out and saying, *"What are you doing and who are you doing it with?"*

"They both looked good," I said, evading her probing question.

"You drink Newcastle? Need a bag of ice?"

That wasn't a bad idea, so I replied, "Yes, please." I ignored the Newcastle question.

She put all of my items in bags. Then I saw the same candy bar O'Fallon brought me and grabbed one, adding to my total at the last minute. Judging by the lady's face, it was a move that was a major pain in her ass.

"Will that be all?" she said sarcastically, but giving me a grin to counteract her tone.

"Think so."

"Big plans this weekend? You need help out?"

"I think I'm just going to enjoy the weather, maybe listen to the ball game on Sunday. I think I can manage."

"I'm sure you can, sweetie," she added as I looped the handles of the bags and headed for the automatic doors.

"Come back now," she shouted after me.

I noticed that O'Fallon's truck was missing from the lot at her dad's garage as I drove past. Had she taken off early, too? That thought excited me.

When I got home, I did a quick run through the house. It was easy to keep clean, mainly because I'd spent most of my time outside, working on the landscaping. I'd even pulled out a few bushes in the back that were overgrown, and, frankly, a pain in the ass to mow around.

I took a shower and gave my face a clean shave. Then, for the first time in my life, I stood in front of my closet—in my boxers—trying to decide what to wear.

What in the hell?

In the city, when I'd take a girl out, I'd wear nice pants and a button up shirt. Here it was all different. We weren't really going *out*. I'd look stupid if I dressed like that to cook on the grill and drive around on dirt roads.

Opting out of the more typical date options, I chose to wear jeans, a nice T-shirt, and I grabbed a zip-up hoodie. It was almost May and plenty warm during the day, but the nights could still get kind of cool.

It was only about five by then and I noticed time had slowed considerably, compared to that morning. I kept myself busy by bringing a pair of the Adirondack chairs from the front porch around to the back deck so we could hang out back there—together—while the food was on the grill. I filled the cooler with the ice and beer, chilled the wine in the refrigerator, cut up the vegetables, seasoned every last one, and wrapped them in foil. I put the steaks in the marinade I'd found on the shelf at the market, and then I looked at the clock again.

Only five twenty. *Dammit.*

I tried to calculate how long it would take me to get to her house, even though I knew it was probably only about two minutes.

Then I had a thought, what if she wanted to stop somewhere on the tour tonight? I quickly went into the living room, pulled the blanket off the back of the couch, and grabbed a few of the throw pillows.

I'd be lying if I denied that just the mere thought of lying on the ground under a sky full of stars—with O'Fallon—didn't get me halfway hard. Thoughts of her often had that effect on me. I was half-hard half of the day, every day since I'd moved here.

And being around her? Forget it. I was a walking, talking erection.

I threw the blanket and pillows in the back of the Escalade.

But I still had thirty minutes.

I sat out back and decided it was as good of a time as any to have my first beer. If anything, it might calm me down.

From the time I'd woken up, until that minute on the back deck with my first cold Newcastle of the night, I'd been anticipating our date.

Our first date.

Me and … Sarah?

Me and … Allison? Megan? Rebecca?

I said a silent prayer that I'd get it. That some omniscient power would show mercy and it would just suddenly come to me.

The sooner the better.

Then, finally, it was time to go pick her up.

Chapter Eleven

Mutt

I took off work at noon. I couldn't focus, and the time was moving about as fast as Highway 106 during harvest. Slow and aggravating.

I'd called Sunny that morning, needing something to wear. Sure, we were just hanging out at his house and then going for a drive, but I didn't feel like wearing my raggedy old jeans and faded shirts. I wanted to look like a woman who might almost pass for someone Vaughn could be interested in.

He was college educated—and so was I, but an online business degree wasn't quite the same.

He was a doctor. Best I could describe it, I was the bookkeeper for my grease monkey dad.

I didn't have many shoes that didn't have laces. Why in the hell didn't I own a pair of slip on shoes? Well, I did, but flip-flops weren't sexy.

I wanted to be sexy, and for him to know I was trying. You know an E for effort?

Mostly, I wanted to know if I was good enough for him. If I'd ever be.

There was something about the way he pushed me out of my comfort zone, yet at the same time made me feel safe and comfortable enough to not push back. No one I'd ever met fostered that type of reaction from me. No one had ever acted like they could see that, maybe deep down, there was more to me than just Mutt. And, if that was true, I wanted to let him find out because then I'd know, too.

I considered texting him my name so he'd kiss me first off that night because then I could chill the fuck out. I'd been a walking ball of electricity all day. Everything I touched seemed to zap me, and I knew the only thing that would give any relief to my nervous system was him.

I needed to kiss him. I wanted to yesterday, but today … it was crucial to my sanity.

"I can't believe you guys are hanging out. This is huge, Mutt!" shrieked Sunny when I showed up at her house, which sat right behind the radio station.

I'd called her that morning to see if she'd be home since I needed to raid her closet and beg her to help me look like—well, a better version of myself.

I wasn't ugly. I was okay.

My body wasn't anything to pin up in a calendar, but I looked healthy. So what if there were a few extra pounds around my hips? As far as I knew there wasn't a whole lot you could do about that. My stomach was flat and I had boobs. More than I'd ever ask for on most days, but they stayed where I put them, so I wasn't complaining.

Although she was a little shorter than I was, Sunny and I were luckily about the same size.

"I know. I'm freaking out," I said in earnest. "He's so hot." This was a situation that was completely new. I'd never chased a man before, and even if I wasn't exactly *chasing* him, I *was* trying to catch him. And that was another reason I needed her help.

"I saw him driving the other day, but that's about it. So what's he like?" she asked as we walked through her small house into her bedroom, Andy Two hot on our heels.

I plopped down on her unmade bed and covered my face with my hands.

"I don't know. He's weird and smart and funny." Then I moved one of my hands to make eye contact with her, hoping it would help explain better. Then I added, "And he's sexy as a motherfucker. He told me he wants to kiss me, but he won't until he knows my first name."

She threw up her hands and scrunched her eyebrow. "So, Mutt, tell him your fuckin' name."

"I know, but now it's kind of this flirting thing we have going on where he guesses … and his face … and, oh my God, what am I doing?"

She straight up laughed at me. The kind that howled and cackled. The kind where she bent over, and with both hands, she did a drum solo on my ass.

"Mutt likes a guy!" she sang. "This is awesome. Okay, so what's your plan?"

"What's my plan? I don't have a plan. I need something to wear, and I could use some tips on how to hide that I'm a freak for not knowing how to act on a date."

"Well, you guys *have* hung out, you said, so just keep

acting like yourself. Plus, he's still guessing your name, so there's that. Obviously he likes you, too. Although, I have no idea why." She winked and then opened the doors to her closet.

I had no idea why either. That was another thing that was making me crazy.

"What are you guys doing again?"

"He's picking me up at six and making me dinner at his house. Then he asked if I could show him around Wynne, like a little road trip around the outside of town."

"Okay, I think you should wear a dress." Her eyes lit up.

What in the description of our plans made her think dress?

"No."

"Why not?"

"Because we're just riding around."

"Smart. Don't give it all away on the first date. Keep some mystery." She tapped her finger against her lips in thought.

"No, that's not it. I just don't want to wear one. I think I walk funny in dresses."

"You walk funny in jeans, your argument is invalid."

"Whatever. What else?"

"Okay, you can wear jeans, but they need to hug your ass. None of those old Levi's you wear." She moved a few hangers around and pulled off a pair of dark blue jeans that looked like they'd only fit around one of my legs.

"Now we need a top. Do you own a strapless bra?"

I didn't. Why didn't I have a strapless bra?

"No. I don't think so." Disapproving of my obviously shitty inventory of undergarments, she shook her head at me. Then she paused and ran into her bathroom.

"Does this fit your boobs? I bought it a while back, but it was a little big. If it fits you, it's yours."

I sat up holding the new bra.

"Are you serious?" Sunny was really saving my ass. I could have kissed *her*. After all, she did know my name.

"Yeah, I'm serious, go make sure it fits before I pick your top."

I jumped up and ran into her bathroom. I threw off my T-shirt and unhooked my bra. I fastened the strapless one in front and then spun it around as I pulled it up and over my boobs.

"It fits!"

"Oh my God. You're going to be so hot in this," she said as I returned, having put my clothes back on. She tossed a really pretty silver knit tube top onto her bed. It was almost white at the top and it faded into a shimmery silver at the bottom. I'd never worn something like that. I had a swimming suit cover up that was strapless, but other than that, I usually had straps, or sleeves, for that matter.

"I don't know, Sunny." I was suddenly even more nervous.

What if the clothes made me uncomfortable and I was more awkward than usual? Oh God, what if it fell down? Or I did something wrong and my tit flew out?

She sat next to me as I folded the jeans and the top.

"Do you like him?"

"Yes," I confessed.

"Do you want to look special tonight? Not that how you look every day isn't special, but Mutt, you'll look so good tonight in this outfit. And here," she popped up and grabbed her white jean jacket out of the closet, "you can wear this over the top, that way you won't be cold. And it'll cover up your shoulders. You can just slip it off when you're eating or something. Trust me."

She was sincerely trying to help me, and she always looked so nice and put together. Not overdone, but fashionable. If there was anyone I trusted to tell me if I looked like a weirdo, it would be her.

"I do want to look special tonight. It's our first real date. Fuck, it's my first *real* date, period."

"See. This is something he sure as hell will remember you wearing." She chuckled a little and added, "And if you like wearing it, maybe then you'll want to go shopping with me in Browning next time I go." Then she clapped her hands and shrieked again.

She was really excited. On the inside I was too, but on the outside it was like my skin was going to rattle right off my bones from the nerves.

"What about your hair?"

"What should I do?" If I was committing to her vision of a *special* me tonight, I might as well go all in.

"I think you should wear it down. I like it when you let it dry all wavy. It's really pretty like that." Well, hell, that was easy. Inside I felt a little bit of pride in knowing that it was natural—just me—and she liked it.

"Really, just let it go?"

"Yeah, I would spend a lot of money for the way your hair looks when you do it like that. No ponytail. Not tonight. You always do that, let it dry, and then wad it up on your head. Leave it alone tonight. And I say keep your makeup simple too. You have great skin and pretty eyes.

Just some smoky eyeliner and mascara and some tinted gloss.

"I don't have tinted gloss." I could probably manage the mascara, but smoky eyes? I doubted I'd look much different than a raccoon. "And show me how to do that eyeliner."

She gave me a toothy smile and clutched her hands over her heart. "Mutt, I'm so excited for you. He must be something special if you like him. He better be a nice guy."

"I think he is."

I hoped I wasn't wrong, but what were the odds of people staying, long term, with their first *real* date?

Slim to none.

Still, I wasn't a pussy. I wasn't afraid to tackle something head on. Putting myself out there for him was dangerous, but deep down I knew it would also be a risk worth taking.

After she showed me how to do the eyeliner—which she said gave me fuck face, but in a good way—she gave me a few different gloss options, shoes, and some perfume I'd always liked.

I went home feeling like maybe, just maybe, he'd like what he saw. If nothing else, he'd have to notice I'd tried to put a little work into it.

I still had a lot of time, and my dad would be at the shop for hours, so I went home and took a long bath, making a point to shave my legs all the way to the tops, and trimmed a few other things. I spent a little more time washing my hair and let the conditioner sit in it longer than I normally did.

As the warm water calmed my nervous muscles, my mind drifted to the night before when his breath was in my ear and his hand on my neck. His lips had been wet and warm, and when he moved them I could feel a coolness where he'd previously been. Like he'd stamped me with his touch.

The way his eyes looked heavy and luminous all at the same time. The way he smelled, and the light scratch of his stubble across my cheek.

What was that saying? Don't go out with a loaded gun?

Well, I doubt it was the same for girls, but I didn't take any chances. For the first time, I touched myself and thought of a man I knew in real life. Not a movie star or singer. A real live person who'd asked me out on a date. It wasn't the first time I'd brought myself to climax, but it was the first time I wished it was Vaughn.

I took my time, applying lotion to every square inch of my body, I pulled all of the out-of-line eyebrows I saw, and I even used a face mask that came in a basket I won at the High School Christmas Bazaar last winter.

It was the single most feminine day of my life. Even before I put the clothes on, I felt good about myself.

The jeans fit like a second skin, but they didn't cut me in half at the waist, so I was happy for that. The shirt fit my curves perfectly and it was actually really flattering. Maybe I *would* go shopping with Sunny next time she drove the hour and a half to Browning.

By five o'clock I was ready. Not only that, I was fucking early.

I paced the house, hoping Dad would stop somewhere after work and miss me leaving. I wrote him a note explaining where I was. Not that he would have said a word, because he knew I could hold my own, but it was strange for me to be gone with my truck still in the drive. I always drove myself.

The note was short and sweet.

Dad,

I'll be out until later. I left my truck here. Love you.

Mutt

Then, after taking one too many laps around my house, walking upstairs to my bathroom over four times to check that I'd done the smoky eyes just right and that my gloss was on straight, I decided to hell with it and cracked a beer. I sat on my porch waiting for him to pick me up. It was just me, Newcastle, and the almost deafening internal prayers that he'd guess my name the second he got there.

At five minutes until six, my dad never showing up, there was a flutter in my stomach as I saw his big, black SUV coming down the lane. I ran inside and grabbed my phone, some cash, shoved the lip gloss in my pocket, and put my empty bottle in the trash.

Just as he was pulling in, I was coming down the steps towards the driveway. The evening sun was a bitch this time of day on the way out to our place, and he had Aviator shades on. Sunglasses looked sexy as hell on him.

The windows were rolled down throughout the vehicle, and I could hear the thumping of some tune on his radio.

He leaned over, seeing that I was already headed his

way, raised his glasses to get a look at me, and the finest smile I'd ever seen crossed his face.

"Kathy? Felicia? Nadine? Melissa?"

Well, he wasn't anywhere close, but he was guessing so I thought that was confirmation my outfit really did look okay.

"Nope. Dammit." I hopped in the passenger side. My hand went to the console for support as I lifted into the seat.

His hand covered mine and gave it a little squeeze.

"Hi," I said, with a smile I couldn't have left at home if I wanted to. "You're punctual."

"You're lucky I wasn't early. I haven't known what to do with myself for the last hour," he said as he backed out of my drive.

"I would have been ready. I've already had a beer."

He looked at me like I'd just told him his head was on fire. "Are you kidding me? I wish I'd known that. I would have come earlier. I just had one, too."

I liked hearing he was at least a little anxious or excited about our night. It put me at ease somewhat, and I let my body relax into the plush leather seat.

"This is a really nice car," I told him as I looked at all of the cool features. The coolest thing my truck had was a pedal on the floorboard that let me dim my brights. Oh, and it sounded like it had glasspacks, even though it was just the deteriorating muffler that was in need of a change.

"Thanks, I like it. I always liked having bigger vehicles when I was driving in the city. They feel safer."

"I wouldn't know what the hell to do in real traffic." The worst I'd ever driven in was Browning, but that wasn't like a major city or anything; they only had four lanes. "The most traffic you'll find here is during the summer carnival. We have a car show and that draws a crowd. But still, it's nothing to freak about."

"You get used to it. When's that summer thing?"

"Not until Memorial Day weekend. So end of the month."

"Do you go?"

"I go for the food." He looked at me as he pulled into his drive. "I love corndogs."

"Do they have those lemonade things?"

"Lemon Shakeups? Uh, yeah. They're awesome. Good with vodka, too."

He turned off the ignition and we both climbed out. I walked slowly to the front of the vehicle, waiting on him.

"You look really good," he said and reached his hand out to hold mine. "Come on."

I didn't hesitate, because I didn't want it to seem like a big deal.

But it was.

It was huge.

The biggest, hugest fucking deal that had happened all day.

He walked behind me as we climbed the five or six steps on his back deck. Then he said, "Really, really good."

Chapter Twelve

Vaughn

O'Fallon didn't look different, exactly, but there were small alterations, and she had a new glow about her I hadn't seen before. There was a sway in the way she walked—and Christ, those jeans.

Those damn jeans.

That ass.

Holy God.

"Jennifer? Chelsea? Samantha?" I guessed as she walked ahead through the back door into my kitchen.

"Keep trying."

I wasn't going to be defeated. I was going to get her name that night. Or I'd be waving the white flag of surrender, and praying she didn't hold it against me. Unless she wanted to *literally* hold it against me, then I'd have to reconsider.

"Still don't want a hint?" she asked, leaning on my island.

Then she saw the candy bar, and subtly picked it up in recognition and aimed it at me before setting it back down. I winked at her, acknowledging that she was pleased I'd remembered the kind she liked.

Tell me your name and I'll share it with you.

"Not yet, but I have to be getting close. Want some wine or a beer?"

"I'll take a beer. Need me to do anything?"

I opened the back door and pulled two beers from my cooler, placing them both on the counter, and I reached behind her for the magnetic bottle opener stuck to my refrigerator.

"I don't think so. I just need to warm up the grill. Everything else is ready to go."

"What are we having?"

"Steak and grilled vegetables." Her smile was all the approval I needed.

I could hardly keep my eyes off of her. Her hair looked so soft, her lips so kissable. Her eyes were sucking the willpower right out of me.

"Nicole?"

"I think you've already guessed that one." She laughed. "You can give up whenever you want."

As she spoke, she leaned forward a little and looked down at the counter. How could a woman who was competent in so many interesting ways be so insecure in these situations?

It didn't matter. I liked that she was independent, and I totally dug the fact that she let me see her look vulnerable, too.

"Carry my beer out and I'll bring the rest?"

She did what I asked and I grabbed the two dishes out of the fridge that had all of my prepped food, ready for the flames.

Again, my eyes found her ass and I realized whether I got to kiss her or not was irrelevant. I could just look at her and be satisfied.

For now.

"I broke my right arm, too," she admitted as we ate, sharing stories of old battle wounds. "Pins?"

"No. Clean break." I took a long swallow of my beer, and decided it was my last.

"Two here, and two up here," she explained as she pulled at the shoulder of the white jacket she was wearing. Her bare shoulder showed off a patch of copper freckles and a collarbone that made my pants tight. There was something so sensual about it, but I wasn't sure why.

I adjusted myself quickly and started packing up our dinner dishes.

"No, let me." She stood and smacked my hand away. "You cooked. I'll clean this up."

"It wasn't really cooking, it was the grill."

"Good, then even less for me to wash."

She put our napkins and silverware on the plates, and I noticed she hadn't eaten any of the zucchini in the vegetables. I didn't say anything. She didn't show any mercy on her steak, though, but neither had I.

Some of my best grilling to date.

"But you can come in and talk to me," she offered as she stacked the plates on top of each other.

I followed like a puppy.

She ran water in the sink and rinsed off the dishes, while I cleaned up the counter and noticed how much I liked having her there with me. And how already I didn't have very many memories in that house without her in them.

When she stopped by that first day, when I was unpacking and trying to get my things situated, it was nice having someone else there. Having her advice on paint and telling me where the furniture would look best was welcome help.

It was changing. I was feeling things much stronger than I had in those first few days. I wasn't just curious about her, I was starting to learn some things. We were getting to know each other, and in some ways it seemed like I was the only one she'd ever been able to relax around. On more than one occasion she'd said that she'd never told anyone this or that. She didn't have to put up a front with me. She was just herself.

I hated the thought that she'd been kind of alone in the past, but I reveled in the idea it was me she'd chosen to take a chance on.

That fact alone made me realize this wasn't just a slow build to sex, it was the beginning of the kind of relationship I'd always wanted. One created from friendship. One that would hold stronger because of a solid foundation. I wanted to protect that.

It wasn't the help or the input she provided anymore. It was the *her* she added to my space when she was in it. Because if the past week proved anything, it was different there when she was gone.

"I hope you have plenty of gas. No pretending to run out with me. I'm smarter than that," she warned as she loaded the dishwasher.

"Full tank."

"Good."

She bent over again and my mouth went dry.

"Leslie?" I started throwing names out again. "Deanna? Gloria? Elizabeth? Katherine?"

"Sorry, Charlie … but Elizabeth *was* my grandma's name." She tugged on her bottom lip with her teeth, like she was debating with herself if that was close enough.

"But you weren't named after her, huh?"

"It's my middle name," she admitted, her eyebrows rising hopefully. I liked knowing she wanted me to get it right as much as I did—or at least it felt that way. Still, Elizabeth wasn't her first name and that's what I was after.

It wasn't too much to ask to know the name of the woman you were starting to fantasize about on a regular basis.

"My middle name is Conrad."

"Vaughn Conrad Renfro. Sounds regal." The way she repeated it was like she was announcing a king. Her hand did this little flourish thing out to her side before she curtsied.

"You *do* know that I'm a billionaire, right?"

She straightened, her eyes as wide as saucers.

"Are you fucking serious?" She was so fun to play with.

"No, but if I was I bet you'd tell me your name."

I leaned on the island counter, facing her as she leaned against the sink.

"That's not true. It has nothing to do with money." She looked down, like I'd seen her do many times before when she was about to say something that made her a little uncomfortable. "And I'll tell you my name whenever you want." Her eyes lifted to mine, and inside of them swam curiosity and temptation and something else that I couldn't put my finger on.

Before the moment got too heavy, and I broke down, we needed to keep moving. Otherwise, I'd kiss her. First names be damned, and I would be breaking my word.

"How about you hop that knockout body up in my passenger seat and introduce me to Wynne? That way I don't have to ask gas station Donnie how to get to you."

The seriousness in her face was replaced by a jovial smile.

Have I mentioned how nice her teeth were?

If I haven't, I'll let you know that her smile was almost flawless. Pretty white teeth, the perfect bite. To anyone else, it might just be a nice smile, but to me—a dentist—it was like mouth porn.

Well, mouth porn is something else, but you know what I mean.

"Okay, so here's the school, if you go to the right it'll take us out to a bunch of gravel roads and farms, if you go left we can either go out to the river or it'll take us a different way out to the lake."

I stopped at the sign and since I didn't have a preference, I said, "You're the co-pilot."

“Okay, let’s go right and I can show you how it loops around back by my house.”

I loved hearing stories about the places we passed. There was O’Fallon family history everywhere. The area was beautiful, but it was the overwhelming sense of community I’d been craving all my life. Where everyone fit, and people helped one another. Where everyone *belonged*.

As she talked about one place or another, it was obvious I’d made the right decision about moving there. For a second, as I looked at her flipping through songs, I realized how lucky I’d been to meet her, too.

We listened to the music I had on my phone, and it was crazy how she hadn’t heard most of the songs I had. She seemed to like them. I saw her looking at the titles and the bands, and then saving some in her phone.

The Escalade handled the terrain well as she showed me where the creek sometimes washed out the road, mentioning for me to be careful if it’s raining—if I was ever out that way.

Most of the farms were squared off and it made a sort of grid that all led back to a road headed to her house, past mine, and back into town.

When we got near her house, and the wye it sat on, she said, “Turn left. This is how you get to the bluffs.” As she pointed, my hand instinctively reached out for hers and I laced our fingers together, placing them on the console between our seats.

“I like it when you do that.”

“Do what?” I asked, hoping it was the hand thing. I always wanted to touch her, and since this was all so new to both of us, I had been taking every opportunity that night to hold her hand when the occasion presented itself.

Something caught her eye, distracting her away from her train of thought. "Look over there. See the deer?" I followed her gaze, and although the sun was setting, I could see the silhouettes of two deer running through a pasture.

"Have you ever been hunting, Vaughn?"

I hadn't.

"No," I answered weakly. I didn't mind the idea of others doing it, and I knew that in rural communities it was a big part of life, but it wasn't for me. I didn't think.

"That's okay. I go, but I don't really like the killing part. I usually only use one tag. That's all I need. Most of the time I let my dad or Dean use my other tags. And, don't tell, but I don't care for deer meat." She sounded like she was confessing to something way worse than an opinion on wild game.

"I won't tell."

"It's funny. I don't mind cleaning fish. I could eat them every day." She sat proudly next to me, head high. "I can fish circles around just about anyone, too. That's my thing."

"Yeah, those fishhooks looked pretty cool."

"Lures. They're lures, or flies, depending on what you're using." I didn't know what she was talking about. Most of it sounded like Greek, but the way she talked candidly about something she loved sounded like a song, and I turned the music down a little so I wouldn't miss a single word. She rambled and chirped on and on about what worked best for which fish and what season you could find them. It was easy to tell she was passionate about it.

"So what do you do? What's your Vaughn thing?"

I had to think about it. I didn't really have a thing. At one time I liked golf, and I still did, but it wasn't something

I got ramped up about. Not like she had about fishing anyway.

"I don't know. I think I need to find something."

"If you turn this way it'll take you up to Johnston's Chute. You came from town on this highway."

Was that a hint? Did she want to go down to the Chute? To her cabin?

"Um, which way?"

Her phone buzzed and she looked at it, then answered. "Hey, Sally, what's up?"

With no cars in sight, I put it in park at the four-way stop and waited for her. I messed with my phone so it didn't seem like I was eavesdropping, but she was sitting right there so it was kind of hard not to.

"He is? Shit. Yeah, I can be right there." Then she listened for a little bit and rested her head back on the seat and looked at the top of the cab. "I'm sorry. I'll be right there. Don't let him leave."

O'Fallon hung up and dropped her phone between her legs, then ran her fingers over her temples like she was irritated.

"I'm sorry to cut this short, but do you mind taking me back to my house?" All of the fun, carefree excitement from earlier was gone from her voice.

"Sure, that's no problem. Is everything okay?"

She looked straight ahead and began to talk. "That was Sally. She owns a bar in town. She said my dad was drunk and didn't want him driving home. She called to let me know it was probably a good idea if I came and got him."

I didn't know what to say. It wasn't my business to pry, but she'd never mentioned her dad had a drinking problem or anything like that, and I hoped it wasn't something that happened on a regular basis.

She didn't return her hand to mine and it sucked. She leaned over against her door and looked out the window as I pulled out in the direction of town.

"Hey, I have room in here. I'll go with you. We can pick him up. It's actually quicker than going all the way out to your house first." It was a long shot, but maybe it would mean it wasn't the end of our night.

"No, I don't want you to have to deal with all of that."

"It's no trouble. We'll just go pick him up." My hand crept over to her leg and I found myself gently rubbing it. "I don't want to take you home yet."

She turned to look at me—finally—as we topped the hill and the town's lights came into view.

"Really? You don't mind? He doesn't usually drink that much. I'm not sure what his deal is."

"No. Not in the least. It won't take that long. He probably just had a few too many. It happens."

Then she picked up my hand and pressed a sweet kiss to the top of it and said, "Thank you."

I knew where Sally's was because I'd driven past it every day on the way to the office. It sat on the square, and when I saw how many cars were outside, I turned down the alley to see if there was a place to park.

She looked embarrassed and thanked me three more times before we ever got to the front of the building. As we rounded the brick wall, we saw Dean helping her dad out.

"Hey, what's going on?" O'Fallon shouted as she ran over to them. I followed, but I didn't want to interrupt.

"I just got here," Dean said to her. "Sally said you were

on your way to get him, but I figured I could drop him off. I was going to see if you were home anyway." Then his eyes landed on me.

"No, I was out," she said and turned to me. "Vaughn and I were riding around."

"Hey, kid," her dad said, lifting his head, obviously wasted.

"Dad, what happened?"

"Nothing. I'm fine," he spoke slowly.

"You're not fine. Look at you. Dean is helping you stand up."

"I'll take him home," Dean offered as he looked at me.

I would almost bet money he had a thing for O'Fallon. From the way she'd spoken about him, I knew they were close. And, as I watched him look her up and down, noticing that she looked different than usual, I was territorial.

Funny, she never seemed to pick up on it. Or at least she never acted like she did.

"Are you sure you don't mind?"

Dean shook his head. "Nah, I'll get him in the house. He's done it for me I don't know how many times."

O'Fallon looked like she wasn't sure what to do, but since Dean really was holding her dad up and her dad was a big guy, it actually was better if Dean took him. She would have been hard pressed to get him home alone. Selfishly, I was glad that maybe we still had more time.

"All right. There's ibuprofen in the cabinet in the downstairs bathroom. Can you give him a few and a Sprite or something? He's going to feel like shit tomorrow."

"Consider it done."

"Thanks, Dean. Dad, go home and go to bed."

"I'm going to bed," he slurred. "All by myself. Night, Astro."

"Goodnight, Mr. O'Fallon," I replied.

Dean walked him across the street to his truck, and we watched until they were both in and he was pulling out.

"Well, we're here. Want to get a beer?" I asked. Might as well take advantage.

She rolled her eyes, embarrassed at the situation, then said, "Yeah. Maybe two." Some of that spark she had was back.

Chapter Thirteen

Mutt

What a weird night.

It all seemed like a dream. One of those really strange dreams you wake up from thinking *what the hell*?

From what I was wearing.

To who I was with.

Sitting passenger.

My dad drunk at the bar.

Dean showing up.

It was one peculiar night.

And to top it off, he still hadn't guessed my name. Even with all of those other things to think about, him kissing me was at the front of my mind, overshadowing everything.

I was happy he didn't dress up a lot. He wore nice jeans and a heather grey, V-neck T-shirt. He sure did like those kinds of shirts, and I wasn't complaining about them either. I liked that I could see more of his chest. He wasn't a muscle-bound hunk of a man, but the way the sleeves of his shirt fit snugly against his arms … it was almost torture riding with him.

We walked into the bar and I saw Sally first.

"Hey, Mutt. Did you see Dean outside? He's taking your dad home. I didn't see him come in until after we hung up."

"Yeah, I saw them. What was my dad drinking?"

"I think he was just having beer. I didn't realize he'd been here that long. I got here about eight."

I walked up to the bar and Vaughn followed. He did that thing with his hand on my back that made me feel like I was short of breath.

It was uncanny how my body responded to him.

"Who's your friend?" she asked.

I looked behind me and Vaughn was already stretching his other hand out to shake hers.

"I'm Vaughn. I'm taking over for Dr. Carver when he retires at the end of the year."

"Oh, the new, hot dentist everyone is creaming over. Nice to meet 'cha." She was a bartender and didn't even pretend to give a shit what anyone thought.

I heard him chuckle a little before he said, "Well, I'm the new dentist anyway."

"What are you drinking?"

"Two Newcastles," I said and reached for the money I'd shoved into my back pocket earlier.

When Vaughn saw what I was doing he tried to push my hand away.

"No, you're not buying my drink. Let me." He looked serious, but hell if I cared. He was about to help me get my drunk dad home, he'd made an awesome steak, and suffered through me talking about fishing for what could have been thirty miles.

"Shut up," I told him quietly, hoping to convey my gratitude. "You can get the next round."

I placed my hand on his chest, just briefly. I wasn't sure why, it just went there on its own.

Then as I turned back around to hand Sally the money, he said low in my ear, "Tammy? Wendy?" He was close enough to me that the rumble of his chest vibrated against my back as he spoke.

Come hell or high water, I was kissing him by the end of the night.

Before too long, he'd bought the next round—and the next and the next—and we'd found two stools at the bar when a few people cleared out. It was kind of slow for a Friday night. The other bar around the corner probably had a band or something going on, must be why there were so many cars in town.

In Wynne, there were enough people to fill a bar, but it was a much better place for having two. If you didn't want to see someone, just head for the other. I wasn't much of a barfly, Sunny could be at times, but I did like going out every now and then. It was nice being at—what I was guessing was—the quieter watering hole that night.

It allowed Vaughn and me to keep talking, which let me look at him all I wanted. Had it been louder in there, preventing conversation, I would have defaulted to staring and looked more desperate than I probably did anyway.

Because I *was* desperate.

With every breath, my chest drew to his. We faced each other on the stools and our legs mingled and bumped, sporadically at first, then my foot was on his chair and our thighs met denim to denim in between us.

"So that's what my first extraction was like," he admitted at the end of his story about the first time he'd pulled someone's tooth. He took a drink from his bottle and, like I was learning he did often after a swig, did this sexy pucker with his lips, reminding me of a kiss.

Fucking beer bottles have *all* the fun.

"I don't think I could do it. I'd be too afraid I was going to hurt someone."

"You get used to that part. You start to trust the medicine—most of the time. After you see how numb someone would have to be, getting their teeth ripped out and still looking at you like *are you going to start yet*, but not feeling a thing, you begin to worry less."

I needed to change the topic. With beer bottles getting to touch him and talking about mouths, I was finding it hard to focus on what he was saying. Only that his lips were moving.

As close as we were sitting, I could smell him and see how long his eyelashes were. On his chiseled, clean-shaven face, with all the power in his jaw, the lashes added something of a gentleness to his otherwise very masculine features.

"One more?" he asked, but he already held his hand up, showing two fingers to Sally down the bar.

One more? How was time going that fast? Looking at my phone I saw that it was already eleven thirty.

Suddenly a rush of apprehension warned me—it could all end before it got good. I needed a minute to get my shit together.

“I’ll be right back.” I excused myself to go to the bathroom. I needed to have a moment. It was hard to think when he was that close.

I wasn’t some flaky girl. I was a woman. And I wanted *him*. I could wait for him all night, all month—if I had to. But I didn’t want to. I wasn’t that patient.

In the one-person bathroom, I looked in the mirror and gave myself a little pep talk.

You look good tonight.

You’re both having fun.

He likes you. Stop wasting time.

Go out there and just tell him your damn name.

I washed my hands and cockily ripped the paper towel from the dispenser.

“That’s right,” I cheered myself on, giving myself one last quick look in the mirror.

I could have used more lip gloss, but—being optimistic—I thought he probably wouldn’t want that all over him in a few minutes.

When I walked out of the ladies’ room, I heard before I saw Randy and Seth, town buffoons, trying to get Sally to sell them a few beers. But since bar time was always fast, it was already last call and I must have missed it in the bathroom.

“I already called it, boys. Besides, Les called from down the street and said he had to ask you two to leave. Can’t you guys just go out and not cause trouble?” She teased, since what she said was true, because they were generally okay guys, but assholes when they were drunk. They never picked on me much, but when they did I always wanted to knock their skulls together.

They claimed it was harmless. They were always just joking. But on more than one occasion, I'd seen people snap after too much. And when they had bellies full of too much beer, too much could happen.

"Sally, his beer's full. We'll take our last call, too," Randy hollered down the bar from Vaughn. "Hey, you're that dentist," he added as Sally caved and handed over a pair of bottles.

"Nice to meet you." Vaughn lifted his beer in introduction.

Seth slapped Randy playfully in the arm as I walked up to them.

"I don't know why you'd ever want to move here. I heard your wife dumped ya because you were moving here. *Smart girl.*"

"Real nice, Seth," I said as I sat on the stool. Vaughn half coughed, half laughed. I gave him a sideways glance and he looked like he was just going to let it roll off of him.

"Oh my God," Randy shouted. "Is that Mutt? You've been to the groomers!" He laughed, as did Seth, and, all of a sudden, I didn't really feel like that last beer. They were harmless, but they were also pricks and it had been a really great night.

I rolled my eyes and turned to Vaughn.

His face was serious and his eyes were raging, a ticking in his jaw told me he hadn't appreciated the slam.

"Let's go," I said quietly, hoping they'd stop after I didn't come back with anything. Vaughn's eyes met mine and I tried to convey that it didn't bother me, and that I was okay. He looked deep into me, and with that one look, made me feel more protected than I'd ever felt in my life.

Over my shoulder I heard Seth say, "Hell, I'd even walk her around town if she wore those jeans."

Vaughn peered behind me and his jaw ticked. The serious look he shot them was almost menacing.

I'd seen the two assholes get into fights before, but that wasn't what they were after. They were just townies who got their rocks off making others feel as shitty as they did. Both of them were divorced, and both of them had kids they never saw. Compared to most, *they* were the two biggest jokes within twenty miles.

He ran a hand through his hair a few times and scooted his stool back as he stood. He appeared inches taller than before, and his chest was puffed. Sexy as it was, I had no time for the altercation I knew was brewing.

I had only one card.

I leaned in, pressing my hand against his chest once again, and whispered, "My name is Hannah."

What I confessed stole his attention, just like I hoped it would. He looked from them to me and back to them, like he was trying to decide which statement to address first. Their dickhead comments, or the key to turning this night from great to … well … kissing.

Quickly, he pulled a bill from his wallet and tossed it on the bar, tipping Sally for the service and paying for our last beers, which unfortunately, went to waste. Then he grabbed my hand and led me toward the door. He didn't say anything, but I could feel the power of his presence as we walked past the pair of knuckle draggers.

"You know I've heard that advice too, Seth," Randy said as we hit the door. "If a woman breaks your heart, you're better off just getting a dog. And look, he went and found himself a mutt, good for him."

It was all so fast, and I spun with the force as Vaughn turned on his heel and punched Randy right in the mouth.

He didn't even let go of my hand.

Seth howled with laughter. "He fucking knocked you one!"

Randy bent over, holding his mouth. Then smiled and wiggled his tooth with first his tongue and then his finger. "What the hell. You damn near knocked my tooth out."

Then Vaughn spoke, his voice rich with promise and threat. "If I ever hear you talking about her like that again, I'll knock them all out." Then he turned us back toward the door, saying on the way through it, "Come in on Monday and I'll fix that tooth."

I was impressed.

I was surprised.

I was turned on like I'd never been before.

My mind raced as he briskly walked us around the building in the direction of where we'd parked his SUV. I wondered if he'd kiss me good night now since he knew my name.

Then I wondered if, with all that happened, if maybe he forgot I'd told him.

I didn't have to think about it anymore because he was wrapping his arms around me and walking us backward to the brick wall, almost carrying me.

I paddled like hell to the top of my consciousness so that I could fully appreciate what was happening.

"What are you doing?"

We stopped when his hand stopped my back from slamming into the surface of the brick. With his other hand he pulled me closer, and he lowered himself just enough to press himself against my middle.

"I don't like it when people call you Mutt."

"I don't like it when you know my name but aren't kissing me yet."

"Your name's Hannah?"

I had to think a second to remember, my heart beating so loud he might have caught that it answered yes in Morse code for me.

"I think so."

"Hannah," he said, his face nearing, closer and closer our lips got. "I've wanted to kiss you so damn bad." Face to face, his nose brushed mine and I could already taste him.

"Then shut up and do it."

They pressed. They parted. Our lips enjoyed their first delicious conversation, pleased to make their acquaintance.

My chest caved and my knees failed. I wrapped my arms around his shoulders, and my hands found their way to his short hair. Then I ran my fingers down his warm neck and I squeezed, needing another outlet to apply myself to him.

A moan danced from his mouth to mine, and I was lost to the moment.

It was furious and graceful. The best kiss of my life, up until that point, and in awe of the moment, I let him lead it.

He was a born kissing leader I learned, and it was worth all of the waiting. All of the cat and mouse. All of the holding back and being patient. It was worth that and so much more.

As I caught my breath, a bittersweet reprieve, he made his way across my jaw, to my neck, and the tip of his tongue lightly licked me before his lips were on mine again.

"We should get out of this alley," he said, raggedly, but pressed himself against me, again proving that he was just as affected by it as I was.

"Okay," I said. But I would have agreed to just about any-fucking-thing he said. "But I don't want to go home yet."

He pulled away from the wall and me and I didn't like the way my body felt, not having him close anymore. He cupped my face, his eyes dreamy and glazed over with a need that I knew mirrored my own.

"Hannah, I just learned your name. We just kissed. There's no way in hell I could take you home yet."

That was all I needed to know.

Chapter Fourteen

Vaughn

The way she felt in my arms. The way she leaned into me when I lost the battle with my cock to rub it against her. The way her eyes were on fire. She'd never looked more beautiful to me than in that moment.

There was no way I was taking her back.

Not yet.

I knew I wouldn't let things go too far—at least not that night. However, I was nowhere near finished touching and kissing her.

I took her slender hand and walked her around to the passenger side of the Escalade; thankful I'd parked behind the bar and not in front. Not that I was worried about anyone seeing us. I was just glad that, for at least that first time, it was just us. Private.

I really wanted to guess her name. That had been my plan all night.

But as I was repeatedly learning—plans changed.

I'd never in a million years think I'd end up punching someone in the mouth the first time I went to a bar in Wynne. Especially since everyone in town had been so nice, up until that point.

I'd fix his tooth, if he came in Monday, but there was no way I was going to let someone talk to her like that. She already took too much shit from people. It was like she never noticed. It was like she was so used to it that it didn't even register to her as being rude.

That was all going to change.

Her heart was too big to let people treat her like that. Treat her like she was less than the wonderful, beautiful, kind woman she was.

I opened the door and helped her as she lifted up into the seat.

When she was in, she ran a hand across my cheek and said, "Thank you."

It could have been for helping her in the SUV, which she didn't really need. It could have been because she'd had a good night. It could have been for dinner or for the beers. But something inside of me knew, without her being specific, that it was about decking that guy.

"You're worth it," I answered.

She sighed and leaned back in the seat with a smile. I may not have earned our first kiss the way I would have liked, but earning that contented smile was just as good.

I closed her door and rounded the front of the vehicle, thinking about where we should go. My place seemed so forward, and I didn't want her to think that was all I was about.

I *was* about that, Christ, I so was, but it wasn't right yet. And I'd be damned if I didn't want to wait until it was totally right. For her.

I'd leave where we went up to O'Fallon … *Hannah.*

"Which way we headed?"

Her knee bounced and she took her time thinking. "We could go anywhere," she said, but her voice was quiet, unsure.

"Is that to the right or the left?" I teased, not wanting her to be so nervous.

She looked at me, and I could tell she was biting her tongue not to say something, as her hazel eyes grew wide and she gave me a fake smile. She didn't know what to do or say and it was apparent, as if she'd never been on a date that had gotten a little heated.

I knew that was wrong, though, because we'd already confessed our losing our virginity stories by the fire at her cabin the other night.

"Hannah," I began, but was interrupted.

"Thank you for calling me Hannah." Then she leaned over and gave me a quick kiss on my cheek, repeating, "Thank you, *Vaughn*." My name on her lips sounded so sweet.

"That's your name." At least it was the name people *should* call her. The more I heard everyone call her Mutt the more pissed it made me.

"I know, it's just that nobody calls me that and no one has ever really cared to. I think they all know my real name, but it's a nickname and sometimes those stick. I don't think they mean it in poor taste. Well, except for Randy, but I doubt he'll act like that again. I can't believe you swung at him. I can't get over it."

And I'd do it again. It was in that moment I wondered if I'd scared her. She was so rough and tumble. So quick to joke and she swore as much as any man I'd ever met. But, I needed her to know I wasn't a violent guy.

Hell, the last guy I punched was in junior high. I looked down at my fist on the wheel and saw that his tooth had caught a piece of my knuckle. Blood had smeared and dried, making it look worse than it was, but I was a bit of a mess.

As I studied my hand, I thought of a way to explain myself, without sounding like a classic asshole. You know? The kind that says they *usually don't hit people*, all the while having just hit someone.

"I'm sorry I hit him in front of you. I've never done that before," I admitted. "Never got into a bar fight."

She laughed. "That wasn't a bar fight. It was just a punch."

I supposed she was right, but that was just semantics.

"Well, it wasn't a very good first impression. Probably not that great for business either."

"First impression? Fuck, Randy and Seth were being jerks. He's fine and you *said* you'd fix his tooth. It was nothing."

Nothing?

"I couldn't allow him to talk to you like that."

She beamed. "You know how you said you didn't have any roots and that you thought this was a place you could grow some?"

"Yeah."

"Well, I think you just broke ground tonight."

She was visibly more relaxed than a few seconds ago, and I hoped it wasn't the kiss that had shaken her up instead of my temper. That wasn't how I wanted people to think I was.

Fuck that. It wasn't how I wanted *her* to think I was.

"Well, I like the way your mind works, but I don't want you to assume I act like that normally."

"Vaughn, seriously. That was nothing. I saw Snapper Jones pull a gun on a guy in there before over a game of cards. That one punch just said, *hey, Wynne, I'm here. And I'm not taking your shit.* How's your hand?"

She pulled my right hand from the wheel to examine it under the dome light she'd clicked on.

"It's fine, just looks messy."

She looked up at me through her thick lashes and said, "Maybe we should go to your place?"

God, that sounded like a good idea. She looked so damn good sitting there in my passenger seat.

To hell with it.

"Are you sure?" Things wouldn't get out of hand. I wouldn't let them—if it was within my power, which I wasn't so sure about. My fear was I wouldn't have much control when push actually came to shove.

We pulled into my drive and I turned off the lights. I decided to leave my keys in the ignition, knowing I'd be taking her home in a while.

Hannah opened her door and walked to the deck, then waited for me.

She was stunning in the moonlight, her hair moving with the breeze. Her lips still a little red from our kiss in the alley.

One part of my brain told me that this was all new, and to take my time. I'd only lived in Wynne for a few weeks. It was a little soon to be jumping into a serious relationship with someone new, especially after Rachelle.

The other part of my brain was screaming, *this feels so right!* She was so unlike anyone I knew. We never ran out of things to talk about.

She was actually interested in me. *Me.*

Not how much money I made.

Not my practice.

Not who I knew at the golf club.

And, although I was still learning about her, I doubted she'd ever be one to concern herself with petty things like that.

Hannah O'Fallon had her own things, and she didn't need mine. She made her own way.

The Hannah way.

For the record, Hannah fit her perfectly. Judging by the way she looked at me when I said it, she liked hearing it just as much as I liked saying it.

"Coffee?" she asked, taking the hand I offered her. I'd never really been a hand holding kind of guy; hers just fit so nicely in mine. As tough as she tried to be, her hands were the exact opposite of that day-to-day tough exterior. Her fingers were long and thin, her palms soft and warm. Her nails were bare, trim, and glossy.

"Do you want me to make you some?"

"It kind of sounds good."

I'd be up all night if I drank coffee at midnight. The thought that she wanted me up all night caused a twitch in my jeans. Maybe I was reading more into it than I should have, but coffee or not, what I wanted to do to her would take hours and no doubt the sun would be coming up long before I was finished.

But not that night.

I'd slept with Rachelle on our first date. We'd been around each other, running in the same circle, but it was our first night out alone. When she invited me up, I didn't really think things were going to progress like they did. Honestly, I thought we would casually date for a while. Maybe.

That whole relationship was doomed from the beginning.

I didn't want that to happen with this one.

It wasn't about being sad or missing Rachelle. It was more about feeling like every year I spent looking and waiting for the right one to come along, was inevitably one year without what I wanted.

A real home. Roots. A family to call my own.

Yet, all of that was *way* too soon to think about. It was too soon to let myself think about making a life with this crazy, beautiful, complicated woman.

It was too soon to admit I hoped she liked me back.

Too soon to want to skip the fucking coffee and lead her to my bedroom. To strip her naked. To lay her on my bed. To kiss every inch of her until she was pink and flushed.

Too soon to *show* her how I felt.

But it wasn't too soon to excuse myself to the bathroom to catch my breath and get some clarity. I was really fucking aroused by all of those thoughts.

She walked straight to the coffee maker and since she knew where all of my kitchen things were, she easily found the coffee packs and started a cup.

"I'll be right back," I said and excused myself.

Was she sending me signals, or did I just want signals? It was possible she wanted the same thing I did, or maybe I just liked everything about her and I got to see a lot more of her tonight. She'd opened up more to me than before.

Whatever it was, it was potent, and as I leaned over the counter in the bathroom and tried to get a grip, I reminded myself to slow the fuck down.

I didn't want to be the first man in history to chase a girl away *with* commitment. However, even if I didn't say it, I could be committed to her, and the beginning of that commitment meant I wasn't going to treat this like a one-night stand. The thought of even being able to refer to it as such would tarnish it.

When I walked back down the stairs, I noticed her through the screen door, leaning over the rail on my deck and looking out into the field that butted up to my property. She was holding a cup of coffee and I saw that she'd fixed me one and left it on the island.

I picked it up and took a sip, enjoying the view before she knew I was watching. Her head tilted one way then the other, like she was having a debate with herself. I didn't know what her points and counterpoints were, but I hoped they had everything to do with me.

Placing her cup on the rail, she shrugged out of the jacket and her bare shoulders were just too tempting, so I placed my coffee on the island and went to her. The sound of the screen door caused her to turn her head, and she smiled when she met my eyes.

Before I could talk myself out of it, my lips were on her

skin from behind. I swept her hair to the side for a better vantage point and my eyes shut, inhaling a perfect Hannah-filled breath. Rightness mixed with her sweetness and something else that was more innocent than not.

Moving with my touch, she rolled her head as I claimed her warm flesh. One shoulder to her neck, to the other side, and suddenly I was under her spell.

She moaned and turned in my arms as I kissed just behind her ear. I think she liked being kissed there; always reacting the most when I hit that spot, a small shiver jetting through her.

I wanted to know everything she liked. I'd commit to memory every sound with every spot and, one day soon, I'd play her body like a guitar. Repeating my favorite chords over and over.

Chapter Fifteen

Hannah

He kissed me breathless on the porch and my coffee cup fell off after he lifted me up in his arms so that our mouths met, my tiptoes barely sliding across the wood boards. I liked the feeling of being wrapped up in him, but it left me no room to explore on my own.

I lightly kicked my feet a little, and without words, he set me down, which allowed my hands to roam his chest. Something I noticed I was always attracted to.

Like they had any claim to it, or invitation, my fingers ran up his shirt, causing his stomach to ripple with the sensation of my cool touch.

My fingers wandered around his back as he deepened the kiss and I almost abandoned my pilgrimage, losing my train of thought. Soon we were turning toward his door, lips locked, hands pawing each other.

The counter on the island met my ass, and the screen

door slammed in our haste not to close it. I heard thunder, which didn't surprise me since I'd seen flashes of lightning while Vaughn had been upstairs.

"You taste so good," he said against my mouth.

I didn't know what to say, so I just kissed him harder. Holding the sides of his head against me as he lifted me to sit on the granite, which he claimed to hate.

My legs wrapped around him and he pulled my ass to the edge so that he could press against me. I was wild and reckless and my want for him changed to necessity.

My body dared me to lean back and see where that move would get me. Half of me wanted to slow down and act like I wasn't a lustful girl who'd never been kissed like that.

Regardless, I was and I hadn't.

The other half of me wanted to fuck him right there in his kitchen with the same amount of heat and humidity that hung in the early summer air. As the sky lit up with electricity and the promise of the first thunderstorm this year, I warred with myself.

I was easy.

If you define easy as a woman who usually only found herself with a man when she wanted one. Therefore, every man I'd ever been with hadn't had to exert much effort. If they were cute, looked like a normal guy and were nice, on one of those nights, I was pretty much a sure thing. Few and far between as those nights were, I didn't want this night to be like that. I wanted something different.

I'd been in similar situations, although none of them ever felt like Vaughn did, pressing against me in his kitchen after our first date.

None had been that potent.

That powerful.

That right.

So I needed to slow down.

I didn't want to be easy with him. I wanted more than just a one-night stand. I wanted another date, and possibly a third. I wanted to know about his family and ask him about three hundred thousand more questions.

Seriously though, the chances of that happening, if I gave the milk away for free this time, were slim. He wasn't the kind of guy who'd want some town Mutt, some easy chick. He'd likely want a lady, and I wanted to be someone he'd be interested in.

I wanted to be *Hannah*. For *him*.

The wind picked up and the unlatched door slammed again, knocking me out of the moment just enough to break the kiss.

"We need to slow down."

No more were the words out of my mouth and he pulled himself up, giving me space, holding himself just above me.

"I'm sorry," he apologized, but he didn't look that guilty. "I lost myself there for a minute."

He placed his forehead to my chest and chuckled, trying to catch his breath. I was chasing mine too.

"So did I."

He moved his face to look up at me, his chin perched on my cleavage. It was a funny sight.

"You're a really good kisser," I admitted, licking my numb lips.

"Well, I know a lot about mouths. You could say I have a doctorate in them."

I giggled and watched his head bounce between my boobs, which only made me laugh harder. I wondered how many chins I had from his point of view. "You look funny down there."

His eyes jagged right then left, noticing where he was.

"I like it here," he teased, then placed a kiss on my neck and lifted both of us up.

"I think it's going to storm and it's getting late." I hated the thought of leaving, but I knew if I didn't get out of that house sooner than later I'd be naked from another kiss like that.

As he stepped back, I hopped down and tried to fix the tube top, which had surprisingly stayed mostly in place.

He had touched me, but he never tried to get under my clothes. I, on the other hand, had had my hands up his shirt and down the back of his pants, not far enough to get a real grab, but far enough to know that his ass was firm as hell. No wonder his pants always looked so good. That ass was no illusion.

I hated feeling like I was being a tease, but the truth of it was, I didn't even have a condom with me. Yeah, he was a guy and probably had one, but these days most girls were on the pill … and the whole *I didn't want to be an easy slut* thing.

When you only have sex once or twice a year, you don't really need a prescription contraceptive anyway. I'd always had condoms with me when I went out on a mission. On those nights when the loneliness took over, I knew what I was looking for and where to find it, but I still always protected myself.

Even if I had been on the pill, my behavior, sleeping

with people I didn't really know that well, really *did* warrant their use.

I'd never picked up anyone who looked dodgy, but let's face it: most guys who go to a girl's cabin after the bar aren't angels.

We walked back outside and as I picked up Sunny's jacket off the porch, thinking about that, I absentmindedly said, "I don't have any condoms anyway." There was no warning, even to me. The words just fell out.

He stopped in his tracks and he grinned salaciously.

"Neither do I."

"Well, Dr. Kissylips, I suppose it's good we're calling it a night then." I wanted him to know that, although it wasn't the right night for it, I was positively interested in knowing all of the other things he knew about mouths and what his could do.

"Think your dad is asleep?" he asked.

I hadn't even thought about him since the bar. What kind of daughter was I?

"Shit. My dad," I said as I picked up speed and hurried to his vehicle. I thought about how nice it was not getting into my truck alone. I'd still get one last kiss before our first date ended. I hoped.

He trailed behind me, and soon we were pulling out of his drive and headed toward my house, just as the first raindrops began pouring from the sky.

My father was going to have one hell of a hangover; he usually didn't drink to that point. I hoped that Dean got him the pain reliever and something to drink like I'd asked him to.

Then, just like that, my brain shifted gears. Back to

what just happened.

One thing was sure, I'd been able to pull back that first night, but I didn't feel like I could hold out much longer.

I didn't know what his plans were for the next day, but I hoped they included me.

As if he was reading my mind, he asked, "What are you doing tomorrow?"

A little creepy, but I liked it and answered with, "Get out of my head."

He looked at me, and, from the light of the dashboard, I saw he had a smile that reached ear to ear.

"What? You want to do something?"

My mind raced with what that something might be. I'd be perfectly fine going out to the cabin and just chilling there, but that seemed kind of forward. Ladies didn't invite guys out to their bachelorette pad for fishing and a run around the bases.

Turns out, I was new at being a lady, so despite myself, I asked anyway.

"I was thinking about getting the boat out, if the weather is good. Maybe troll around and fish for a while. Test out a few new lures. Do you want to go?"

"I was hoping you'd say something like that. I had a really good time tonight, Hannah."

And there it was again.

My name.

It was weird. Hannah had always been my name, but it felt foreign and familiar all at the same time when he said it. He'd never called me Mutt.

I wondered how long it would have taken him to get to Hannah, had I not broken down and told him after Randy, the town dick, had earned the business end of Vaughn's fist.

I knew I'd always be Mutt, and there wasn't a whole lot I could do about it, but at least there was one person who saw me as Hannah. And, if I had to choose, I was glad it was him.

"I had a good night, too," I said as he pulled onto the gravel lane at my house. The rain was beating down so hard at that point I knew for sure I'd be soaked by the time I reached my door.

"So you think you like me a tiny bit more than just a little yet?"

I laughed. He had to know better. My hard-to-get game wasn't that strong.

"I don't know. What do you think?"

"What do I think?" He repeated while putting the SUV in park, after pulling as close to my front door as he could get it, driving up in our grass. That alone made me warm on the inside.

"I *think* you looked so good tonight that I couldn't keep my eyes off you. I *think* every time you laugh a timer starts, and I tick down the seconds until I hear it again. I *think* that I'm going to need a serious cold shower when I get home. I *think* I'm really glad, regardless of how I got it, that I know your name now. I *think* it suits you—if I didn't tell you that already. I *think* that I like that granite in my kitchen more than I did before. I *think* I miss that van," he said, looking in the back of the Escalade, which was a whole hell of a lot nicer than Dad's old Astro van. "There's a lot more open space in the back of that classic. And let's see ... I *think* there are too many hours in between now and tomorrow."

My mouth watered, wanting to taste his lips, as he grew

closer. Lips that were saying some of the most simply perfect things. He adjusted so that he could get closer, apparently I was frozen in place, and I appreciated his struggle, liking that he did something about it when he couldn't reach me.

I wasn't sure if I knew how it felt to fall in love, but if it was anything like that moment, I'd been a wise fool to wait that long. At the same time, I'd been so blind, believing I didn't care about having someone *all* my own, and I was loving the discovery. Glad that I'd waited for something better than a town leftover. Because I was so pleased in that moment to be there—*with him.* It was almost validation that good things *do* come to those who wait, and maybe that was just what I'd been doing all along.

He went on. "I *think* kissing you is better each time. I *think* your eyes look even prettier when I'm this close. I *think* I could go on, but I'd rather you kiss me goodnight."

I didn't care anymore if the things he said sounded cheesy. It's not cheesy when it's real.

I leaned closer, the only inch he gave me, and traded it in for his mouth on mine. It was a good trade.

This kiss was slower and it made my neck weak and my shoulders slump forward into it. Leisurely, he proved that although our previous kisses—like pushing the throttle forward on my boat, wind rushing through my hair—were exhilarating, slowly floating along in the warm sun felt just as nice.

For unrushed minutes we floated together, the rain pounding down on the roof, me in his passenger seat, dressed up like a woman on a mission, praying that it wasn't all too good to be true.

When I finally went inside, I saw my dad in his recliner, snoring like a bear, and a can of soda next to his chair. I grabbed the blanket off the couch and covered him up.

He blinked a few times, still drunk and more than half asleep.

"I miss you so much, Katie," he said, his voice lenient and sad.

"Good night, Dad," I said and kissed his forehead. He must have been pretty drunk to call me by my mother's name. I couldn't imagine how much he missed her, or even why he'd still be thinking about her after what she'd done.

I wished he'd move on and find someone who'd love him like he deserved. It killed me to think that he'd be lonely forever.

Upstairs, I got in my bed and thought about everything that had happened, but it all came back to one thing.

I liked Vaughn a lot.

I liked *me* with him a lot, too.

For as late as it was when I went to bed, I rose with the chickens. Well, we didn't have chickens, but you know what I mean. I slept well, not waking once, and popped out of bed, hitting the ground running, like it was the first real day of summer.

And since I was getting the boat out for the first time that year, it kind of was.

I was showered and dressed before seven.

I'd packed an overnight bag and grabbed some clean towels for the cabin.

I had about an hour before the store opened. There were things I needed to grab for my day, and hopefully night, while I was in town.

As I put my to-go mug under the coffee pot, I heard my dad stir in the living room, pushing the forever-broken-foot part of the recliner into the chair.

"Morning?" I asked more than offered.

I peeked in there to see what kind of state he was in. I could count on one hand how many times I'd seen my dad that wasted, and I was sure he wasn't going to be very good company, at least until after lunch.

Again, I was glad to be heading to the river.

He was still groggy and puffy-eyed as he reached for his glasses, which sat on the end table beside him.

"I survived another night," he said weakly, repeating the stupid thing he'd said almost every day of my life.

"Yeah, and that one was a rougher one than most. What were you doing at Sally's last night?"

He slumped forward holding his head, noticing his shoes were still on from yesterday.

"Oh hell, I don't know. I guess I got bored or something."

I was right. He was going to be a bear.

"Want some coffee?" That always helped me and it reminded me I'd need to grab some for the cabin. I mentally added it to my list.

"Do you mind? I'm going to wash the stink off," he answered.

He stood on fresh legs and didn't wobble like I'd expected, taking his time getting reacquainted with gravity.

"I almost feel sorry for you," I teased as he passed me on the way to his room.

When my cup was full, I slid one under the maker for him, making sure to change the setting to strong. He was going to need the caffeine more than I did.

I was bright-eyed and downright bushy tailed.

I was spending the day, not only on the water—which was normally reason enough—but I was going to be with Vaughn.

Maybe he'd kiss me again.

Maybe I'd kiss him first.

I grinned into the sink waiting for his cup to fill, and when it was done I doctored it up real nice. Just the way he drank it. Although he said he hated so much shit in his coffee, he made it the same way for himself. I'd watched him do it a thousand times.

"So what did you do last night?" he asked when he came back fresh from the shower and looking eighty percent better.

"I went out on a date."

"With who? Astro?" He stood stock-still in front of me and watched my expression.

I kept my mouth closed despite the smile that was crawling around on my face.

"Maybe?"

"Maybe?" He kicked my foot. "You got a thing for that tooth yanker?"

"I don't know." It wasn't like I was ashamed of it—it was just so new. Or weird. Or awkward to talk about with him. We'd never talked about anyone we were seeing. Mostly because neither of us ever saw anyone.

"You don't know? Looks like you know. What did you do on your big, fancy date?"

I sat down at the two-person table in our little kitchen and drank my coffee, thinking of what I wanted to tell and what I wanted to keep for myself.

"He made me dinner, and then we took a drive." I smiled thinking about it. "Then Sally called and said you were shit-hammered and you needed a ride home. He was going to help me, but Dean got there first."

"Yeah, I suppose I need to go get my truck. You headed into town any time soon?"

"Yeah, in a bit when the store opens."

"What did he make you?" he asked, sipping carefully so he wouldn't burn his mouth.

"Steak."

His eyebrows shot up and he challenged, "Better than mine?"

"It was pretty damn good. I bet he'd give you a few pointers. *If* you were nice to him."

He laughed and sipped his hot coffee.

"You're a real turd, you know that, kid?"

"I get it from my dad."

"I think someone needs to warn Astro about you. Poor feller."

Chapter Sixteen

Vaughn

I didn't sleep that well. Thoughts of our night together kept replaying. Don't get me wrong, it was no hardship.

The way she tasted.

The sounds she made.

The way she looked, and hearing her confess her name to me. It was so much more than just telling me her name. It was a gift. Something about it was almost pure because she'd never given it to anyone else.

I was still smiling when I woke up. Because I knew she was giving me part of herself no one had ever even seen. It was all mine.

After a quick shower, I walked outside to grab the paper that showed up on my sidewalk every day, even though I wasn't sure how I'd subscribed to it.

The sun was out and it would be nice and warm.

As I was standing up, paper in hand, a rabbit ran past

me, followed by a dog running full speed.

"I'm gonna kick your ass, Smokie. You little shit," yelled a guy chasing behind them.

The Dalmatian, Smokie, abandoned the chase when he came across me and instead rolled over for me to pet his belly.

"You mind holding him there for a minute?" the guy asked from about half a block away.

"No problem."

I bent down and gave the runaway a scratch. "You're a troublemaker, aren't you?" His leg ferociously kicked when I found a special spot on his white and black coat.

"Sorry about that," the guy said. "He's a good dog, but he's still very much a puppy."

I stood and he clipped a leash onto the red collar around Smokie's neck.

"That's okay."

"You're the new dentist? This is your place, right?"

He was about my age, I guessed. He wore a Wynne Fire Department shirt with the sleeves cut off and basketball shorts.

"Yeah, I'm Vaughn."

"I'm Aaron. I live a few blocks that way, and this is Smokie." He gave the dog a stern look that I'm sure the runaway pup had seen before, considering the way he slunk down guiltily on the grass.

"How are you liking it here so far? Not much to do."

"Wynne's a good little town. The people are friendly."

He glanced toward my porch and said, "I noticed you're doing some work on the house. I always liked this bungalow."

"Yeah, I've mostly been working inside. You know, getting unpacked."

"Well, if you ever need any help, just shout. I work at the station, but I'm off quite a bit, too. I'm good with a hammer. My dad was a builder."

"Thanks. I might take you up on that."

I looked back at my house, which obviously needed a lot more work. Namely, a roof, a new deck in back, and a few new windows. I'm sure Hannah would help, but she didn't need to feel obligated.

Plus, I didn't really know any guys in town that well. I could tolerate having a guy friend.

"I think by the end of the summer I'm going to get a new roof on her. Maybe some paint."

"Sure. Just let me know."

I heard her truck coming, my ears tuned to everything *her*. And, like I knew I would, I saw her old pickup coming down the highway toward town. Distracted, I watched as she got closer and noticed she wasn't alone. Her dad was sitting passenger.

Aaron noticed what I was watching and said, "Her truck is getting louder. I bet you get sick of hearing that thing go by all the time."

He couldn't be more wrong. The only thing I didn't like so much about it passing was when it didn't stop.

"You'd think her dad would fix it, or at least Dean would. You know them? They own the garage uptown."

"Yeah, I've met them."

"I think when Darrell retires he'll leave both the shop, and Mutt, to Dean." He laughed. "I know Dean's ready for that."

I bet he is. Not going to happen though.

As she passed, her boat behind her, she honked and we both waved. It was odd how much this town knew about her and her family, but at the same time knew nothing at all.

"Well, it's nice to meet you. I better get moving. I need to be at the station in a few hours." He stuck his hand out to shake mine and I took it. "Thanks for grabbing Smokie for me. I live on Hyde Street, drive a black truck that's usually parked out front if I'm home. Otherwise, I'm at the station. You ever need some help, just let me know."

"I'll do that. Good to meet you too, Aaron."

Even though he was totally wrong about the O'Fallons, I couldn't hold it against him. He seemed like an all right guy and I didn't have many friends in Wynne yet. Then again, after I met Hannah, I hadn't really felt like I'd needed any.

Still, if this thing was going to work out, I didn't want to smother her, or have her feel obligated to keep me entertained.

"Hey, do you golf?" I asked as he started back down the sidewalk.

He turned around, stopping best he could, while Smokie pulled him back the way they came. "I'm not that good, but I like to play."

"I was thinking about going to the driving range sometime this week if the weather is good. Hit a few, drink a few beers."

"Now you're talking. I'm great at drinking beers. If my truck is home, stop by on your way out. First bucket is on me."

Finally, a possible friend. Things were looking up.

After a bowl of cereal and a workout in my new gym, which was also known as my garage, I couldn't hold out any longer and called her.

"Good morning," she sang over the line.

"Good morning. How's your dad feeling today?"

"Better than he deserves. Hey, do you like fried fish?"

"I grew up Catholic. It was almost a requirement, but I haven't had it in a while."

"Well, I don't mean to brag, but mine is the shit. I think we'll fry some later if you can catch any." She was teasing and challenging me; I could hear it in her playful voice.

This would be where she had me at a disadvantage. I'd never been as an adult, unless you called deep-sea fishing where the pole is anchored to the boat and there's a guide who does everything for you, the same thing.

"I'm going to warn you. I'm not a fisherman. That's a lot of pressure, you know. If I can't catch our dinner we'll go hungry?" I was playing along, but everything I'd said was true.

She loved fishing and I was going to look like an ass.

"We'll see. Ever hear of beginner's luck? That's a real thing, you know. Anyway, I'm heading out to the cabin, so whenever you get around, that's where I'll be."

"Need me to bring anything?"

"Not that I can think of, but, Vaughn?"

"Yeah?"

"Hurry the fuck up. Okay?" I loved how she said exactly what she wanted, the precise way she wanted to.

I needed to get a quick shower and run by the store, but I didn't want to make her wait. I knew how excited she was about getting out on the water for the first time this year.

"I'll hurry."

"Good."

Like I said I would, I rushed through a shower, foregoing a good shave that I probably could have used, and I threw on a T-shirt, some cargo shorts, my old tennis shoes, and a ball cap. I grabbed my sunglasses and my wallet, wondering if I should throw some other things in a bag, on the off chance that I'd be staying, but then decided that was a little too presumptuous.

I walked into the small grocery store and headed straight for the aisle where I knew I'd find what I wanted.

I was a grown ass man.

I could buy condoms.

But son of a bitch, the whole town was there. The. Whole. Damn. Town. The parking lot was fuller than I'd ever noticed before. All twelve spots were used.

"Morning, Vaughn. You're up and at it early," said Dr. Carver as I walked in. He was checking out, which I was thankful for, but it didn't make me feel any better.

"Good morning. Just picking up a few things. See you Monday," I said quickly with a wave as I passed him and headed to the far end of the store to scope out the aisle three situation.

I passed a patient I'd seen the past week and gave her a friendly smile that she returned without any hesitation.

A few weeks ago, none of the faces registered, but now, as I was getting more familiar with the people of the small town, everyone seemed like someone I knew. Or someone I at least recognized from somewhere.

I rounded the back aisle and began walking toward the

one I needed to hit up before I made my getaway.

Like my prayer had been answered, it was empty. I marched to the section where I'd seen the condoms before and decided I wasn't going to hang out that long. I'd find the ones I wanted and be out of there in no time.

"Hey there, Astro. How's the Caddy running for ya?" I heard the gruff voice from behind me.

Fuck. Hannah's dad.

I spun around to face him, hoping to block the contents of the shelf I'd been hastily browsing.

"Hi, Mr. O'Fallon. It's good. Thanks."

"Whatcha lookin' for?" he said, a mischievous twinkle in his eye.

I coughed, being taken by surprise with his question and said the first thing that came to mind.

"Athlete's foot cream."

"Oh, ya got a little crook foot, huh?"

He walked around me and pulled off the box of lotion that was positioned right under the box of prophylactics I desperately wanted to buy. Even if I wasn't going to use them that day, I didn't want to be unprepared again.

"Here you go. I used a mess of this a while back and it cleared right up. You don't want to mess with that stuff. Gets nasty. Smelly."

"Right," I agreed, taking the box from him.

"Busted knuckles? You one of those cage fighters? What's your ring name? Captain Cavity?" He gave a few pretend punches to the air.

"No, sir," I answered, looking at the injury from the bar. I didn't want him to get any ideas that I'd hurt his daughter, which was exactly where my mind would go if I were him, knowing I'd been out with her last night. "I kind of took a swing at a guy in the bar who was being rude to your daughter."

That was the truth, I couldn't hide from it, and he'd probably hear about it before the day was over anyway.

He smiled and rocked back on his heels, sticking his hand in the pockets of his bib overalls.

"I might like you after all." Then he looked behind me again and cocked his head to the side. "Anything else I can help you find? You know I've been coming here since they opened. I know where *everything* is." His tone was teasing, but still a tad warning.

"I don't think so, just the cream."

"Good. Good. Did you know they sell bullets here? Do you have a gun, Astro?"

He was my height, but he was bigger than me. I didn't want to be on his bad side. I was picking up where the conversation was headed and thought it wise to steer it somewhere else.

"I don't. I hope you're feeling okay this morning. Hannah was worried about you last night." I knew it wasn't my business, but then again, maybe it kind of was.

He stepped back a little, losing the momentum he was trying to gain with the shit he was giving me.

"I'm feeling pretty good. Pretty good. That's right, you were on your date."

"Yes, sir."

"She told me. Are you headed out to the cabin?"

"I am. She asked me to go fishing with her."

That made him genuinely smile and I liked it, feeling more at ease.

She didn't have a lot of family, pretty much just him, and Dean—if he counted. I wanted to get to know her more and that meant I'd probably be spending some time with Mr. O'Fallon in the future. It would be nice if he liked me.

Also, I didn't have much family and I liked being around them. They always seemed to have a good time with each other.

"You know she doesn't date a whole lot. Never has."

I didn't know what to say, so I nodded and looked at the box in my hand.

"You treat her good and she'll treat you good. But she likes her space, too. One thing I know about women, as much as they like having you around, if you corner 'em, they'll fly away."

His bloodshot eyes showed a flash of something that looked awfully painful.

"Yes, sir."

"All right, I'll leave you alone so you can get some rubbers."

My mouth hung open. He punched me in the shoulder.

"I'm just kidding. You get that cream on those feet. Mutt will tease the piss out of you if you get to smellin' like high noon in hell. She can be unmerciful."

He walked off chuckling.

I left the store with foot cream.

Then remembered I had an Amazon app on my phone, which would allow me to buy whatever the hell I wanted. *Privately*.

Problem solved.

Well, problem solved … Monday when they'd arrive.

I pulled into the lot at Johnston's Chute and took the gravel road on the far side of it, just like I had before. It looked different in the day and my Escalade was a much smoother ride than the van had been.

The road was muddy from the small storm the night before, but it wasn't too bad. When I pulled up at her cabin, she already had the boat in the water and was carrying a cooler down the small dock.

"Can you grab that bag by the stairs and my tackle box?" she shouted to me as I hopped out of my vehicle.

Hannah was eager to get out on the water, and I was just pleased she wanted me there.

Even more than that, I was excited to have a whole day of looking at her in those shorts. That tank top. She had a ball cap on too and her hair was threaded through the back in a ponytail that swung behind her as she walked around the boat.

I did as I was asked and picked up the bags by the stairs and headed down the newer-looking dock. It swayed gently under my feet, and I did my best not to look off kilter.

"Do you know how to swim?" she asked with an accusing grin off to one side.

"Yes. I can swim. Thanks for the confidence."

"I was just checking. I have life jackets here, but we'll be along the banks mostly. If you should happen to fall out—or get pushed in—you'll probably be able to touch."

Was she planning on pushing me out of the boat? Or was that just a warning...

"Permission to come aboard?"

She rolled her eyes and said, "Get on here." I didn't miss the way she looked at my lips before she threw her shades on, like she was seeing me in a new light and didn't know how to react.

Hannah took the bags, shaking her head at me. I thought that was what you were supposed to say before you got on someone's boat.

The small vessel had two seats that were more like bar stools, tall and swiveling, and the boat was shallow and wide. There was a bigger motor in the back and a smaller one lying on the floorboard at the front.

"Why does your boat have two motors?" I asked as she untied the ropes tethering us to the dock.

"Ah, good question, Doctor. The one in the back is an outboard; it's the main motor. The one up there lets me putter around in shallower water. It's quieter when I'm fishing and it allows me to move around while I'm doing my thing."

She took this seriously. Two motors. *Shit.*

If I was going to learn how to fish, I was glad to be learning from a professional.

"Interesting."

"Not been on many fishing boats, huh?" She lowered the motor in the back and turned the key, causing it to roar to life.

"No. Not that many. I've been on bigger fishing boats in Cleveland. They'll take you out to fish on the lake, but they're nothing like this. I think this boat is quieter than your truck," I teased.

"I don't care how loud my truck is, but I care a lot about how quiet my boat is."

She pushed forward on the throttle and we slowly

moved away from the dock by her cabin. The morning sun was strong on the water and I was glad for both my hat and glasses.

She didn't drive fast, taking her time to show me all of her favorite haunts. She called them her "honey holes" which I thought was cute.

What wasn't cute was the look she gave me when she threatened my life and my balls if I ever shared the top-secret information.

Okay, that was pretty adorable, too.

She pulled into a narrow piece of water off the main channel and it was peaceful and calm, the current barely noticeable. Green buds sprouted on the trees, but not quite big enough yet to shade the water from the sun. Their branches arched over us like a tunnel made of wooden lace.

"It's beautiful back here."

"I know. I love this spot. It's my favorite honey hole. It's great bass fishing."

I wasn't sure what that meant, other than that's what she planned on catching, but I admired her zest for all of it. It lit her up.

"How do you know where to go to catch different kinds of fish?"

She cut the engine and turned in her seat, swinging her feet into the middle of the boat. She licked her lips and her neck stretched out towards me just enough. Again, it was obvious she wanted to kiss me, but she held back. So I did, too.

I wanted her to give in to it. To take what she wanted.

She blew out a quick breath, like she was shaking off the urge to touch me, and spoke.

"I'd like to say experience, but my dad taught me most of it. I've been fishing this river, and the lake outside of town, all my life. Some of it is trial and error, and some of it is just fact."

"Don't you just bait a line and throw it out?"

"Yes, but there's more to it than that. Remember what I was talking about last night on our road trip?"

I remembered she was happily chirping along about fishing, but most of it was Greek to me. Scratch that, I knew some Greek. It was more like Japanese.

"Yeah, but to tell you the truth, I didn't get most of it."

She smiled. "You'll catch on."

She slid her poles out from the side of the boat she sat on and propped the ends up on her lap. "I'm going to bass fish. Do you want to try?"

"Yeah. What's first?"

Her eyes were hidden behind her shades, and I so wished I could see them. She smiled and laughed at me quite a bit, but her eyes always let me know how I was really doing.

She handed me one of the poles; immediately, I noticed they were different. The one she gave me had string coming out of a compartment, where hers was open, the string exposed.

"Is this some sort of beginner's pole?" I accused, only half joking.

"No. It's just easier if you're not used to an open cast. Don't feel bad though, it took me years to get my cast to come out right using them. I still make a huge mess from time to time."

She opened the tackle box, and moved the top shelf

over to get something from the bottom.

"I like fishing with these when I'm back here. They look like bees." She held the lure thing in her hand, letting me get a good look. "I don't know if bass eat bees for real or not, but the ones back here like these little fuckers."

She handed one to me. It was a little heavier than it looked and had a triple hook on it.

"So I get three hooks? What is that—backup?"

She chuckled and shook her head.

"*No*. Those are treble hooks. I use them too. Relax, you'll catch something, I promise. Now, watch how I tie this and see if you can do it." She paused and lifted her glasses to the bill of her hat. "And that wasn't a cheap shot about you not being able to do it. My dad has a hard time and he's been fishing twice as long as I have. You just have big hands and they're small lures."

Here was where I could shine, if I watched carefully enough. I was a dentist, and, therefore, used to small, fine details.

I studied her fingers and watched her loop the line in and out, then pull it tight with her teeth, which made me cringe. She snipped the extra line off and proudly said, "Voilà."

"Okay. I've got this." Meticulously, I repeated what she'd done and much faster, since I wasn't demonstrating like she'd been.

In seconds I had it tied, and then I wrapped the line around my finger to give me a better grip for pulling it tight. I wasn't about to bite it. No, thank you.

She clipped the excess off for me.

I looked up into her eyes and they looked at me in wonder. I'd impressed her. On her boat. Point for Dr. Kissylips.

"Nice job. Are you sure you haven't done this before?" She was skeptical now and squinted at me like she might be getting hustled.

"I'm sure."

She was wearing hardly any makeup, but she was still just as pretty. Her bare skin revealed the freckles she had on her cheeks and nose.

I noticed I didn't have a preference when it came to her. Only that I always adored what she looked like.

Chapter Seventeen

Hannah

"Yeah. Just like that. Cast and then sort of jerk it as you reel it in slowly. You got it."

He was a natural. Why had I expected anything less? He followed instruction and didn't get the least bit shitty with me when I corrected him.

"So where are they then?" he asked as he threw his line out once more. This was a hopping little spot and I trusted that within minutes one of us would get a bite.

"Just be patient."

I threw mine out in front of the boat. Having put the trolling motor in the water, my foot rested on the pedal, happy where we were for the moment. The nice thing about this Chute was, it went on for a good little bit and it would be late morning by the time we made it to the end of the island where it divided from the shore.

He fell into a nice rhythm with his pole, and from

where I stood I was only able to give my line half the attention I normally would.

The way his shirt fit tight across his shoulders did something to me. Or maybe it was the way he shook his ass as he reeled in his line.

He looked so good in my boat. I'd wanted to kiss him on more than one occasion, his mouth was hard to keep my eyes off of, but I wasn't sure how any of it worked. I figured it was best to let him lead.

Besides, I could watch him fish all day. *Every day.*

"Whoa. Whoa. I felt something," he stammered.

I dropped my rod and went to stand on his open side, away from his pole.

"Got a nibble, huh? Okay. When you feel that, don't reel as much. Just give it a few light twitchy pulls. Give him a chance to hit your lure."

He looked at me and nodded quickly, concentrating on doing it just right. His line reached the boat and he gave it a nice clean toss right under a limb about thirty feet out.

It was such pretty cast.

Then, he worked his magic. Pulling at the right times. Reeling when he should. Like magic, a fish hit his line.

"There's a second where you don't want to move. Then yank and set your hook. Crank like hell back to the boat," I whispered, not wanting him to lose his fish—our first catch of the day.

His pole bowed under the weight of the fish.

"I got it. I *think* I've got it."

I grabbed the net and crouched down to pull the fish out for him.

It was a nice one too. A keeper. Just like him, I thought

to myself as I looked up at him. He was in the zone and it was sexy as anything I'd ever seen.

I grabbed the bass by the mouth, careful not to catch my thumb on the hook.

"Look at you. Real nice catch. We're keeping this bad boy."

I went to hand him the fish so I could get a bucket to fill the well, and the pliers. Those hooks weren't anything to mess with, in my experience. There's no amount of fishing you can do to keep one of those from ruining a perfectly good day. They're bastards no matter who you are.

"Okay. Just hold him like I am. Put your thumb in his mouth. It's rough, but he can't hurt you. Watch that hook."

"I'm used to getting bitten. I'm a dentist."

I chuckled, he was probably telling the truth.

He took it, again following my instruction without any hesitation.

I filled the well and found the tool.

"Okay, do you want me to do this or do you want to try?"

"I want to try," he answered adamantly and lifted his shades to the bill of his hat. I prayed he'd leave them there. I'd missed seeing his eyes.

I had to respect a man who didn't want a woman taking his fish off the hook.

Impressed, I handed him the tool and he skillfully unsnagged it from the lip of the fish, much gentler than I'd been known to do, by the way.

"Throw number one in there," I told him. "See I told you you'd catch something."

I liked that he took to it so well, and even though I

hadn't been going easy on him by not catching anything first, really I'd just been distracted.

He'd caught one and all bets were off. I was about to get my fish on.

"So you think you'll catch any or you gonna let me have all the fun," he challenged, a cocky grin spread across his stubble-covered face.

"You sit back and watch a pro," I countered.

I loved the competition. There was no way to know for sure if he was having fun, but by eleven thirty in the morning we'd each caught about nine, and we'd already cracked open our first beers while we took a little break.

"You're pretty good, Vaughn. I'm wondering if it was a mistake to show you all my sweet spots. You'll be back here without me, cleaning them out."

"Your sweet spots? I think there are a few more I don't know about yet." He winked and I almost choked on my beer.

"Are you hungry?" I asked before I attacked him on my boat.

"A little, but I'm not really that ready to head back yet. I think we should try to fill that tub up."

Goddamn, how I loved the sound of that.

"We don't have to go back," I assured him. "I packed us a couple sandwiches."

"You did?"

"Oh, yeah. I had the deli make us some turkey subs and got a thing of pasta salad."

I found the small cooler I'd set down in the large tote bag to keep it out of the sun. Then realized I'd forgotten one important thing, after all of that planning.

"But you know what? I don't think I brought any forks. Shit."

Our hands were dirty from fishing. The sandwiches wouldn't be any trouble; they were wrapped in paper, but the pasta salad would be nearly impossible.

"Wait, I have toothpicks," I suggested.

"We'll make it work."

So in the middle of the Chute, with a cooler for a table, we ate our sandwiches and used toothpicks to stab the creamy shells. Laughing and talking about the one that he claimed got away, just like a real fisherman.

It was the best lunch of my life.

The day grew hot on the water, and soon we were just looking for the shady spots, puttering around along the bank on the way back to the cabin.

"So you think you're ready to clean all of these fish?" It was the worst part, but it had to be done. If you caught fish, and you wanted to eat them, there was no way around it. Guts and all.

I was used to it, and I'd found a way that was fast, but I still didn't love that part.

"It has to be done, right? I'll help, maybe it'll go faster with two of us."

Other than my dad, and on occasion Dean, I'd never had someone help me clean my catch. Never in a million years did I ever imagine I'd find, not just a sexy, well educated, funny man, but one who *wanted* to help me clean fish—that we'd caught together, no less.

If I wasn't careful, I was going to get in way over my head with him. Honestly, there wasn't a damn thing I could do about it.

After we tied the boat up and cleaned up our mess, we hauled the cooler and bags back to the cabin. Then we went back and pulled out the well, and, each carrying a side, we hauled it over to my fish cleaning station.

I uncoiled the hose I had under the shack and snuck it through the contraption I'd made to hold it. Quickly, I ran upstairs to get my fillet knives and said a prayer that this went just as smoothly as … well, *everything* had gone all day.

I showed him my trick to cutting the fillets and he quickly caught on. Maybe it was because he was a doctor, of sorts, and therefore had a great attention to detail, or maybe he was just a great learner, but after he did the first few, he was flying through them at about the same speed I was.

After about an hour of some really gross stuff, we were finished and glad for it.

"Thanks for helping. It sucks, but it's worth it. They'll taste good, I promise."

I bagged up the last of the fish for the freezer, keeping some aside for us for dinner later that evening.

"It wasn't that bad. I've been inside some really gross mouths. I have a strong stomach. It was pretty nasty though."

I laughed at the face he was pulling. Even covered in sweat and fish guts, he was oh, so fine.

"So the cabin has a shower, but the hot water tank is kinda small." I knew I needed a shower, but I wasn't sure if he'd want to take one here or if he'd go home and clean up.

"That sounds like an invitation."

God. Had it?

My insides dropped as he stepped closer, his voice taking that tone again. The one I didn't yet know how to react to. The one that was making me doublethink everything I'd ever thought about relationships. The one that could easily talk me into a shower, cold water be damned.

We were both disgusting, hands only cleaned by the running water out of the hose.

I leaned against the makeshift sink under my cabin, and in front of me he stepped closer and closer.

Excited nerves controlled my words and I began to ramble, something I was sure he'd be sick of sooner than later. How was I supposed to be in a mature relationship? I had zero experience. I was no smoother than a thirteen-year-old. It wouldn't take him long to get sick of trying to have an adult situation with someone so inexperienced in those ways.

"No. I didn't mean it like that. I mean, if you want to share a shower, I'm game. I'd love to see you naked. Wait, did I just … ignore that part. I didn't know if you brought out anything clean to wear or not. I figured we could clean up and maybe have another fire or something."

If he was annoyed with my awkward rambling in those moments, it wasn't showing. He was smiling and nodding, looking amused and full of life.

I was a jackass.

"I wish I'd brought a change, but I didn't. How about you take a shower and I'll run home, but there's one thing that's really been bothering me all day."

Here it comes.

I'd been waiting for the shoe to drop and now was the time. I was too much of a tomboy. He was looking for someone more sophisticated. I was too crude, and he wanted someone who could hold a worldly conversation, or at least one that didn't have anything to do with Wynne, or construction, or guts for that matter.

I was covered in fish slime.

I'd pulled my own boat in the water without waiting for him.

I'd been too bossy when we were fishing and I'd emasculated him.

Just like Sunny had told me I did to the kid who took me to prom. I'd picked *him* up because it was raining really hard and I had better tires. I didn't want to wreck on our way to the dance. And I certainly didn't want to change a tire in the only dress I'd ever owned that had a zip up the side.

Men wanted someone delicate they could take care of and protect. They wanted someone who made them feel powerful and needed.

And I'd never be a woman who couldn't take care of herself. A girl who couldn't survive if left alone.

I'd been left alone before.

My mom left both of us. I'd watched my dad struggle with trying to teach me things a mother would have. From baking when he'd rather have been hunting. Or making Christmas decorations when the game was on.

He'd fallen in love with a woman who couldn't sit still. A woman who would abandon her child and never come back. I knew he struggled with it. I knew it broke him. He was lonely, and often he'd apologize that it was him I was doing things with when it should have been her.

That's what stuck in my head. I never wanted to feel like I was left lost. Wandering around, needing someone else to save me.

I could save myself.

Ironically, he saved me *from* myself at that moment by saying my name.

"Hannah."

It snapped me out of my worrisome thoughts and my eyes locked on his.

"Lost you there for a minute."

"Sorry," I said and laughed to pretend like my thoughts weren't getting much deeper than I wanted.

"That's all right. You want to talk about it?"

"Nothing to talk about. Now what were you saying?" I could hear the change in my voice. Normally, around him I spoke much softer than I usually did. In that moment, I sounded like I was talking to anyone in town. "You wanted to tell me what I'd done all day that bugged you?"

Time to face the music.

He got closer and it shocked me when he wrapped his arms around my waist and pulled me into him.

"You haven't kissed me all day."

That was it? He'd wanted me to kiss him?

"What?" I wasn't sure I'd heard him right.

"Before I go I wanted to let you know that I want you to touch me, to kiss me. I saw you today—you looked at my lips more than my eyes. You licked your lips after I lifted my shirt to wipe sweat off my face—which I did as an experiment. You want to touch me."

Where does this stuff come from?

Where did he get the balls to say things like that?

Right as he was, I'd never known anyone who could just say whatever was on their mind the way he did.

It was one of the things I liked about him the most. His sincerity. He never let me wonder where I stood with him for too long. Never left me hanging.

Still, he hadn't kissed or touched me either. What was that about?

"I don't know. I guess I've just never been a touchy feely kind of girl. I'm sorry."

"Sorry? Do you want to do those things?"

"You just said you knew I did." I wasn't following?

"What I'm trying to say is, I know this is new for you—and I really like that—but if we're seeing each other now, then that means a few things. If there's something you need, or want to do, then do it. I want you to grab my hand, or kiss me, or touch me. It lets me know I'm doing all this the way you like it. It lets me know I'm treating you well if you want to be near me. It's not about being clingy or anything like that. It's your body communicating to my body it likes it, too."

My body was all over that and I kissed him, without holding back.

He made me feel so good about being me. Which made things a bit trickier. I didn't want to *change* for anyone, but for Vaughn, I wanted to be other things that I wasn't sure I knew how to be.

Gentler.

More attentive.

Sweeter.

It wasn't something I had to think about doing, somehow I was already starting to behave those ways. And that part of me, a part I didn't know was even there, sort of existed when he was around.

He'd magically turned all of my rough edges to silk when he touched me. Made all of the empty and lonely spots full with his attention. When his fingers moved over me, everything male in him spoke to everything female in me, and I felt beautiful. Fragile and vulnerable.

I loved how he knew he should take his time and be careful with that part of me. Because obviously I did not.

When my swollen lips almost abandoned my face to take up residency on his, I pulled away, slowly breaking the kiss.

"Thanks for the invitation."

"I mean it. I want you, Hannah. But I'm going to take my cues from you. I won't rush this. Won't rush *you*."

"But I want you, too," I admitted, not much louder than a whisper. I wasn't used to saying things like that. I knew for a fact that those words had never left my mouth.

We stood there, the late afternoon sun sneaking under the cabin and warming me from behind, the front of me warmed by him and his romantic words.

The light was in his eyes and they shimmered like brilliant, glowing ripples on the water.

"I like hearing that. I'm going to run home and clean up, and I'll come back, if you want. Then, instead of looking at my lips, you better kiss them."

"And I'll touch you," I added to let him know I understood what he meant.

He groaned a little, but it was more of a tease. "That doesn't sound like too bad of a time."

"Yeah, but what if, after I start, I can't stop?" That was something I should have thought to myself.

"Then I guess it's going to be a long night." He placed a kiss on my forehead. "Need anything from town?"

I didn't, but I didn't want his offer to be empty.

"5-hour Energy," I said, then silently prayed to the gods of sexy dentists who said all of the right things that I would blissfully need two.

Chapter Eighteen

Vaughn

I needed a shower.

I needed clean clothes.

I needed the gas station to have condoms.

I wasn't being forward, and if she still wasn't ready, she'd never know that I had them. But if—*IF*—she was ready, I had to be ready, too.

All day she'd been looking at me in a different way. I loved that she never shied away when I caught her. She'd just smile and then go back to what she was doing. Almost like she hadn't the faintest idea she'd been staring at me.

After I said what I had, I would never want to slow her down. I'd seem like a liar. Like I'd been all talk and I wasn't all talk. Even as I pulled away from the cabin, my all-action dick was still hard.

5-hour Energy.

Yeah, you'll need a few of those if you start something

entirely too fun to finish before I'm done with you.

The fucking gas station better have some damn condoms.

I showered and didn't skip the shave, glad I'd waited until then. Her poor lips were red and I didn't want kissing me to feel like sandpaper, because there would be a lot more kissing that night than there had been that day.

Sure, I'd told her I'd follow her cues, but there's only so much a guy can take. Especially, when I'd been watching her all day working and laughing and closing her eyes, face up to the sun, enjoying the moment.

She was becoming irresistible to me.

I wanted to tackle her there in that boat, and I'd decided on the next trip, we'd have to carve some time out for the occasion. Now that I knew how good she felt in my arms, tasted on my lips, I only wanted more.

I'd had so many fantasies of taking her clothes off in the middle of that river and kissing every square inch of her. Seeing all of her.

The view when she bent over nearly drove me insane. The way her skin looked warm and inviting. The way her mouth would part when I spoke to her. Her body sent all of the right signals to mine, even when she didn't know she was doing it.

There were almost two different Hannahs. There was the girl the town knew, the capable, hands-on, do-it-herself character who had a wall up so high nobody ever bothered to climb it.

And, oddly enough, it's like with me she was this other person. Someone who was confident in their skin, yet still breaking out of it a little more each time we were together. Someone who never let anyone get close to her, but was brave enough to try. Someone who never let herself get close to someone else, but was tiptoeing her way inside me.

She was a woman who knew more duty than desire, more perseverance than passion, and more acquaintance than affection.

I wanted to show her what she was missing. I wanted to be the man that could handle her strong will and headstrong ways. I wanted to be what she needed, what she desired. Someone she could rely on for anything.

I wondered if I was changing a little myself.

It would be cooler when the sun went down, so I wore jeans and a T-shirt, grabbing a zip-up hoodie on the way out the door.

I ran by the damn gas station and the stupid condom machine was fucking broken.

As I drove back to Johnson's Chute, I was disappointed, and then again I wasn't.

There were plenty of places to take the night that still ended with her being satisfied, even without sex. I'd let her steer me there.

I stopped where I was on her road and pulled out my phone. Finding I had three glorious bars of service in the middle of nowhere, I opened up my Amazon app and ordered two more boxes of condoms.

At least, I'd never *not* have them again.

Good thing I was a silver lining kind of guy. There were many worse ways to spend a Saturday night than finding all of the ways I could bring Hannah to orgasm without selfishly seeking my own.

That was going to happen. I couldn't wait any longer to witness it. Imagining what that would look like … I was surely going to arrive the same way I'd left the cabin earlier.

Hard.

When I finally reached the spot in the road, which ended at her place, I put the SUV in park and watched as she flapped a white tablecloth over a small table she'd set up on the deck overlooking the water. She had on a pair of jeans and a tank top; her brown hair was wavy and moved with the breeze as she finished straightening the fabric.

She'd looked so good the night before, and then again that day, but—and I knew it sounded crazy—she was even more beautiful that evening. I was more and more attracted to her the more I got to know her.

"Well, are you getting out or staying in there all night? Hurry up," she shouted from the wooden rail that ran around the cabin.

So I got out and climbed the stairs as she waited for me at the top.

"Took you long enough," she teased when I stood on the last step, which made her my height.

"Trust me, I went as fast as I could."

She ran a hand over my smoother face. Touching me like I'd invited her to do. It was a mystery to me why a woman, who was so damn stubborn, would do whatever I wanted, and all I had to do was ask. It was a manly feeling and, oh, so rewarding.

"This looks good."

"You like that?"

"I bet it feels good, too."

Then she kissed me. Her lips were warm and soft and welcoming, and her hand lingered on my neck. Everything about the way she kissed me made me want her to do it again and again.

The way she'd sweep my lip with her tongue. The way she tipped her head to kiss me deeper. The way she pressed her chest into me to get closer. And the way her quiet little sounds, which played on repeat whenever we were apart, always sounded fresh in my ears.

"Can you peel potatoes?" she asked when the kiss eventually faded.

"I think I can manage," I assured her. Even though I didn't want it to end, I wanted to get dinner over with. The sooner, the better.

She put me to work, setting three large potatoes in front of me inside the small kitchen. I peeled them as she made tartar sauce and prepared the fish.

I enjoyed working with her. Actually, it wasn't what we were doing at all. It was that we were doing it together.

"I know it's not good for you, but it tastes so good this way," she told me later as she dunked the metal basket into the fryer outside.

We filled up on potatoes, fish that we'd caught ourselves, and dined beside the river as the light slipped away. Earlier, she'd said something about having another fire, and I liked that idea. What I didn't like so much about that plan though were the chairs.

Her chair.

My chair.

It wasn't close enough.

Apparently she felt the same way.

After we cleaned up from dinner, she asked, "Want to go hang out on the boat? Listen to music?" She cocked her head to the side, being both a flirt and a shy vixen. Then she admitted, "Maybe I'll touch you."

"Maybe?" Her words alone gave me enough pleasure, but I was seriously interested in how she was planning on doing this touching. That thought alone made my dick twitch.

"Your odds are very good, Doctor."

Very good was good enough for me. I'd let her lead this round since she was going for it.

Stupid fucking no condom having gas station.

I didn't know how fast she could shower, but in the time I was gone, she'd gotten a lot done. Walking down the narrow dock behind her at sunset, I saw that she'd put a quilt down on the floorboard of the boat and added a few pillows. I noticed a cooler. She was prepared.

"What if I would have said I *didn't* want to get in the boat?"

She chuckled as she stepped onto the boat. "I have more than one trick up my sleeve."

I found a place to sit and propped one leg up against the side of the boat. She knelt on the quilt and pulled two glasses out of the cooler and a chilled bottle of wine.

"Wine?" I asked, surprised that it wasn't her customary Newcastle. She'd passed on wine at my house.

"I like this kind. It's from a winery not too far from

here. I like it because it's not too sweet and not too dry."

I thought, sounds about right, just like you. A perfect blend.

I liked wine, and it was just another fun element about her I hadn't expected. Another thing in common.

"You have a nice little picnic down here."

"I wanted to do something nice to say thank you for last night, and for going out with me today. For everything."

Last night wasn't the best, most thought-out first date in history. I would have loved to take her out on the town somewhere, maybe see if she liked to dance, or even take her to a nice place to eat. Wynne only had one nice place that I knew of, the golf course by the lake, but it was all so new and I'd wanted her to be comfortable.

The fact that she'd had a good time and needed to thank me for it only proved how no one had ever taken the time to show her a proper date.

And today?

I couldn't remember a day where I'd been more out of my element, but enjoyed it nonetheless. She was in her element, and damn, did she shine.

"You don't have to thank me, but I like this."

She reached up and flicked on the radio, turning the volume only loud enough to hear what song was on. Then she kicked back and sat close to me with her wine.

I wrapped an arm around her and we sat there for a while drinking and enjoying the fiery sky.

When our glasses went dry, she refilled them and came right back to my side. Her warm body fit next to mine like it was made to go there.

She drank her second glass a lot faster than the first,

which led me to believe she was looking for a little courage.

After she emptied it, she said, "Last night, when you said all of that stuff, I didn't know what to say, Vaughn. I know I'm a little strange, but hearing you say what you did really made me think."

I didn't want to interrupt. So when she paused, I just rubbed her arm and gave her time to get it all out.

"I don't know how to do this. I like you, and I think you like me, but I've never been someone's *girlfriend*. Hell, I don't even know if that's what you want. I just know that I like the way you make me feel, and I like the way you look at me."

She sat her empty glass down, not caring that it tipped over and rolled away.

"And I'm not very good at talking about this stuff, and you are, but I want to try. When you kiss me, or when you look into my eyes, I don't know what to do with myself, and I get worried that I'll make a mistake, or say something stupid. Which you've already witnessed. I don't want to mess this up."

I stretched my arms out to her.

"Come here," I said, and she moved to my lap, facing me. The boat rocked gently against the bumpers, separating it from the wood of the dock. I moved the hair from both sides of her face and held her gaze.

"You don't have to worry about any of that. I wouldn't want you any other way. I've yet to find anything about you I'd ever want to change. I think you're sexy because you don't have a clue you are. If you're not comfortable putting a name on this yet, we don't have to. But I want you to know I'm not going to see anyone else. I'm a one girl at a time kind of guy. I can't tell you what to do, but I know inside I don't want you with anyone else either. I won't say we're just having fun though, because I don't think that's what this is."

Her blinking became slower and her breathing shallower. My hands ran up her back caressing her warm skin, causing her to lean into me even more.

"Then what is this, Vaughn?" she whispered.

"It's the beginning of *everything*."

She leaned forward and her mouth found my neck, her wet lips kissing me. My hands found her ass and pressed her into me so she was straddling me exactly how I wanted her to.

As good as she felt on my neck, I wanted her mouth. I led her there by leaning down to meet her lips with mine, earning an appreciative moan when I did.

She rocked into me and I moved my legs together and bent her forward so she leaned back on my knees.

I wanted to see her.

She followed my lead and relaxed on my legs as I pulled the bottom of her shirt up and over her head and arms. I was lucky it hadn't gotten as cool as I'd expected, because it was incredible being outside in the open with her like this.

Her perfect skin glowed in the dark for me. She wore a simple white bra, no lace, and without any words she leaned forward and removed it. All of her curves and valleys given to me in one movement. She shivered, not from a chill, but under my touch as my hands roamed the uncharted nakedness of her breasts.

They were full, and in the twilight I could see perfectly round nipples that stiffened under my caress. She moved against my zipper searching for something more than my touch on her chest.

I let my hand wander to her button fly and I leaned against the pillows propped up behind us as she rested against my legs, allowing me to explore her.

When there were no more buttons to work apart, there was a moment where I thought it was too much for her, her body shaking like she was nervous.

I had to know if she wanted me to go any further, before I did.

"Hannah?" I asked as I ran a hand over her center above her jeans, along the denim seam between her legs. "Do you want this?"

I selfishly applied a little pressure with my hand to her, needing to feel her, even before she agreed.

She didn't say anything, but her hand covered mine and led me into her. Past her panties. Past a soft patch of trimmed hair to where my fingers were met with wetness and her obvious arousal.

I took my time feeling her, learning her, finding my way. When my hand reached the top of her, she bucked in my hand and leaned forward, giving me a much better angle to use.

She hugged my neck tightly as she rocked against my luckiest hand, while my runner-up hand pulled her into me.

She sat on her knees and kissed me even harder from slightly above me.

I slipped a finger into her and she released a beautiful sigh. I stopped the kiss to watch her face as I gave her a second to get used to me there.

Her mouth fell slack and her eyes danced in the moonlight as she rode my fingers.

It surprised me when her hand slipped atop mine, mingling with my fingers, feeling them go in and out of her.

I could feel her thighs begin to shake as she pushed harder against my palm and then, as she said, "Vaughn," in the most sensual way I'd ever heard, she removed her hand to hang onto my shoulders again.

I moved my head in a way that she'd touch my cheek, and when it was close enough, I sucked one of her fingers into my mouth just as her core tightened.

The taste of her on my lips, combined with the sound of her pleasure, made my erection almost painful.

As she came down, she rested her head on my shoulder, her index finger still in my mouth. She relaxed against me and found her breath.

I leaned back, putting our full weight on the pillows, and held her. And my hand, which was still inside her jeans, stroked her sensitive skin.

Something powerful, and almost possessive, swelled inside of me as we lay there.

Soon she was lazily kissing my neck.

Was it possible she wanted more? Because I was perfectly happy giving it to her. As many times as she liked.

I wanted to come more than just about anything, but not necessarily more than I wanted her to again.

"I liked that," I told her, the words almost getting caught low in my throat.

"I really liked that," she said dreamily. "A lot."

That, my friends, is what victory feels like.

Chapter Nineteen

Hannah

My body was boneless against him. His hand was still in my pants and keeping the fire alive after what had happened. And what he'd done with his hand was better than most of the sex I'd had my whole life—combined.

If he could do that with his fingers, I had to believe the other things he could do would be just as good, if not better.

I wasn't willing to wait very long to find out.

I craved more and wanted to touch him. So, as I let the rhythm of his rising and falling chest reenergize me, my hand wandered between us. He shifted a little and I heard the sharp intake of breath pass his teeth.

I felt him through his jeans, incredibly hard. I followed the length of his erection to the side of his lap and then back to cup his balls. A strong desire to please him surged through me.

"Vaughn, I want you to have a good time, too," I quietly admitted between kisses near his ear.

"Oh, believe me, if you keep doing that I will." His voice was low but had a weakness to it that sounded so sexy. I had him, literally, in the palm of my hand. Which was fitting because I'd just been putty in his.

I stroked him over his pants, and then I couldn't stand not actually touching him anymore. Wandering over to his button and zipper, I gave them a little time off and made my way to him.

"You don't have to do that, Hannah," he assured me. "That's not why..." and then he trailed off and gave up on chivalry. It made me smile.

I wanted to tease him a little, so instead of making my way under his boxer briefs, I ran my hand on top of them until there was not enough room to fit my hand and him in the space between his hip and his pocket.

His head falling back on the pillow, I took pity on him and tucked my hand inside his underwear. His skin was hot, and he flexed against my palm when I gripped and released him from the confines of his clothes. Freed, he fell stiff against his stomach and my mouth watered at the sight.

His hand was still in my pants, and as I started to stroke him, he began teasing me a second time.

Quickly, he sat forward and brought his shirt over his head.

There we were: two shirtless people making out on a boat for the first time. Mouth on mouth, chest against chest. Hands feeling their way around, testing out what the other might like, only to find they pretty much liked everything the other had to offer.

I'd push forward and he'd give, his hips would rise when I'd tighten my grip just enough.

"I'm not going to last like this," he said around my lips. "That feels too good."

I was feeling it too, but I had a suspicion he was going to get there before I did. I liked that idea. I loved feeling like I was the source of his pleasure.

"That's okay. I drank that 5-hour Energy you brought me," I joked, even if it wasn't the best moment for it, but seeing him come apart under my will made me spunky.

"And it's still early," I added. I had no plans of ending the night anytime soon. "I want you to stay."

His breathing became rushed and quickened. He pulled me hard against him and moaned against my neck. His teeth grazed my skin and he tensed, his erection flexing in my palm. Once, twice, and then he made a sound so erotic I found myself moaning in unison with him.

His wet orgasm was slick on his stomach.

He removed his hand from my pants and wrapped both of his arms around me, kissing me so passionately, all of the cockiness I was feeling jumped overboard.

I was totally consumed by him.

Yes, I'd just gotten him off, but that wasn't enough. I wanted to give him more. Wanted him to have more of *me*.

I leaned back and he moved to follow, falling in between my legs and grinding himself against me, mimicking what I really wanted.

"I want to be inside of you so badly, but I don't have anything with me," he confessed between kisses.

"I have condoms."

He stopped and held his weight above me, looking me

straight in the face.

"You do?"

"Yeah, I bought them this morning."

"You did?"

"Yeah, they have them at the store. I just went early and got them."

"I wanted to buy some, but your dad showed up and started talking to me." His face was adorably frustrated remembering what had happened.

"Oh my God. What did you do?"

He answered matter-of-factly, eyebrows raised, like there'd only been one option. "I bought foot cream."

Foot cream? I began laughing—the thought of Vaughn getting caught by my dad while buying protection was hilariously uncomfortable.

"Well, I guess the early bird gets the worm."

In the moonlight his face twisted, not liking my joke. "That wasn't good."

"No. Pretend like I didn't say it."

He laughed and I leaned up to kiss him, I was tired of all the talking.

"Wait. Wait. Wait," he repeated, and then he sat back on his legs. "Are you sure you want to do this?"

Waiting no time to answer, or for him to sense any hesitation, I said, "I'm sure."

I was *damn* sure.

"We don't have to yet. This is only our second date, Hannah. I'm not in any hurry."

I considered that maybe I looked a little slutty, but it was also thoughtful that he was worried about rushing me. "Will you think less of me if we have sex tonight?"

"God, no. That's not what I mean. I don't want you to think you're not worth waiting for, is all. I'm not in a hurry. If—and only if—you're ready to go there with me, that's what I want, too."

How did he always know exactly what I needed to hear? How to make me forget how nervous I was to make the wrong move? How to make me feel like it mattered to him as much as it did to me?

There was no doubt I was ready to be with him.

"Then take your pants off and grab that bag." I kicked the small tote I'd carried them down there in. Then, I scooted out of my jeans and underwear, as if it were a race. Like I had to do it fast before he changed his mind. *Sluts be damned.*

"Hey, whoa. What's your rush? I wanted to do that." He'd taken his pants off, but left his underwear on. In that moment, I did feel kind of slutty.

Was I ever going to get this right?

"I don't know. I just really want you." How embarrassing. I scrunched my eyes together, wanting to disappear.

Vaughn's tone changed, softening almost. He cajoled, "Hey, I want you, too, but I want to look at you. Remember this. Take my time. Just relax and let me make you feel good. I don't have anywhere to go."

The look in his blue eyes was full of tenderness and heat, trying to comfort me and reassure me that this was where he wanted to be. Again proving how much he thought about my feelings. It touched me. In places I didn't know occupied so much of my heart, he aroused something deep inside me much stronger than my desperate body.

"You'll stay then?"

"I said I'm not going anywhere," he answered, as he kissed my belly and then my hip. "Except maybe here."

He moved my legs, opening me up to him, and placed a kiss at my center. "Yeah, I think I'm going here first."

"But…" I began, only to realize I didn't really have anything to say. I wanted him to do what he was about to. It was just that I'd never let anyone do that before. It had always been too personal. Too intimate for a one-night stand.

"Is this okay?" he asked as he kissed the inside of my thigh. Of course it was okay, I was just a little anxious. I'd never felt so laid bare, as if I were surrendering all of me.

"I've just never…" I said to the stars.

"May I?" His tongue flicked out and touched me, my sensitive skin too aware of what he was doing, and I jumped a little, my hands tapping down against the boat with a jolt.

I didn't know if I could handle it.

I didn't know I would feel like that. So equally vulnerable and turned on.

I didn't know what to do with my hands, and suddenly I was really aware of them. My fingers fidgeted from my nervousness.

"Give me those," he said and reached for one of my hands, and then held out for the other. I did what he asked, and he held my them together on top of my stomach with one of his.

His lust-filled eyes blinked slowly at me as he looked up from below. Then I watched him look back down between my thighs, and like he was overcome with what he saw, he moaned and took another lick. Then said, "If you don't like it, I'll stop. If you do, I won't. That simple."

Was it that simple?

He gave me a minute, time to decide, but the kisses he was peppering on my legs were very persuasive. I would trust him.

"I want you to."

He didn't say anything, taking one long lick up the center of me. The sensation was new and made my toes curl, and my ass left the bottom of the boat.

"Oh my," I panted and he did it again. That time he'd moved slower and my eyes damn near rolled around to the back of my head.

Every time I bucked, he held my hands tighter, and something about that added to the experience. The control he had, the control I gave him. He was gentle, but strong. He found what I liked, and when my hips rolled he hummed his gratitude.

I couldn't say anything, all of my focus on this one extraordinary sensation, and everything else drifted away with the gentle rocking of the water.

Just as I thought I was going over the edge, he'd slow and take it easy on me. Then he'd bring me right back.

It was exquisite and maddening. My feet and my shoulders holding my weight, I pushed myself against his mouth as he flicked at the most perfect spot. The last thing I remember thinking was *those are the most beautiful stars I've ever seen* and I didn't know if they were the real ones or not.

I didn't care either way.

Was there anything this man wasn't good at?

Every ragged breath shook my whole body, and before I knew it, he was crawling up my tummy with kisses and saying over and over, "You're so beautiful."

When he reached my mouth, he said, "I know I'm

sounding like a broken record, but it's important to me. Are you sure you're ready to do this?"

I nodded and my hand reached for the bag he'd brought closer, and I pulled out a condom as he pulled off his briefs.

He took it from me, leaning up to put it on, and I reveled in the way he looked. With the reflection of moon dancing off the water and the dim light that came from up on my deck, I studied the ripples on his stomach and the muscles in his arms. As he rolled the condom on and gave himself a few strokes, the fire inside me came roaring back to life, like fresh air on smoldering coals.

He was a sight. His skin slick with fevered lust. His lips still wet from my climax.

Then he returned to me, and my hands ran desperately over his taut muscles and ribs, wanting more.

He gave pause, and said, "This means something to me, Hannah. I've wanted you since the moment we met." With one hand he guided himself to my entrance, then let go and held himself precisely there with the most tantalizing pressure. Just the tip of him inside of me. His hand found my breast; then his mouth found my nipple. The overwhelming rush of sensation brought my hips to his, causing him to enter me fully.

"Ah," I breathed, becoming acquainted with the fullness of him. I'd never had someone take so much time on behalf of my pleasure. I'd never been with someone who made me so desperate and wild with need. I'd never been with someone who fit into my life like he did in every single way.

"Oh, Hannah."

My fingers moved across his shoulders as he held still

inside me, almost like he was waiting for me to make the first move again. His hips only slightly pressed against me where we met flush in the middle.

He licked my breast once more and sucked my nipple into his mouth one last time before coming up to kiss my shoulder sweetly. Then he met me eye-to-eye.

It was almost too much. He was too handsome. Too good for me. But there he was, and I was lost in him, helpless to know whether I was awake or dreaming.

The friction he made proved too much as, impatient for more, I moved and he pulled away only to come right back. So began our first time together.

The first time our bodies, together, moved towards climax. The first time, together, all the walls and all the pretenses I'd tried to hide behind were gone.

I felt more like a woman than I ever had. My body's purpose was to gain and give pleasure with this man, while he showed me how it incredible it was to be made love to.

Another thing I'd always thought was cliché. How when it was with someone special, it was more special, and, apparently, that had always been true. Vaughn was that special piece I'd been missing all along.

The way he moved in and out of me at the most divine pace and pressure, while whispering how I was making him feel and how badly he wanted me to come for him, it was unlike any other sexual experience of my life.

Even the sweat on his skin was intoxicating, and it only proved how all of my senses were being tantalized.

Although I tried to hold off as long as I could, and we'd slowed ourselves down as many times as our bodies would tolerate, I couldn't fight it longer.

"Vaughn?"

"Hannah, don't hold back."

"Oh, yes. Yes," I gasped, over and over, as my body rocked itself against him, grinding out my orgasm.

"There you go, beautiful. There you go."

My back arched, head tipped back, his mouth on my neck and his body moving furiously into me, he chased his orgasm and caught it just as I wrung out the last of my release.

"Jesus, Vaughn. Oh."

He grunted as it hit him and he pushed one last time, with such force, it hit a spot that almost set me off again. His ass clenched tight, my hands held him to me.

He moved the hair stuck to my face and he tenderly kissed my lips. "You're incredible."

I laughed, because it seemed like he'd done most of the work, but it was not time to argue.

We ended up lying there, propped against the pillows naked, and finished the bottle of wine.

It had been one of the best nights of my life.

"I still can't stop picturing you and my dad at the store. Where did he run into you?" I watched as he climbed out of the boat, prepared to help me carry things back up.

"Right in front of the condoms. Like *right* in front. He even teased that it was funny he ran into me next to the *rubbers*."

I handed Vaughn the cooler with the blanket folded on top of it, and picked up the last of the stuff to take to the cabin. Then I had to stop because I was laughing too hard. I didn't want to fall off the boat.

"Priceless," I countered when I caught my breath.

"Yeah, so my *rubbers* won't be here until Monday. Thank God for next day shipping."

My side hurt, but it was amazing watching him joke about the whole thing. Then he winked, and I almost fell again.

"Bet you never thought when you signed up for that you'd be buying those with it."

"I didn't, but I'm sure glad they sell them. What do people do around here? It's fucking awkward."

It really was, that's why I was sure to be the first one through the door before anyone else showed up that morning. I had never even thought of ordering them online. That was genius, but it still wouldn't have helped us that night.

"Are you really staying?"

He stopped and looked at me like I was nuts. "Of course I am, if you still want me to."

"That was before. You know. I didn't know if you'd want to go home now or not." I wasn't proud of asking that, but I'd rather know sooner than later. What if he wanted to go home?

"Hannah, are you serious? I wasn't just saying those things to have sex with you."

I felt guilty saying that to him, but in my experience, guys say a lot of things, either just before sex or right after, that may or may not always pan out.

"I was just checking." Then as an apology I reached up and gave him a quick kiss on the cheek.

Sometimes he was just too good to believe. You know?

"Well, trust me," he said and put the cooler down on the deck as we got to the sliding back door. "I won't ever lie to you like that. I won't manipulate you. And, I'm really sorry, if in the past others have. That's really wrong. I don't want you to sleep with me because of something I've promised or said I'd do, I want you to be with me because—and only because—it's what you want. That went for tonight and it goes for every time we have sex—if I should ever get so lucky again." His face was serious, but kind.

I hoped that whatever we were doing would last a little while, because the more he said things like that, the more I believed him.

We went inside and I used the bathroom to wash up. Our adventure on the boat had been a little messy. What I really wanted was another shower, but decided I'd rather get back to him.

I didn't want the night to end. Something in my mind always told me I needed to take advantage of the time he was there. Even though, over the past few weeks, whenever I wanted to see him all I had to do was say the words.

But I was realistic and knew it couldn't last forever.

It was only ten o'clock, but after the boat, I was ready to settle down. Ready to crawl up next to him. Ready to listen to him talk to me as I fell asleep.

I found him sitting on the deck, so I grabbed the blanket off the cooler and wrapped it around my arms. It was still warm, but the breeze was a little stronger and it was cooling off.

I went to sit on the other chair, but stopped when Vaughn said, "No. Please, come here." He sat back and opened his arms for me, and I couldn't deny him.

Would I ever get used to him wanting to be close to me? Probably about the time he would change his mind.

Chapter Twenty

Vaughn

Hannah climbed on my lap sideways. It was funny, sometimes she seemed so strong and powerful, and then, in times like that, she seemed so fragile and small. She curled into me, laying her head on my chest, and I stroked her thick, wavy hair, enjoying how she let me care for her.

After a little while of watching the water go by and listening to her breathe, she said, "Vaughn, tell me more stuff about you."

I thought and thought. There wasn't that much to tell, but maybe I could kind of explain what I was looking for in Wynne. Why it was important to me.

"When I was a kid, I had a best friend named Pete. He lived close to me and we hung out together a lot. In the summer, I'd go with him to his grandparents' farm. They lived near a small town just like this one. That might be why I like it so much."

She lay there quietly as I began speaking about my favorite childhood memories.

"We'd ride our bikes all day and build real tree houses and forts with extra wood his grandpa had around. They had dinner every night at five thirty and went to church every Sunday. We were Catholic—or bad Catholics as my mom used to say—so we rarely went.

"I'm not a really religious guy. I believe what I do, but I always liked going when I was at Pete's grandparents'. They'd go and then usually everyone would end up at someone's house and we'd eat and play in town until it got dark.

"I guess that's what I wanted my life to look like." She looked up at me and I could see she was listening—really hearing—what I was telling her. Her eyes roamed my face and a lazy grin bent the corners of her lovely lips.

"I know times have changed, and life is busier and more complicated than it looked at seven or eight, but they were a *real* family.

"My parents got divorced when I was nine. My dad moved to Columbus, and my mom remarried pretty fast to a guy who didn't have kids. They travelled a lot and left me with sitters. My dad worked too much, so if I spent time there, it was usually by myself. Both my parents were only children, so I didn't have cousins I could go spend time with.

"Then in high school Pete moved, his parents got a different job or something—I can't remember now—and I pretty much just studied and played sports to keep busy."

I could tell she didn't like that part; compassion mired her features. Her bottom lip making an adorable pout.

"His grandparents still invited me there that next summer, but I think we both had some kind of sports camp we had to attend and the dates didn't line up. Even after all of those years, I still think of them."

I wanted her to understand, that even though she thought her town might not have much to offer, the sense of community and belonging was what I wanted.

"What happened to Pete?" she asked, with curious eyes before she yawned.

"He lives in Houston. Has a wife and a couple of kids. We still talk every once in a while. I was in his wedding." I think the fact that we were still friends made her smile.

She said, "Good," as she lay her head back down. And then she wrapped an arm around my back and covered both of us with the blanket.

"That's really why you moved here. The job worked out, but I'm sure you had other options."

I had, but she was right. I'd been waiting until there was a little town, where I could move. Fix up a house and start a *real* family.

One that I could hold together.

One that was mine.

"I think you're right."

She fell asleep in my arms, and I sat awake in the chair on the deck for a long time and let her rest. The soft rise and fall of her chest and the way her hold on me never weakened gave me a new feeling. Something peaceful and something worth working hard to keep.

I realized I wanted her to love me, and I wanted to love her back, but also knew we had some time to kill between now and then.

In just those few short weeks, she'd already become

someone I cared about. Someone who made time go faster together, and slower when we were apart.

I had a desire to give her things, show her places she'd never been, make her laugh and hear her say my name thousands of times, like she had on the boat.

The hunger to build something with this woman was powerful and new to me. I didn't want the *idea* of the perfect life, I really wanted it, and it was so easy inserting Hannah into all of those future thoughts. It was the most natural thing picturing her by my side.

I wasn't going to come on strong, even if everything in my being told me to hold on to her. What we had was new and exciting and fun. Completely unexpected, but so welcomed at the same time.

There was no place I'd rather be. I wasn't going anywhere, and, I thought, neither was she.

I woke up early in the cabin in my boxers, still holding her, just as I'd fallen asleep the night before.

I didn't want to let go, but I wanted to stretch out. Careful I didn't wake her, I tried to pull my arm out from under her, not realizing she was already awake, too.

"Remember that day you asked me *why do you keep coming over here*? And I asked you *why don't you ever tell me to leave*?"

I did remember. I was frustrated and annoyed, and there she was. The only person who was trying to help me and the only one around to take it out on. It wasn't that I missed Rachelle, because I didn't. It was that all along I was trying to force something that wasn't right. Then, when she showed up, it made me question why it never felt wrong with her there. It was confusing.

"I'm sorry I was so rude that day."

"I'm not."

She rolled around in my arms, looking sleepy and fresh faced. Her hair wild and messy. I took a moment to memorize exactly the way she looked. A mental snapshot, knowing there would be a time when I'd think back to this second and be thankful for the clarity.

She'd been half asleep when I set her in the bed last night. I didn't want to wake her, but when I sat her on the bed, she stirred. Then she kicked off her flip-flops and pulled her jeans off, choosing to sleep in her underwear and tank top. Her bra never found its way back on after the boat.

"Want to know why?" She quirked a conspiratorial eyebrow and puckered her lips to hold her secret in a little longer.

"Why?"

"When I was little I remember asking my grandpa if my mom and dad fought a lot. I always knew she left, but I never really understood why until I was older." She propped herself up on her hand, her elbow pressing into the bed.

"Anyway, from time to time I'd ask my grandpa if it had been this or that which had caused my mom and dad to split. On this day, it was fighting. I wanted to know if they fought all the time and I was shocked when he said no so fast.

"He said, 'Never, Mutt. Not one time did I ever see them fight and that's not good.' Now I was probably ten or eleven when I asked. So his answer confused me. I thought that people fighting was bad in a relationship, not the other way around, so I asked him to explain. He told me that when I grew up I'd understand it a little more. Then he told me the key to having a long happy life with someone was finding someone you *liked* fighting with.

"That day, after you asked that, and I said what I said back, on the way home it made me smile. Don't get me wrong—I don't want to fight with you—but I don't think I'd mind it either."

I wanted to kiss her, but held off for her to continue.

"You're hot when you're pissed. And, for those first few weeks, even though you didn't say anything else that was rude, there were days when you were working things out in your head, and you had every right to. It was your home. You were going through some changes. But being around you like that, if that was what you were like when you didn't feel at your best, I knew you were worth hanging around a little more. I knew you were special."

Where had she been my whole life? Here. She'd been here, as if she were waiting for me.

Hannah shrugged as I watched her grin like she was confessing something scandalous.

"And the hot thing. One time I saw you get so mad you clenched your teeth, balled your fists, and looked like you were going to scream, but then you scanned around for me, and didn't make a sound. Pissed and fine as they come."

I had to agree with her grandpa. Rachelle and I never fought. And at the very end, when we did a little, I didn't like it. I didn't like that side of her.

That morning when Hannah fired back, then kept right

on working on my house—in her free time no less—even when I wasn't the best company, said a lot about the kind of person she was.

Also, I really liked hearing that she thought I was hot.

I couldn't hold back anymore. If there was more to the story, it could wait. I kissed her, because that's what you do when someone looks as sexy as she did lying in that bed.

While she kissed me back, I thought about the night before and how it had been exactly what I'd wanted. What I'd needed.

Her body was made for me. Every soft curve. Every corner and bend, I wanted to touch and claim for my own. I wanted it all. The freckles and scars, the whimpers and moans as she fell apart in my arms. The look of wonder in her eyes when I tasted her, and knowing that I'd been the only man to please her in that way.

I'd had sex, and I'd done my share of fucking, but it had never been like we were together.

Never that powerful. Never that intense. I'd never craved for more as bad as I did in that moment with her.

That morning was the first of dozens.

Well rested. Satisfied from the night before, but ready to go again.

I learned she was very affectionate as soon as she woke up, and often that was when she was the sweetest with her words. She was always pleasant, but catching her as soon as she woke up was like she hadn't turned her sarcasm on yet.

It wasn't that I didn't like the smart-ass side of her, but

I especially loved the mornings.

Sometimes we were at her cabin, other times we were in my bed. I liked both, but there was an element of having her in my bed with me that made it feel more like home.

She got into a habit of leaving me notes in my SUV if she had to leave earlier than I did, to go home, or to open the shop.

Some were sweet, because she'd just been asleep and was still only partially awake.

Things like:

> *V-*
>
> *I'm so glad I was running late for dinner the night you moved to Wynne.*
>
> *H*

Or,

> *V-*
>
> *I'm thinking about a sunset boat ride, but the boat is out of gas. Don't buy any. I'll get the wine. ;)*
>
> *H*

That was the day she'd gone shopping with Sunny in Browning. That night I found her waiting for me on her boat wearing a pale pink silk thing that made me ask her where she'd bought it, in case I was just too careless and ruined it completely on purpose.

The sex got better and better. She was bossy, and totally in control in everyday life, and so beautifully and confidently submissive to my every wish, my every move. Which only fueled me to please her more. Making her come harder. Louder. And over and over again, even when she swore she was wrung dry. When she'd say she could barely handle it, I pushed just a little further and she'd melt into my mouth, or my fingers, or my cock.

Our conversations were just as fun as they'd always been. She'd argue with me, or I'd argue with her, and then she'd wink, mouthing the words, "You're so hot."

She said she didn't want to label us, and I didn't push it, but she ended up being the one to call me her boyfriend in public first.

Sunny had a friend in town, from a different radio station, and we ran into them at the summer carnival.

"Hey, this is Julia, the friend I told you guys about," Sunny had said as she walked up to us just as we'd finished eating our second corndogs.

Julia was petite and cute, but she had nothing on Hannah. And even though I hated that she was insecure at that moment, I also liked how she'd needed Julia to know I was hers.

"Nice to meet you, Julia. This is my boyfriend, Vaughn." Then she grabbed my hand and didn't let go for the rest of the night.

That evening, up against the shower wall in my bathroom—which she'd helped me tile—when I asked her whose boyfriend I was, she said, "You're all mine, Vaughn, and I'm all yours."

I lost it right then, pushing harder and harder into her until she said it over and over again. "I'm yours. I'm yours."

Things changed after that night.

Up until then, we laid kind of low. We didn't go up to the bar together on the weekends, not that either of us really wanted to. We tended to stick to ourselves.

We'd never talked about it, but it was fun and there wasn't anything wrong with spending time getting to know each other in private. And as fast as our sex life took off, it was important that we spent just as much time out of bed as we did in it.

The weeks passed in a blink.

The days were hot; the nights were blistering.

We boated, and like it was the most natural thing, we began spending time with other people.

Together.

As a couple.

It was almost like she finally realized I really was hers, and it was safe to share. Safe to let people know she cared about me and brave enough to show people that she let someone care about her.

I was learning that in a small town, you protect what you hold sacred. For Hannah, what she protected the most was her feelings.

We'd been to Browning a few times with Sunny and it was great watching her interact with someone who was so completely different. At the same time, Hannah was changing a little, but enjoying all the new things she'd never tried.

Her dad still called me Astro, but he came fishing with us on a few occasions and we'd had a good time.

Dean still wasn't warming up to me, but I couldn't blame him. It was easy to see he was in love with her and was realizing that he'd lost his chance.

Hannah cared for him like a brother, so I made an effort to pretend I didn't notice. I never thought it would ever come up, and, honestly, if he was kind to her, what did it hurt me? He wasn't making her uncomfortable, from what I could tell, and he wasn't a dick to me. He just didn't say much of anything.

So when I'd asked Aaron to help me with the roof, and Hannah said Dean would help too, it caught me off guard.

The work went quickly that morning. Dean and I scraped off the old shingles without much trouble. And after catching up on some sleep, Aaron came around noon.

The roof didn't have too much going on, which made it a pretty straightforward job.

The three of us worked, talked about baseball, and then the conversation turned to women.

Well, one woman.

My woman.

Hannah.

She'd just pulled away, heading back down her road to get caught up on some flies for orders she always said she was behind on. So it was just us three, sitting on my porch eating the sandwiches and drinking the tea she brought us.

"You know what's funny?" Aaron asked, then kept talking, not waiting for an answer. "I always saw Mutt getting with you, Dean. Sorry, I know that's fucked up to say, but, Vaughn, you guys look like things are going good. She seems happy. I think that's cool."

Yeah, it was awkward and I still hated hearing her called Mutt.

Dean didn't say anything, filling his mouth with the ham and cheese with mustard she knew he'd like.

That had to be the most challenging part for me.

She cared for him, just like she cared for her dad. From the sandwiches he liked, to his whole life story, they had shared holidays with each other, and even though I knew deep down she felt one way and he might have felt another, I couldn't deny they had a lot of history. Somewhat of a shared past. One I wasn't a part of or could ever change.

Hopefully, I was her future. As long as he didn't try to change that, and as long as she wanted to be with me, I would respect their friendship.

Plus, I respected her dad and Dean's relationship, too. I knew what it was like to be a surrogate family member. I got it.

So, I was the first to speak up.

"I care a lot about her." Then I wadded up my napkin and baggie, and went around back. That was all I needed to say that mattered anyway. It was the truth and it wasn't debatable.

How he felt about it wasn't my business, and if he wanted to talk to Aaron about that, I didn't need to hear.

Hannah didn't want to be with him, otherwise she would have been. The fact was, she was with me and that was all I needed to know.

Chapter Twenty-One

Hannah

I'd promised myself that I wasn't going to go over there bothering them while they worked. Besides, I really did have a shitload of lures I was behind on, so I only let myself drive to Vaughn's on new roof day twice.

The first time was that morning to make sure there wasn't anything he and Dean needed before they started. Dean and Vaughn hadn't really ever spent any time together, especially alone. I didn't want them to be uncomfortable around one another.

I knew Vaughn wanted to get to know him, he'd told me as much, but every time I invited Dean to do something with us, go out on the boat, or cook out, it was always *maybe next time.*

It kind of shocked me, when I was telling him about Aaron helping Vaughn with the roof, how Dean was the one who chimed in that he'd be willing to help.

Things at the shop had been good, but a little tense. My dad was still slacking on office things, and Dean and I were picking up extra duties we'd never been responsible for in the past.

It was like my dad was kind of silently handing things over, but he never came out and said why. We didn't know if it was intentional or by accident, and it was getting to a point where I needed to talk to him. I simply didn't know how. The time was never right.

Dean even agreed that something was up. Things were changing all over the place.

When I dropped off some food and tea around lunchtime, everything seemed like it was going okay. Like they were getting along.

The old roof was stripped off and they were already putting the paper down. Undeniably, they, too, worked well together.

I didn't kiss Vaughn in front of them, even though I really wanted to. Instead I asked him to look at something in his kitchen and pushed him up against the refrigerator for a quick kiss before I left.

"What is wrong with me that I can't go without kissing for too long?" I asked as he grabbed my ass and pulled me harder to him. He was sweaty and dirty and so fucking hot I wanted to strip his clothes off and lick him clean myself.

A full-on Vaughn smile pierced my heart as he said, "I don't know, but I think I've got a little bit of that too?" Then he playfully bit my bottom lip.

"Stop," I demanded, but wanted no such thing. "I need to go. I just wanted a quick kiss."

"Hannah, there's no such thing as a quick kiss when

you walk in here with those shorts on, slinging roast beef on rye at me." His spoke into my neck before attacking me with his mouth. The delicious scratch of his stubble made me declare those jean shorts my most prized possession.

It went on a little longer than it should and we had to stop before it got wickedly out of hand.

Seeing them getting along made me happy. Dean was my family, and I didn't like wondering if it would ever get to a point where they would spend time together.

My dad, Dean, and Vaughn.

My dad. My friend. And my boyfriend.

I thought about a lot as I blew through the lures and flies on the order sheets that were coming almost every day at my dad's shop. I didn't even have time to make more to display there, always trying to get through the ones people wanted special for themselves.

Later that evening, I was surprised when Vaughn hadn't come over or called when I thought they'd be finished, but I just kept working, happy with my progress.

Then it happened, and I knew the second that I'd done it.

Just like Vaughn told me a hundred times. I was going to break my tooth. And I did.

I broke the shit out of it.

Trying to get this one stubborn band tight around this specific piece, my tooth gave out and I bit down hard as it cracked.

I sat there having one of those *did that just really happen* moments when you hope your mind is playing tricks on you.

My mind did no such thing.

Untricked and chipped, I needed to call my dentist.

He answered, "Hey, I was just about to hop in the shower. What are you doing for dinner? Want to run up and split a tenderloin?"

That had become something we did about once a week. Then, we'd usually get a piece of pie for later and eat it in bed.

Half a tenderloin and bed pie sounded a whole lot better than anything this conversation was leading towards.

"Well, depends."

"Okay, depends on what?" he retorted as I heard him turn on the shower. He was probably naked. *Yum.*

"Depends on if you want to be seen out with me sporting a chipped up tooth?"

"Tell me you didn't." The sound of the water stopped, like he'd turned it off to listen.

"I did."

Vaughn would never yell or shout at me, I knew this for a fact, but he was going to tell me how careless I'd been. He would have been right to do so. But instead, he didn't do any of that because he asked, "Are you okay? Does it hurt?"

I was okay, but, also, it did kind of hurt. I hoped it was because I'd bitten down so hard, and not because I'd done some real damage.

"It hurts a little, *not too bad*, but I did a pretty good number on it."

"I'll shower then I'll run out there and look at it. Hannah, if it's throbbing, tell me."

My mouth wasn't throbbing, it was only if I pressed my teeth together that it was slightly tender.

"No, I'm okay. I'll be in my garage."

I heard the slide of his shower curtain along the metal bar and the shower came back to life. I looked down at the sliver of tooth in my hand and thought about driving like a bat out of hell to catch him in the shower instead.

"What? You just chipped your tooth."

"It's still going to be chipped in the house and I'm almost done with this one. I might as well finish before you get here and distract me anymore."

He grunted and laughed.

I was getting pretty fond of his grunts. They were more like a growl when I frustrated him, but he always looked so good doing it. I tried to get him worked up about something at least every other day. It kept things interesting, that's for sure.

"*Anymore*?" he fished.

"Yeah, I know you're naked."

The sound of his warm laughter soothed my fractured ego.

"How's that?"

"I can hear the water over the phone. You always take your clothes off in your bedroom by the hamper before a shower and walk in the bathroom, dick swinging."

"Oh, my dick isn't swinging right now. It's more like … well, it's hard."

"See distractions everywhere. Hurry up," I said and then hung up. I'd just chipped my tooth. Picturing him naked and erect getting into the shower would surely give me a hook through my finger.

It was a safety issue.

"Well, I can't tell if you cracked it above the gumline without an X-ray, but it wouldn't surprise me if you did, Hannah. It's split right up the side."

My lips seemed so huge with the gap left from the missing splinter of my right front tooth. Up until that night, it had always been my loyal and trusty biting tooth. It really let me down.

"I know. It was dumb, but I do it without even thinking." *Kind of.*

"Move over here and let me see it in this light?" He walked to where I had my desk lamp and he twisted it up to shine in my mouth. "Open up."

Oh, I'd open up.

My mind went in one direction and my body went where it always did when he told it what to do. Yielding to my new hussy-like tendencies, I shoved all of my smart-ass quips aside and opened up. I was already in a little trouble. Anymore and I'd be asking for it.

"Ahhh," I sang as he took a closer look in the new light.

He pushed a little on my gum and said, "I think we better go in and fix that, Hannah. Before it does get sore. I don't see any pulp though. I hope it's just superficial."

I tried to answer, but he was still inspecting me and his finger was still in my mouth, which I usually really liked.

"Ha-kai," I agreed. "Ah go."

He drove us to his office and it was weird being there with the lights off, at night. I waited in the almost dark room, while he walked to the other side where the front doors were, to turn on the overhead lights.

"Let's get a quick X-ray," he advised as he held out his hand for me to follow him down the hall and into the room where they did them. I put the vest on and he handed me the things to bite as he got the machine all set up.

"I'd rather be getting a tenderloin with you," I admitted with my teeth clenched.

Even though Vaughn wasn't exactly thrilled with me, he flashed me a forgiving smile as he prepared the X-ray thing.

"I'd rather be picking out pie, but I think I have some ice cream at home." He kissed my forehead, and I knew it wasn't the end of the world. I was dumb, but he rolled with it pretty well.

I always enjoyed watching him work on his house, but this was different. He was so focused. So in his element.

After we looked at the X-ray and saw I hadn't done any damage above my gumline, he was satisfied with giving me a cap made of this composite stuff. I didn't even have to get numbed or anything.

I was lucky, and he told me that probably ten times.

"If this doesn't feel strong, or gets loose, we'll have to give you a different crown or a veneer," he said as he walked around collecting the tools he was going to use and moving the light around to a spot that suited him.

As he worked on my mouth, I watched his eyes, and every so often he'd catch me and he'd wink then go back to work.

He couldn't wink enough. I loved it every single time.

My boyfriend, the dentist, was so handsome and, probably because it was just me, he didn't wear a mask like Dr. Carver always did. So I studied his mouth, too. That talented son of a bitch.

Finally, the last time he put the ultraviolet light on the work he'd done, he spoke.

"I was going to ask you about something tonight. Yesterday, a lady from the country club was in and said they have a few plates left for the charity dinner they're having next weekend. I didn't know if you'd want to go or not, but I went ahead and bought two plates."

His eyes met mine, looking for a reaction. I wasn't sure what my reaction was. So it was a good thing I still couldn't talk.

"It's fine if you don't want to go, but I thought it would be a chance to do something different and have a nice meal. Maybe a little dancing. Maybe a few drinks. I *want* to take you. I'd wear a suit and clean up real nice."

That almost made me laugh. He didn't need a suit to look good to me. The more he talked about it the more I could tell he genuinely wanted to go.

"But I know it's short notice, and you might already have something planned for next weekend."

Meticulously, he tested the last thing he'd done to my tooth before flipping off the light above my head and pulling out the spongy worm things he'd shoved in the corners of my mouth.

I stretched and moved my dry lips around and then ran my tongue over the cap. It felt really close to what my tooth was like before. A little smoother in the back, but overall, it was good.

He handed me a little cup of water. "Feel okay?"

"Yeah," I answered and took a drink, which I desperately needed. "Feels good. Thanks for fixing it for me."

"Sure. We can't have you hiding that smile, beautiful." Then he quickly kissed me, remarking, "Feels the same to me."

"I'll go with you on your fancy date, Dr. Renfro." I'd never been to the charity dinner before, and, so far, all of the new things I'd tried with Vaughn were wonderful.

More than wonderful.

I often questioned, if I'd never met Vaughn, or if Rachelle hadn't ever left him for his friend, would I have ever been that happy? That invested in someone else?

I was glad there was no way to know those answers.

Being with Vaughn had made me braver. I'd been shopping with Sunny twice that summer, and the closer Vaughn and I got, the more I wanted to look as beautiful as he made me feel.

For me *and* for him.

I was still me, only I was changing. And, in my opinion, all for the better. For the happier, anyway.

"Good. We can just go and eat, or stick around and see if it's a good time. Totally up to you. We can leave whenever you want."

"You'll be there, it'll be fun."

I even had a dress I could wear for it already. I'd found it on sale in Browning but hadn't had any reason to wear it yet. A pretty light peach color, which would look awesome with the great tan I had.

I leaned in and kissed him, knowing how he liked when

I did. "So are you picking me up or what?"

He looked up at the ceiling with a smirk. "I don't know. Maybe you could just bring clothes with you Friday night and get ready at my place?"

I'd gotten ready at his place a few times, but not ready-ready. Like doing nice hair and taking my time with putting makeup on-ready. That was his house. I couldn't imagine what it would be like to have all of my things there.

I didn't dress up a lot, so I had to go a little slower than most. Sunny would have to help. It takes a village, people.

"You know what? How about I spend the night Friday, then go home Saturday afternoon for a while and get dressed there? You come and get me, and after I'll go home with you."

It wasn't as large as I liked, but that got a little grunt out of him before he clicked back the chair I was in and proceeded to give me a real-life doctor/patient fantasy come to life.

"I'll let you win this time, but you're mine both nights," he told me in a seductive, rumbling tone.

Suddenly my heart raced, knowing we shouldn't be in there. The look on his face wasn't to be taken lightly as he threw a leg over me and pulled my hands up over my head, biting his lip.

"Are you going to be a good patient now and not use your teeth to bite things you shouldn't?"

I snapped my teeth at him, just to rile him up.

It worked out for me just fine though.

After my mouth on him wasn't enough for either of us, I was bent over a dentist chair begging him to stop torturing me when he'd brought me so close to too many orgasms before backing off each time.

"I won't do it again. I promise. Just, *please*, don't stop," I begged.

"That's right, beautiful. I can't stop now anyway," he said as he grabbed my hips and thrust even harder into me. We found a new level of ecstasy in a procedure room under fluorescent lights, knowing it was totally wrong for us to be doing it there.

It wasn't until we were finished and he was cleaning the chair down like our genitals were radioactive, did he start really giving me shit about the tooth.

"Seriously though, do you think you learned your lesson?"

"Shit. What lesson? Crack a tooth and my dentist will give me orgasms? Lesson learned." I hoped he'd never get sick of my sarcasm.

"I wondered if you were going to be upset about the blowjob for payment arrangement I was making with you," he teased.

As he shut the lights off and walked out after me, locking the doors on his way, he asked, "So you still up for ice cream?"

I was.

I hadn't eaten since lunch and I was always ready to see what he did with his share. Let's just say the good dentist liked to play with his dessert.

I stayed at his house that night and he had to get up early to take me home.

There was no way to hide what was going on from my dad. Not that I felt like I needed to.

I walked in the next morning, wearing what I'd been wearing the day before and one of Vaughn's hoodies.

He sat at the kitchen table, drinking a cup of coffee.

"Things are going pretty good with Astro, huh?" he asked. As I tried to walk invisibly past him on my way to the shower.

Caught, I stopped.

"Things are going really good, Dad."

"You're spending a lot of time with him."

He was right. I was hardly ever home anymore, between Vaughn's and the cabin. I'd been leaving him all alone.

I took a deep breath and found some spine. I'd never lied to him, and not saying anything was the same as being dishonest.

"I'm not sure what's going on, but it's new and fun. I've never felt like this."

"I know, kid."

"I hope I don't screw it up."

"It's not the same without you around as much…"

I interrupted, "Dad, I'm sorry."

"You didn't let me finish." Then like he was about to say something else, he got up and kissed me on the forehead. "I just miss you is all."

Then he walked out the door.

I knew I'd see him at work in an hour and he wouldn't bring it back up. That's just the way he was.

While I was getting ready for work I got a text from Vaughn.

Vaughn: I'm glad you're going with me Saturday.

Me: I can't wait to see you try to dance with a boner. My dress is gonna kick your suit's ass.

Vaughn: I can do a good many things with this boner. I have yet to hear of any shortcomings from you.

I laughed. He was right. I couldn't give his penis all of the credit though. Vaughn, as a whole, was one completely skilled package. Always knowing what I wanted and how I wanted it, and then he'd deliver. Every time.

Me: You got me there.

Vaughn: Come over at noon and I'll make you lunch.

Me: Okay.

I loved that things like that were becoming our normal. We had lunch at his house every now and again, or sometimes we'd meet somewhere. But knowing if I wanted company at lunch, and it was there for the taking, was special. It was something I'd only done with him.

I didn't want anything to change. I liked us just the way we were.

No pressure.

No expectations.

It was perfect and I wanted to bottle it up and keep it

going that way forever.

The days moved fast and by Saturday afternoon, I was actually really excited to go home and get all dolled up for him.

Sunny dropped by, offering to help curl my hair, and I agreed that would be best.

He was going to love the dress. It landed loosely above my knees, and held me tight through the middle, criss-crossed over my shoulders and down my back, where it was mostly open.

My hair was just exactly how I'd wanted it with big, fat, smooth waves, almost like something out of 40s or 50s Hollywood. She'd helped me with my makeup, too, and I looked like a movie star, to be honest. My body filled out the dress just the way I wanted, and my skin looked even tanner in contrast with the creamy peach color.

"Well, I'm going to get out of here, but you look like a million bucks. I'm serious. I've never seen you this happy and it shows."

That was a compliment I was proud to take, because that was exactly how I felt.

Happy.

"Thank you, and thanks for helping me," I added as she packed up her things.

"I didn't do much; you didn't need much. You look perfect. Call me and tell me how it goes. Have fun."

She gave me an air kiss, I guess so she didn't mess my face up.

I wasn't about to fake kiss with Vaughn later. Ladylike or not, makeup be damned.

As time grew closer to my big, fancy date, I sat down in

the living room, where my dad was, and put on my shoes.

If I had any worries about the night, the only one I could think of was the damn heels I'd bought to go with the dress.

I could count on my toes how many times in my life I'd ever worn shoes like that. It was less than a shoe's worth.

I'd just be careful. Besides, he said we could always leave. If shoes ended up hurting my feet, we could go back to his place where I'd take them off. Take all of it off.

When I had strapped up, I looked at my dad who I could feel was staring at me.

"You look like your mom," he said.

I was used to hearing digs on my mom, but it wasn't very often I'd heard anything positive about her. She'd really been an asshole to do what she'd done to my dad. To both of us.

"I do?" I asked as I smoothed a hand over my hair. I'd never seen any pictures of her wearing it like that.

"Not the hair, your face. You look like you're in love." He'd definitely never said anything like that.

"In love?"

He gave me a weak smile and answered. "It wasn't all bad with us, kid. There was a time she loved me and she looked just like you do right now. Excited and scared." He ran a weathered hand over his mouth. "You look more excited, though. Either way, that's how I remember her the most. The way she looked when she loved me. When she wanted us."

Then he made a face like he was shaking off the memory.

How she could ever leave a man, who loved her as

much as he did, was beyond me.

"Dad," I said, not knowing what else to say.

"I'm sorry. You just look so pretty." He stood and I stood and then he hugged me, kissing the top of my head.

Don't misunderstand—my dad hugged me plenty growing up, but after you reach a certain age that kind of fades away. And that week he'd kissed me twice and there he was squeezing me like I was leaving forever.

I hugged him back, hoping he knew he was a huge part of the reason I was so happy. He'd *never* made me feel like I had to pair off. It never felt like he was in too big of a hurry to have an empty nest. He never pressured me to move, and I never sensed I'd worn out my welcome at home.

I knew it was unrealistic to think that I'd be roommates with my dad forever, but he really had been a good one. Anything that would change that was pretty far off anyway. No matter how right he'd been about my feelings for Vaughn.

That was about the time I heard tires pulling in and a door close on Vaughn's SUV. Suddenly, it was feeling a little bit like prom. There I was at twenty-six, watching my boyfriend climb the steps with a corsage, while my dad waited to open the door for him.

Vaughn knocked and Dad opened right on cue.

"Hey there, Astro. You look nice. Taking her to a funeral?" he joked from behind the screen door.

"No, sir. Taking her dancing at the country club for the night."

"Well, come on in, Fred Astaire," my dad instructed as he held the door open for him.

"What happened to *Astro*?"

“I don’t think Fred had one,” my Dad said, toying with him.

Vaughn looked confused for a second then relented. “Fair enough.”

I stood there like a sixteen-year-old hoping my dad didn’t embarrass me, but on the other hand, hoping he gave him a little more shit. It was funny, after all.

Vaughn looked sharp. He wasn’t wearing a jacket, but he wore dark grey dress pants, a white collared shirt rolled up at the sleeves, and a thin black tie, paired with a fitted grey vest. He’d combed back his hair, making him appear powerful. I’d never seen him look so good. Then almost overwhelming pride swept through me, knowing I was his date.

That paired with how I felt dressed up for him and our night out, it was like something out of a fairytale.

“You both clean up real nice,” my dad said as we both stared at each other.

I hoped Vaughn liked my dress.

Then, probably sensing he was three’s company, my dad patted me on the shoulder and walked out of the room.

“I can’t take my eyes off you,” Vaughn whispered, stepping closer, opening the clear package with the flower bracelet inside without looking. I held out my hand and he slipped it over my wrist, then kissed my palm. “You’re perfect, beautiful.”

I wasn’t a blushing type of girl, but my face heated like a dashboard sitting in the sun and I assumed a blush was like that.

“Thanks. I like your vest.”

He looked down and gave the bottom of it a little tug to

straighten it, although it was fine before.

"Well, if we're both ready..." He offered me an arm and I took it, feeling so classy and sophisticated.

I was thankful to have his arm as I walked through the grass on my tiptoes so the heels wouldn't sink into the earth.

He'd washed and waxed the Escalade and it looked shiny and new.

Before opening the door, he turned me in his arms and kissed me. It was one of those kisses I'd seen in movies where the guy dips his girl, damn near sweeping her off her feet.

My feet were swept, and I'd never been safer than I was there in his strong arms. He wouldn't drop me like I always thought I'd feel like that. His hand behind my neck, holding me steady and his other arm wrapped around my waist, I knew he'd never let me fall, and so instead of worrying about it, I concentrated on kissing him back.

"I wanted to kiss you in the house, but I thought it might be weird for you. Then I thought about kissing you when we got in the car, but I wouldn't be able to hold you. Then I just couldn't wait any longer." He explained as he pulled away.

"I didn't want you to."

I was grateful that Sunny reminded me to pack the lipstick in the tiny clutch she'd let me borrow. No one had to know that all I had in there was my phone, mints, and lipstick.

When I was back on my feet, I ran my thumb over his lips to wipe away the color.

We pulled up the lane leading to the golf course's main

building and country club, and I noticed they'd hung lanterns in all of the trees that lined the drive. It was still too light out to really enjoy them, but they'd be pretty on the way home.

Even though I didn't let myself dwell or focus on it all day, I was nervous to walk into the club. I knew most of the people who were members there, and I got along just fine with everyone, but I hadn't dressed up like this since once in high school. Not even close.

I'd tried not to think about it, and, instead, decided that the night was just for us. Vaughn and me.

As we walked in, Sandy Shaw, the chiropractor's wife, met us, and I smiled as she covered her heart and told me how lovely I looked.

In fact, after showing us to our seats, she took a minute to tell me again how pretty my hair and dress was. "Okay, I'm done. I just wanted you to know, Mu…"

But before Mutt left her lips, Vaughn corrected, "Hannah."

She smiled apologetically at him and then knowingly beamed at me. "That's right. Hannah, please enjoy your night, dear, and the company of your handsome gentleman."

I felt beautiful.

Normally, I would have thought most of the pomp and circumstance was a little over-the-top for Wynne, but I couldn't find anything negative about it. Even busybody BethAnne stopped to tell me how happy I looked in the ladies' room, and for once I didn't feel like being a bitch to her.

Funny how when you're content, things like that seem

silly and a huge waste of time. I didn't want to spare a single second I didn't have to away from him.

The auction began with happy hour, which was a little boring, so we strolled around the deck sipping wine—the same kind we liked to drink on boat nights. I liked the naughty feeling it gave me when he brought me a glass, wondering if he was thinking about our secret spot, too.

I was careful not to spill on my dress and to stay upright in my shoes. I walked slower than usual, but Vaughn didn't mind and strolled at my pace.

"It's a good night for this," he said as we looked out on the golf course, the sun falling over the hills.

"It is. I love it out here."

"You do?" he asked, taken aback.

I wasn't a high society type, obviously, but there wasn't much of a high society in Wynne anyway, so to hell with it.

"I know it's strange, but I love how pretty the grass is and how it all looks like it's been perfectly colored neatly in the lines. I think it's cool."

"Well, I'll have to bring you out here more. I didn't know that."

He didn't have to *take* me anywhere and we both knew it. If I wanted to be out there more, I would be.

"To show me your swing?" I was teasing at first, but then I thought about watching him golf and I was genuinely on board. "I think I'd like that. A lot."

He shook his head, knowing where my mind went.

"Vaughn, here's a fun fact. Did you know when the water is up a little, you can take a boat all the way from my cabin to the golf course?"

"Really? To the lake?" He squinted like he was trying

to remember the river, trying to navigate how it was true.

"There's a creek that runs between the two. It's usually not deep enough, but sometimes in the spring it swells a little and you can make it here just fine. If it rises we'll do it next spring."

"All right."

He looked so peaceful and satisfied. Vaughn wasn't a man who let life stress him out too much, but in that moment he looked carefree, and I liked knowing some of it had to do with me.

"I like when you make plans in the future with me."

"What? It's just a boat ride, man."

"No, it's not. It's a boat ride *next spring*. Just like yesterday you said something about Christmas or Valentine's Day. Valentine's Day is *next year*."

He had me thinking.

I had said that.

I'd decided to get him an open cast reel as a present. He's really good. Freaky good, to be honest. He had a Midas touch for sure.

But he was right. I had been thinking out a bit farther than I was used to. I'd already bought him some things when I was with Sunny a few weeks back.

Was I getting ahead of myself?

It didn't feel like it.

He smoothed a thumb over my brow, and I relaxed a little from my thoughts.

"Stop that. I said I like it. I want all of it."

Chapter Twenty-Two

Vaughn

After the fantastic dinner, I thought about taking her straight home for purely selfish reasons.

Hannah wasn't like other girls. Getting dressed up wasn't high on her list of priorities. However, when she did, she was sensational.

She had it all.

I wanted her all to myself and I'd expected she'd want to leave early, but, to my surprise, that wasn't the case.

Through bidding on a few items and feasting on the meal, never once did that look of confidence leave her face. She mingled and introduced me to people I hadn't met yet, and each time she thoughtfully referred to me as her boyfriend.

She claimed to love things the way they were. Each and every time I tried to steer the conversation in the direction of the future, she got somewhat anxious.

I was learning her well and I could pick up on her tells.

The wandering eyes when she was looking for a way to change the subject. The way she paced when she was irritated. How she rambled when she was looking for the right thing to say. The hypnotic look in her big, hazel eyes when she wanted me.

I knew them all.

In theory, the thought of having a future with me scared her. But in practice, she was right alongside me. We were spending nearly every night together. Eating lunch with each other most days. Talking about next year and things we could do to the house. Only when she was met with talking about actual commitment stuff did she really show how nervous it made her.

Things were moving forward whether she was willing to admit it or not.

Hell, it made me nervous, too. I'd thought I'd found someone who wanted all of that with me, and it turned out she hadn't. Who knew? The pressure of it might have been the reason she ran straight into the arms of another man.

I didn't want Hannah to feel forced, but I wanted her next to me at night. Every night.

I wanted to share the bathroom and not have to plan times to see her. I wanted her with me, and if that made me some sort of crazy person, then I was one hundred percent crazy.

We'd only been together a few months, but it was so right.

And, if it caused a fight trying to talk to her about it, so be it. We'd argued before. It was worth the risk.

"One more dance and then I think I'm going to need

to get off these feet," she said with her head on my chest, another song ending, after over an hour of dancing.

That was all I needed to hear. Of course, I wanted to get her to my place, but I wasn't ever going to leave while she was enjoying the night.

"Let me take you home," I said.

"I don't want to go home. I want to go to your place." Her voice was laced with disappointment, misunderstanding what I'd intended.

I placed a kiss on her lips. It never got old hearing that she wanted to be with me.

"That's what I meant. Trust me, I'm not letting go of you all night. And maybe not tomorrow either."

Just like that, the peril in her relaxed, and she sweetly kissed my neck as she hummed her agreement.

We walked to the front, arms around each other, not caring who saw or what they thought. She didn't want to let go and I wasn't going to suggest it.

"The black Escalade," I said to the young guy who was acting as valet for the night. He couldn't have been more than sixteen. The golf course was probably his first summer job.

It didn't take him long and he hopped right out, rounding the Escalade to open the door for Hannah.

"Ms. O'Fallon, you look real, real pretty tonight," he said, squeaking a little on the first *real*. I loved that he didn't call her Mutt.

He held the door for her, and I took a second to watch as she followed his lead and got in.

"Thanks, Joey. I think standing next to Dr. Renfro makes me look better. His good looks rub off."

"No, ma'am. I think it's the other way around," he replied, no squeak, and shut her door.

He might be young, but that little dude had some game.

Inside, I shut my door and teased her, "I might have some competition."

"Did you hear that? I think you're right." She shined under kindness and compliments. I loved how this town treated her that night, like they were seeing what I'd been seeing all along. A strong, beautiful woman, who didn't *need* to be with a man, but *chose* to be with me.

"Well, before you go riding off into the sunset on a golf cart with him, I'd like to remind you of that thing you like me to do with these." I slid my hand up her bare leg, and we drove slowly through the lights they'd hung down the stretch of gravel leading to the highway, which she seemed to be enchanted by.

"I'm not remembering exactly," she countered. Being facetious, she spread her leg, just enough, to tempt me. "Help a girl out."

I had two options, help her out on the way home, or make her crazy and drive a little too slow.

I chose the latter and she was almost climbing out the window before we pulled into my drive.

I heard under her breath as she hopped out. "I bet Joey drives faster than you."

Before I was out of the SUV, she'd already marched inside, shoeless. I decided to make her wait a little longer, just for fun.

She was already upstairs when I walked through the kitchen door, and I took my time, taking off my vest and hanging it on the back of a chair.

As much as she acted like she hated anticipation, she thrived on it. I got off on making her crazy.

In an old house, you could hear all of the sounds. I listened to her bare feet pat across my wooden bedroom floor and I heard her hop into the bed.

She was still playing with me, too. "Do you need help getting up the stairs? You're killing me," she said loud enough I could have heard her outside.

I laughed to myself from the stairs where I was quietly making my way to her.

She didn't know I was as close as I was. Didn't know I could see her down the hall as I climbed to the second floor.

She lay in my bed, the duvet pulled back, exposing the white sheets underneath. Her flawless tanned skin contrasted with the sheet and the white lace thing she was wearing.

Whoa. Where did that come from?

Things quickly changed. I didn't feel like wasting time anymore and almost fell up the last step.

I sauntered down the dim hallway, and when she finally noticed I was coming, she sat up on her knees, letting me see her.

The lace was sheer, and I easily made out all of my favorite spots. Her excitement obvious, two perfect nipples pebbled under the material.

I loosened my tie and watched her lips part the way they did when she liked what she saw. I unbuttoned my shirt, then took it off and threw it on the chair next to the closet door, all the while stalking nearer.

Just as I was close enough to touch her, the lust in her eyes cleared a little and she said, "Vaughn, I'm in love with you."

Her shoulder shrugged a little with her confession, but her words sunk into my chest.

She'd taken me by surprise. *Twice.*

Looking like a vision in white on my bed, her hair still perfect as the second I'd picked her up. Her lips a perfect color of pink. Telling me she loved me.

I'd never been that lucky in my life.

I rushed her and lifted her into my arms, laying her back on the bed. I needed her.

Had to have her.

She felt it, too. Holding onto me like I was a life jacket and she was being swept away by a current. I was what she needed and she was so brave and amazing for being so honest with me.

My mouth claimed hers from above and my hand pulled her closer to me with a solid grip on her thigh.

We moved with each other, not caring where we rolled, only caring that we were connected.

Lips on lips.

Skin on skin.

Our clothes somehow vanishing in the heat of the moment.

I couldn't stop, nor did I want to.

She moved down the bed, greedy and hungry. When she took me into her mouth, she lifted a finger to mine. Wanting me to suck on her, too. I loved that naughty quirk of hers; she'd done it many times.

Before I couldn't hold back any longer, I lifted her up and rolled her over, losing a battle of will with my patience. Wanting to taste her for myself, I slipped a finger in her mouth and she moaned as she loved on it, just as she'd been doing elsewhere only seconds before.

I licked and bit at her, using my tongue to make her back lift off the sheets and then using my finger to coax out her beautiful orgasm.

"I love yous," poured and poured from her lips as she rode my fingers and touched her breasts and pleaded with me for more, saying, "I can't take it."

She was wrong.

She could take it, and she took it all as I made love to her with my hands and mouth until she came again.

I loved being inside of her after she came, or came twice, as the case was. She was so sensual like that, almost lethargic and drugged from lust.

Our kisses were passionate and slow, and she held onto me so tight.

When she relaxed from her climax, I pulled away to roll on a condom and watched her legs spread open for me, swaying in the light from the lamp on the far side of the room.

Unashamed.

Brazen.

Hungry for more, touching herself in my brief absence.

We liked it hard and fast, and I was only too eager to get to that, but I looked at her and remembered I hadn't even said a word back to her after she'd told me she loved me.

Heedlessly, I couldn't wait to be inside her either. My body did what it needed, positioning itself where I belonged. I brushed the hair from her face, holding my weight on an elbow. Still wet, she lifted her hips, impatiently pushing herself on me.

"You're all I want, beautiful." The way she was grinding her body against me was clouding my thoughts. Our hips grinding together, perfectly in sync. Deep and intoxicating.

I had to get to my point before I lost myself in the moment, to the way my body was already starting to accelerate with hers.

"Hannah, I love you, too."

"Yes," she whispered and moaned.

When the necessary words were out, new energy exploded in my veins and I buried my head in the crook of her neck and gave her everything I had. Her legs wrapped around my waist and her arms found the iron bedframe above our heads.

She held on and I let go, pushing even myself to a limit of rawness and power I'd never experienced. She writhed under me, the sounds of her pleasure filling my ears.

"Yes, everything. Give me everything, Vaughn."

As she hung onto the rail, I sat back a little, taking her perfect ass in my hands and with every thrust into her, I pulled her to me just as hard, until we were both panting and shouting. I collapsed backward and she followed me, curling up on my chest.

"Move in with me," I requested, out of breath. I didn't want to be without her and I had to ask, not wanting to waste any more time.

"What?" she asked, looking up at me, and moving to straddle my legs. I reached down to pull the condom off and tossed it in the wastebasket near my bed.

"You heard me. Move in here. Live with me."

She was still panting and swiping sweat-soaked hair off her face and her neck. "Isn't it too soon? I mean…"

I pulled her back to me, wondering if I'd made a mistake by blurting it out like that.

"Just think about it. You don't have to say anything right now," I assured her and rubbed her back. "Just think about it, and if you're ready, or when you're ready, come be at home ... with me."

"I do love you, don't think I'm not..." she anxiously began to ramble.

"Shhh. I said *think* about it. I'm not thinking anything."

We fell asleep at the foot of the bed, her on my chest moving her finger around my skin in little circles and me running my hands through her hair.

Later that night, she woke me up my favorite way, nudging her ass into me until I was getting another condom and sliding into her on our sides. It was before the sun came up, and we took this round slow. I kissed her neck and used my hand to touch the front of her as she pushed back against my deep thrusts.

Before long we were coming again, and then we settled back into the sheets and off to sleep I went.

When I woke up again, she wasn't there.

Chapter Twenty-Three

Hannah

I couldn't fall back asleep. My mind was too busy.

After Vaughn's breathing leveled off and he was sleeping, I got out of bed and found some of his clothes I could wear, a pair of mesh shorts and a T-shirt. Then, when I reached the kitchen, I put on his flip-flops and went straight out the door and walked home.

If the shoes would have fit better, I'm sure I would have ran.

When I got to my house, I forfeited the rest of the night and decided to take a shower instead. I thought about working on some fishing things, but then changed my mind, and after filling up my coffee mug, I headed to the shop.

I would tackle Monday's paperwork a day early.

It wasn't so much that Vaughn's invite scared me. It was just such a huge change.

I'd never lived anywhere but home. I'd never *not* lived

with my damn dad. Could I go straight from his house to Vaughn's without ever even living on my own? Could I be another woman who left him alone?

Sure, I had the cabin, and I knew how to live on my own, but that was so different.

My mind raced on for hours.

By the time the sun was heating up the shop and the sound of cars driving past on their way to church alerted me to the fact that I'd been there for hours, the invoicing was ready for the post office, and the following week's appointments were sorted for their reminders.

My stomach rumbled and I decided I'd look in the break room for a snack. I opened the garage doors, letting the sunshine in so I could see across the shop. I was heading into the small kitchen area when I heard tires pull into the lot.

I expected it to be Vaughn, so I was shocked when it was Dean instead.

"What are you doing up this early on a Sunday?" I asked as he hopped out of his Cherokee.

"Getting breakfast. Want a doughnut?"

I knew there was little chance of anything better than a granola bar or a speckled, half-brown banana in the break area, so I quickly accepted.

"Yes, please."

He reached across the seat, pulled out a box, and walked inside.

"Question is, why are *you* up this early? Didn't you and Vaughn have a big night on the town?"

He kicked out one of the braces on the truck lift and raised it to the perfect sitting height, something we did all the time.

"We did."

"And you're here?" He looked at his watch. "At eight thirty on a Sunday? What's up with that?"

It was weird talking about it with him, but he was there and he had doughnuts. Plus, I'd already sat down and started eating one. I was kind of obligated to give him something. Besides, I really needed to talk about it with someone. I'd just expected that someone would be Sunny. Not Dean.

"Do you really want to talk about this?" I asked, giving him my no-bullshit look.

"Yes. I do." He answered then cracked his knuckles, taking a deep exaggerated breath before going on. "Look, I don't know if you know this, but I've always kind of had a thing for you."

I looked at the glazed doughnut and shook my head. Chewing and not knowing what to say to that. We'd always been close, and there were a few times I sensed he'd wanted more, but he'd never come out and said it.

Then he continued, "But I also think you're happy. Vaughn's not a bad guy. He seems to treat you right. So I guess I'm just a fool who missed his chance."

I looked at him and now he was the one studying his doughnut.

I still didn't speak.

"I guess what I'm trying to say is … yeah, at first I didn't like it. Now, I just have to chalk it up and get used to it. I think he's good for you."

That was why I loved Dean. To me, he still felt like my family, and what he was saying didn't sound romantic, it sounded brotherly.

"Dean, he is good to me. He treats me like … like … like I want to be treated. He doesn't give me too much shit, and he takes just enough of mine. You know? He's different."

"I know."

Finally, we made eye contact and he repeated, "I know. So then tell me why you're here. I'm not stupid; something happened."

"I told him I love him." I popped another bite in my mouth and chewed.

He took another deep breath. I considered maybe I screwed up and should have talked to Sunny instead, but he'd asked for it.

"I asked if you wanted to talk about this and you said yes," I stated matter-of-factly. I couldn't take it back now.

He shook his head as he chewed and swallowed about half a doughnut. "I do. I just didn't expect that. Go ahead."

"What? You didn't expect I'd tell him?" I was confused about what he meant. Wasn't that how things went?

"No. I didn't. Has he told you that before?" His expression showed he really couldn't believe what I'd done.

"No. I said it first. What's wrong with that?" Was that weird? Didn't people just say it when they felt it?

"Wow," he said and bobbed his head looking at the ground. Looking maybe a little impressed. "There's not a *damn* thing wrong with it. Good for you." Then he laughed and relaxed a little.

"I don't get it." Why was he being so weird?

"No. You *do* get it. That's what it's all about. Having the balls to say it. Telling someone how you feel."

It was getting clearer.

He continued, "I never had the balls to do it. Good for you."

"I've got big balls, *Dean*." I tried to lighten the moment, and he chuckled a little so I went on. "Anyway, that's not the reason I'm here. After I said it, he said it. *Then* he asked me to move in with him."

I waited to see his reaction. I expected him to have the one I thought I should have. That shocked, it's-too-soon look.

Because it was, wasn't it?

And when he didn't react that way, I thought I'd lost my mind.

"So what?" he asked.

"So what? What about my dad? I live there. That's where I've always lived. And the way Dad's been lately. I'm worried about him being alone. I can't just leave him."

"He'll be fine. You can't stay with him forever just so he isn't lonely, Mutt," he argued.

"It's just too soon and I hate the thought of that."

He stood and grabbed one more pastry. "Know what? I can't even believe I'm saying this. I think you *should* move in with Vaughn."

Hearing that come from Dean's mouth was insanity.

I needed another doughnut.

I stuffed a good half of it in my mouth and plopped back down on my half of the lift.

"Are you shitting me?"

"I shit you not, girl. You said yourself you love him. He loves you. What more are you waiting on? What can't you figure out along the way?"

It was more complicated than that. I needed more time. I needed to think and I knew the best place for that.

"Okay, these doughnuts are good and all, but I got shit to do." I hopped up and kicked his foot. "Get out, or lock up for me."

"I'm gonna fuck around here for a while. I'll lock up. Go."

I ran in the office and grabbed my keys then ran back into the garage to say goodbye.

"Dean, thanks for breakfast."

He'd picked up a broom by then and propped his chin on it as he said, "You're welcome."

The store wasn't too busy when I pulled up. Everyone was at church. I walked in past a woman about my age in white pants and heels, who I'd never seen before, and thought, "Excuse you," when she shuffled past me with her one grocery bag and huge purse, putting her designer sunglasses back on her head.

I ran past the counter, heading straight for the coffee. I was out at the cabin.

When I got to the register, Rhonda was giving me a funny smile.

"Good morning, Rhonda."

"Oh hey, Mutt. How are you doing, honey?" she said strangely. Almost sympathetically. She was being weird.

"I'm fine, thanks. How are you?"

Perplexed and surprised at my answer, she said in a hushed voice, "Don't you worry about that woman, Mutt.

There are plenty of other men in this town who would knock a bull over to get to you these days."

What the hell had she smoked? *And what fucking woman?*

She read my what-the-hell face correctly and added, "Well, honey, that woman just told me she was *Dr. Vaughn Renfro's fiancée*. I hadn't heard she was in town."

Oh no, she did not just say that.

Was "excuse me" bitch with the bag *Rachelle*?

"That was her?" I screeched and pointed to the door where she'd just walked out five minutes earlier.

"Yes, Mutt. That's what she said?" Then Rhonda hit her top speed in checking shit out, knowing she'd just made a huge mistake and that *obviously* I didn't know she was in town either.

"I think I said something about you to her too, Mutt. I'm sorry I didn't know. She asked if I met him and I said how cute you two were."

I didn't say another word.

I paid and left.

Then I barked my tires for a good solid block on my way to Vaughn's.

When I got there, just as I'd expected, her vehicle was parked in the driveway. An ugly red Prius.

What a bitch.

By the time I got to the front door I heard them talking. Mostly, I was concentrated on Vaughn using a tone he'd never used with me.

"I don't care if he went back to his wife, Rachelle. That has nothing to do with me."

"It does, don't you see? I'm back and I'm sorry."

"You're back? You were never here! It's been months and now you just show up? What do you expect from me?"

I stood on the bottom step listening, knowing he probably heard me pull up anyway. Frankly, he probably heard me barrel ass out of the store parking lot. My truck was still too damn loud.

"The lady up town said you were with some Mutt girl."

That's when I said, from outside the door on the porch, "He's been with me." I opened the door and walked inside, head held high.

"Her?" she asked him, her voice thick with judgment. "You're with her? Your name is Mutt?" she shouted in my direction.

I looked at his face, disgust from hearing her say Mutt all over it. He hated Mutt, but his reaction gave me a little hope.

Then I realized it wasn't my fight, and he really only needed to deal with one crazy woman at a time. Everything was up to him.

I couldn't sit around and watch. I wasn't supposed to be there. I'd just been impulsive. Besides, what was I to say after all?

I'd left before he woke up, leaving without a note or a goodbye. I was no better than my fucking mom. And if I couldn't leave my dad yet, maybe he'd want to be with her anyway.

It was all his call. Still, I loved him.

"You, shut up," I said to Rachelle, because I didn't give a shit. Nobody gets away with talking to me like that. Never have.

Then I spoke to him. "Vaughn, I'm going to my cabin.

When you're done here … well, that's where I'll be."

"You can't tell me to shut up. This is *my* house."

Yeah. I definitely needed to go or they were going to see a woman come unglued. But first, *first* I was going to tell her what I thought of that statement.

The house was hers? My ass.

"Your house, huh? Where do you keep the silverware? What breaker keeps Vaughn from getting the fuck shocked out of him when he plugs too many things into the backsplash by the refrigerator? Where is the extra toilet paper? The clean towels? How many coats of paint did we put on this wall? Or that one? When was the last time the sheets were washed on *your* bed? This isn't your house. *And my name is Hannah.*"

My adrenaline was making me feel like I was about to fly around the room, like a bird set free from a cage.

"Are you going to let her talk to me like that?" she asked Vaughn.

"She's not wrong, Rachelle." His tone was neutral.

I didn't need to hang around for what was about to go down. I'd said my piece.

I just hoped that whatever he felt for her really was long gone. For his sake.

Also, having seen her I wondered, if he'd ever wanted her, how could he possibly want me? We were polar opposites. I'd never be like her, and she was nothing like the town tomboy I was. If that was what he was looking for I'd only be a disappointment when the newness wore off.

He could do better than both of us.

I got back into my truck and headed out to my cabin.

On one hand, if he didn't show up, at least I'd have coffee to cry into, and my work was caught up so I could just wallow out there alone.

On the other hand, I could lose everything. Including things I wasn't sure I was even ready for. Things I'd carelessly ran away from that very morning.

Chapter Twenty-Four

Vaughn

How had I ever thought she was what I wanted? The look on Rachelle's face as Hannah asked her about the house was ugly in every way possible.

The way she sneered at Hannah as she spoke. As my strong, beautiful woman stood up for *me.*

The way Rachelle ignorantly looked down at her, having no clue how much she lacked in comparison to Hannah.

Every single point Hannah made was true.

"I'm sorry you drove all this way, but there isn't anything for you here," I told her. I didn't need to be mean or callous toward Rachelle, I simply wanted her to leave. Just the same as she'd chosen to do months before.

"You'd really choose her over me?" she asked, her tone much calmer.

"I don't have to choose. There is no you *or* her. It's just her. *Only* her."

She rolled her eyes, a truly unattractive trait of hers I never did like.

Leaned in the doorway of the kitchen, looking at her standing in my living room, I didn't hesitate. "I think you better go."

She gave me a doe-eyed, silent plea to reconsider, and it only made me shake my head.

After the moment passed, she huffed and marched toward the door, then turned around. But, before she could open her mouth to say whatever the hell she thought she needed to, I said it for both of us. "Goodbye."

The door hadn't even shut before I had my phone out dialing Hannah, but the battery died and my phone dropped the call.

Shit.

I went to find a pair of shoes to throw on, but the ones I usually left by the back door were gone.

She must have worn them earlier; she did that sometimes.

Wait.

I'd only been up a few minutes, but suddenly things weren't adding up.

If she was just getting breakfast, then why didn't she take my Escalade?

Where were my shoes?

Had she *walked* home?

After pulling my running shoes on, I ran out to my SUV.

It was dead. No clicking. No nothing.

"What the fuck is with all of these dead fucking batteries!" I shouted in frustration, pounding my hand off the wheel.

I thought about charging my phone and then calling her, but that just wasn't fast enough.

I needed to get to her now, and find out if she'd left me this morning because she was freaked out. Or if—God forbid—she decided it was all too much. If I'd pushed her too hard, too soon. I had to let her know that Rachelle was gone and never coming back.

The Astro van.

It was only a few blocks uptown to their shop, so I decided to run there, hoping the van was where I'd seen it last.

It didn't take me long to round the corner in front of O'Fallon's garage and the door was wide open with Dean inside.

"Hey, I'm grabbing the van real fast, my battery is dead," I said, not really asking for permission.

"Sure. I can take you back and jump it though." Then asked, "Where's Mutt?"

I took a deep breath, either I was going to have to get used to people calling her that, or I would have to take out an ad in the paper saying, "Knock it the fuck off."

"*Hannah* is at her cabin. That's where I'm headed."

"Yeah, sure, man. Keys are in her office on the wall."

I hadn't even thought about the keys. What would I have done if he weren't there?

"Thanks."

"Sure." He waved and went back to what he was doing.

I ran inside to get the keys off the hook, then around the other side of the building and pulled the handle on the van.

The fucking door jammed.

I smashed my shoulder against it, just like Hannah did the day when her dad first loaned it to me. The handle unstuck and the door came open. It turned right over and I was headed out to her cabin, just like I had the first time.

I tore out of the parking lot and down the roads. Only to get slowed down by Wynne's slow ass Sunday drivers. Who's to say small towns didn't have traffic?

The Astro van wasn't the quickest vehicle on the road either, though, and I tapped the steering wheel like it would help things go faster.

Finally, I flew down her lane and threw it in park next to her truck before jumping out and running up the stairs. Two by two.

"Hannah? You up here?"

Nothing.

An irrational flood of worry hit me, but I knew she had to be close.

I opened the door, but she wasn't inside. I walked around to the far side, the one closest to the water and slowed as I noticed her there on the dock, sitting on the end, looking out at the water.

I wondered if I should give her some time. Maybe she was angry, which I could handle. I could deal with her frustration. Rachelle had been awful to her and I'd pretty much just stood there.

What if she changed her mind about being with me altogether?

There was only one way to find out.

So, as I played out different scenarios in my head, I walked down to the water where she was, willing to fight for her. Willing to plead our case if I had to.

I heard her sniffle as I got near, and the mere thought of her crying squeezed at my heart.

"Hannah, are you all right?" I asked from behind her.

She swiped her cheeks and blew out a long breath.

"Did you know she was coming?" Her voice shook, but it was clear she was trying to hide her emotions.

"No." What a terrible thing for her to think.

Then she asked, "What happened?"

"She asked me to take her back. To choose between you and her."

Her shoulders slumped forward.

I couldn't take it. I knelt down and sat beside her, hanging my feet off the dock with hers.

"I told her there was no choice to make. I want *you*."

Her head spun to face me.

"You do?"

"Of course I do, beautiful," I said. Even though there were no tears to be seen, all of them wiped away, I could tell by the way her eyes were red-rimmed they'd been there. "I'm in love with you. *Only* you."

"Really?" She smiled and her chin quivered just enough to make me reach out and touch her.

"You have to know it. I told her to leave."

"I was kind of a bitch." Her eyebrows rose guiltily.

"She deserved it. Everything you said was right and I told her that. I want that to be our home. It already feels like you belong there. You're in every room. Every step I take in that house has a memory of you in it."

She threw her arms around me, almost reflexively.

"But there's more we need to talk about. Something

happened even before Rachelle showed up."

As if she knew, or remembered, she pulled away and straightened, a complacent look fell upon her pretty face and her hazel eyes dulled.

"I know. And I'm so sorry. I came down here to think, and then it really hit me. I left. I ran." Her voice got strained again, but she swallowed it down and cleared her throat. She was trying to be stronger than the emotions she was feeling.

Again, how had I ever found a woman so brave?

"That's what she did. You know?"

I wasn't sure what she meant.

"Who?"

"My mom. She just left. I got up this morning and I ran away. You deserve much better. A real woman won't freak out and leave."

"How could you think that? You're everything I want. Every. Single. Thing."

"I want you too, but I can't handle the thought of hurting you like that. Like she did my dad. Like Rachelle hurt you. I don't think I can do this."

She turned away from me and faced the water.

I didn't like how it felt.

And I *hated* what it was beginning to sound like.

"You can do this. We can do this."

I reached out to touch her, but she pulled away. I saw a tear fall from her eye before she knocked it into the water below.

"I just don't think I can be what you want me to be. I tried, but some things in small towns like this really don't ever change. I think I'm one of them."

"You're wrong," I countered. How could she think that? After all of the time we'd shared. After she told me she loved me. "You said you..."

"I know what I said last night, Vaughn. But maybe I just said it because I wanted you to hear it? What do I know about love?"

My stomach tightly knotted, I couldn't believe what she was saying.

"You're just scared. You don't mean that."

She couldn't.

"I think I need to be alone." She pulled her feet up and rose, standing over me. "I just don't see how this will work. You want more than I can give you right now. More than me." Where her face had shown emotion just moments ago, there wasn't much showing anymore.

I scratched my head and gave my hair a frustrated pull. "What can I say to make you realize..."

"Just stop," she said, and held up her hand. "I can't. Don't follow me. Go *home*."

Then she walked away.

Chapter Twenty-Five

Hannah

It was the right thing to do. How would I *ever* have made him truly happy? I was my mother's child, born to leave. If anything, that morning had proven it.

And what about my dad? I'd be another woman he loved who abandoned him.

I called him after Vaughn finally pulled away to let him know I was going to be at the cabin for a few days, and that I was taking Monday and Tuesday off.

"Are you sure you're okay, kid? You sound a little low."

It was unlike me to mope, and I was in the middle of Mope-a-palooza. Even though I'd tried to sound normal, he easily picked up on it.

"I'm fine. I just want to spend some time out here. Clear my head."

Avoid seeing Vaughn and changing my mind.

It was better for everyone if I took a step back for a few

days.

After promising three more times I was fine, he told me to call if I needed anything.

Vaughn had sat on the dock for a while, then a while longer in the van, before he left. I didn't get why he'd had the Astro out there anyway. Something must have been messed up again on the Escalade, and if he was going to be in the shop, I didn't want to see him.

I was pitiful, not even fishing the whole time I was there. I lay in bed and cried like one of the girls I always swore I'd never be.

I did love him, but I loved him enough to want something better for him. Someone better. Someone who knew how to be the woman he wanted.

I'd miss him—miss everything—but I'd been alone before. I could handle it.

The hours ticked by.

Then the days did, too.

It was going to take time for things to get back to normal. For me to go back to the same old Mutt I was before him.

He'd move on.

Hell, he moved on with me pretty fast after Rachelle. He'd surely move on even faster from what we almost had. They'd been together for years. We'd only had the summer.

I tried to rationalize it that way. It was a summer fling, and I'd have to think of it like that. A falling star that burned out fast. A summer thunderstorm here and gone before we knew it, leaving damage in its wake. A bite on the line, that as cliché as it was, got away from us both.

I ignored calls from Sunny and Dean, but finally went

home on Wednesday, taking the long way around town so I didn't have to pass his house. I guessed that was just the way I'd be going into town for a while until I was sure I could handle not pulling into his drive.

Until I was confident I could keep my selfishness at bay.

Until I didn't think about his hair when it was messy. Or his hands and what they could do. Or the way his voice sounded commanding and tender at the same time in my ear. Or, more importantly, that he'd said he loved me, too.

I still didn't go to work though; instead, I found myself in the shed working on lures and getting beyond caught up on orders. I made dozens to have on hand.

Then, when I was finally tired enough, I was content to fall dead asleep. Instead of lying in bed reliving the passion and time we'd shared, I climbed under the blankets and closed my puffy eyes. Sleep came fast.

It didn't matter.

I fell asleep quickly only to be cruelly reminded of him in my dreams.

I woke up on Thursday, after surrendering to the thought of him all night, deciding I had to start moving.

Work needed me.

My dad needed me.

I needed me to start moving on. Or, honestly, move back. Things were easier when I was just Darrell's daughter in the shop and the girl who made the fishing lures. Plain old Mutt O'Fallon.

"I saw Vaughn the other night," my dad said one night a few

weeks later.

I'd seen him too. We passed on the road and he waved. I pretended not to see him and messed with the radio in my truck. Then I got drunk and cried in my shed.

Not my finest, but I had my days.

I had days when I didn't see him, didn't hear his name, and didn't sit in the Astro van. Days I couldn't taste his lips in every sip of Newcastle I drank. Days when the radio played only songs that didn't remind me of him. Days I didn't think about all of the things that were still at his house and wonder if he was sick of looking at them, or if he just threw them away.

Days I didn't wish I wasn't someone else.

Or at least I pretended pretty well.

"Vaughn? Since when do you call him that?" I asked. If I acted like it was no big deal long enough, maybe it would become the truth.

"*Van*. Vaughn. *Astro*. Whatever. I saw him. You too cooled off a bit, huh?" He passed me a can of cheap cheerleader beer from the cooler he was sitting on.

It was becoming a nightly thing. Me. My dad. Sitting in the back of the shed drinking shitty beer.

I had a new respect for him. As I licked my self-inflicted wounds day after day, I realized just how tough he was.

Love is a bitch, even for Mutts like me.

I swung my feet off my lowered tailgate as I wondered about what to say, if I could actually talk about it, and if we had enough beer.

"Yeah, didn't work out." There. Short and simple.

"That's a shame. You got on pretty good there." His expression kept talking when he stopped. Wrinkled, brown eyes rooted around for information and his puckered mouth waited for more.

"We did, Dad. It just..." I paused.

Talking about that shit made me sound so stupid.

"...I don't know. It was too much. He wants different things than I do."

"Things like what?"

An adult relationship. A woman who could stick around. A lady who looked good on his arm. Someone who knew more about culture and the world than she did about open cast fishing poles and stink bait. *Someone good enough.*

I took a drink from the ice-cold can.

"Just things."

"So. Want different things. What's that got to do with being together? Want whatever the hell you want."

"Doesn't work like that."

"I know how things work—and I sure as hell know why they don't—I'm a mechanic. It's my job, kid." If only it were as simple as replacing a few parts here and there and everything would work fine.

"There's just too much shit."

"I doubt it."

He doubted it? What did he know?

"You know, we've been needing this talk for a while now. You know I'm not one for rambling on about shit. I was taught actions speak louder than words." His right hand lifted his cap, wiped the bald spot on his head, and replaced it with a few jerky adjustments. He was nervous, but went on. "Sometimes I wish I would have said more to ya, dammit. Talked to ya."

I tightened my ponytail and took another drink. I didn't know what he was talking about.

My dad continued, "I figured if I was there for you, provided for you, made sure you had everything you needed, then you'd be fine."

"I am fine."

He stood and looked me dead in the eye.

"No. You're not."

Well, maybe I wasn't at that minute, but I was okay. I wasn't falling apart.

"You're drunk." That had to be the root of all of this.

"Oh, kid, I'm sober as a rock. I messed you up."

"You did not. Sit down." I wasn't in the mood to deal with him. I wasn't in the mood to deal with anything.

"I thought if I started slacking off at the garage, you'd get sick of it and finally start on your tackle shop. You didn't say anything though. Just kept on going. You just take it and take it and take it some more. Always have. From everyone." He sighed and added, "I think I'm selling it to Dean."

Selling the garage? What the hell?

"Dean? Are you losing your mind? I don't have a tackle shop!" I shouted, feeling so out of control.

"No, but you could, if you weren't stuck there all the time. Dean wants the garage and, frankly, I'm tired of hassling with the business end. I just want to work on cars and go home."

I didn't know how I felt about that. It was *our* garage.

What if I'd wanted it?

I didn't have to think long though because I knew deep down I didn't.

I looked at him dead in the eye. "Have you really

thought about this?"

"Damn right I have. You don't want that place. Do you?"

"Not really, but are you ready to give it up?"

"I love the work, I do. But I'm not cut out for all of that other stuff anymore. I did it while you were coming up because I needed to, but I'm sick of fussin' with it."

Where did that leave me? Surely Dean would want me to work there. Wouldn't he?

"So what's going to happen?"

"Things are going to change. I know what's going to happen with me, but, kid, you need to figure out an answer to that for yourself."

He hopped up on the tailgate and put his arm around me. I still didn't know what to say. It was all so much to process, but it explained a lot about the past few months.

"I never meant to clip your wings when your momma took off, but I did. And I love you more than anyone I've ever loved—her included—God knows it's true. But I'll be damned if I'm gonna watch you let your life pass you by, thinking you have to take care of me."

He gave me a squeeze. I was confused and a little scared.

"So what are you saying? I have to leave?"

"No. You don't have to leave, but I want you to. *Eventually*. I want you to do whatever you want, not what ya think this old man needs you to do."

I could hardly believe what he was saying.

Dean was buying the shop.

Dad wanted me to move out.

Everything was coming down on me. A knot tightened in the pit of my stomach and clambered its way up into my chest.

"I don't want you to be lonely," I said quietly. I'd never said that to him out loud.

"I'm lonely by choice, kid. That's not your problem. Your problem is you're making the same damn mistake."

I looked up at him and admitted, "Dad, I left him."

"Whatcha do that for?"

"Because he deserves better."

He tipped his head back and argued, "Ain't no better."

"I ran like mom did."

His arm fell off my shoulder and he turned a little, the rivets in his jeans scraping the metal on the tailgate, then he shook my shoulders.

"You did not. You're still right here."

"Yeah, but I just up and left. Then I told him I couldn't do it. That I didn't want to be with him."

"Well, you never were a very good liar. I've never known you to fail at anything you put your mind to, and by no means have I ever seen you happier than when you were with him. So what's that tell ya?"

"He wanted me to move in with him, but I couldn't do it," I confessed.

"Yes, you can. I love having you here, and you're welcome as long as you like, but you ain't gonna be content here forever, kid."

"I can't make him happy."

"Well, I think you're wrong. Do you love him?"

There it was.

I fidgeted with the aluminum tab on the can. "Yes."

"Does he love you?"

I didn't answer and he gave my shoulders another good

shake, telling me to cough it up.

"He said he did, but that was before."

"Then what's there to worry about? Go say sorry."

Sorry? I almost laughed.

"It's not that simple. I can't just break up, and then say *sorry*."

"Why not?" he argued.

"Because … I don't know … I just can't." I had to make him understand. "If my mom came back here tonight and said she was *sorry*, would you just forgive her and take her in?"

"If she loved me like you love him? Damn right. You're. God. Damned. Right."

I almost dropped my beer. I didn't know how many times I'd heard him curse her, or cut her down for what she'd done to us. How could he possibly be telling me the truth?

"Bullshit. That's bullshit. You'd tell her to fuck off."

"That's not true. If she loved me, I'd move heaven and hell to keep her. That's how my love is. I can't turn it on and off. If there's love, what else do you need?"

What else did I need?

"What if he changed his mind?"

His expression said he wasn't sure. "You'll never know if you don't ask him."

"What if I mess it all up?" I asked, knowing that was my biggest fear.

"What's wrong with messing it up? You were raised better than that. We're small town folk, we don't throw something away just because it's broke. We fix it, *Hannah*."

He'd never called me that.

"*Hannah?*" My voice cracked repeating my name.

"See? It's never too late to make things right. I'm so sorry I let them call you that." Then he gave me an apologetic smile, his eyes a little glassy, and I lunged forward into his big arms.

"It's okay, dad," I said into his chest.

"Did you know I named you Hannah? I thought it was such a pretty name for my sweet baby girl. Should have always been Hannah."

I forgave him because I loved him. What else mattered?

My dad was right.

God, I hoped he was right.

I knew exactly what I had to do.

Chapter Twenty-Six

Vaughn

Mr. O'Fallon's way was only getting about one more day. I couldn't wait any longer. My phone didn't ring. Her truck had barely even driven by in the past two weeks.

The day I returned the van, Mr. O'Fallon came over to my house to change the battery in my Escalade.

"You know Mutt's out at the cabin. You heading out there later?" he asked.

All I'd heard was *Mutt.*

I was sick of it.

Sick of everything. The idea she really didn't want me. The idea she didn't love me. The idea that it could really be over.

To put it mildly, I'd been in a mood.

"Why don't you *not* call her *Mutt*. Shit. At least around me. Her name is Hannah."

I didn't care if I went too far. I didn't give a fuck if he

was her dad.

I'd hit my limit.

He'd popped the hood and took out the dead battery. I'd expected him to fire back at me, to be offended, but he kept his head down and continued working. A few minutes later he looked up as he pulled it out and set it on the driveway next to the new one.

Then he rose and I was sure he was going to deck me, his breathing heavy.

"Who in the hell do you think you are?" he asked his tone severe. He'd had a right to tell me off for *how* I'd said what I did, but he didn't have a leg to stand on when it came to *why* I'd said it.

"I'm someone who loves your daughter, and I'm tired of everyone in this town treating her like she's something she isn't."

"Well—if you know so much—what is she?"

I was getting even more riled up, instead of cooling down. It was damn time someone stood up for her.

"She's a woman. A beautiful one. A hard working person who deserves better than what she gets. Her whole life she's been reminded that she was left. It's been rubbed in her face. And you know what? She can't leave you. She can't stay with me. All because she's had to carry all of that shit around with her. She's so damn tough, walking around like it doesn't matter, because what can she do about it?"

I should have dialed it in, but I was done holding back.

"You think calling her Hannah would change anything?" he retorted.

"It would for her," I deadpanned, not budging.

He took steps toward me, but I was far from backing

down. Not on that. I stood my as he grew near.

His voice raising, he argued, "So then why is she out there by herself?"

He had me there. If I only had a good answer for that.

I deflated some and answered, "I wish I knew. She told me to leave."

His stance relaxed as he leaned against the radiator and took his hat off. "What did you do to piss her off?"

"I asked her to move in with me."

His grey eyebrows rose almost like he'd been shocked to hear it.

"Guessin' she said no," he said, scratching the stubble on his chin. "Right?"

"She told me she can't," I replied, and leaned under the hood next to where he was staring at the engine for no reason that I could tell.

"Don't you see how she feels so responsible to you? That name just reminds her of it. She's never going to be my Hannah as long as she's this town's Mutt."

"That's bullshit. You probably just pissed her off," he said. Then, like he was in a hurry to get out of there, he picked up the battery and set it in its place.

He quickly hooked it up and told me, "Start it up."

I hopped in and turned the ignition, the Escalade started on command.

He slammed the hood and picked up the old battery, while I sat in the driver's side with the door open.

"Want some advice?" he offered as he was passed.

I didn't know what he could possibly tell me that I didn't already know, but I was willing to do anything that might work. Might make her change her mind.

"Give her a little while. If she doesn't come around, just let her be. Might take a day, maybe a month. Wait on her."

Wait?

How was that going to ever get her back? What if she thought I didn't want her?

I didn't want to wait.

"I don't know."

"Just trust me," he'd said before he walked away. "Wait for her."

So, I did.

A day. A week. No Hannah.

I passed her on the road and she all but ran off the side to avoid me. Her number was dialed up in my phone and ready to go at all times.

By week two, I was losing my mind. I spent a lot of time in the garage. The house didn't feel like my home without her in it.

I slept on the couch more nights than not, and that's where I was when I decided I wasn't going to wait any longer. The next day I was abandoning the *wait for it* plan and implementing the *get her back* plan.

I awoke to the sound of someone outside, and as soon as it registered, I kicked off the sleeping bag I'd been using and sprung from the couch.

I didn't see anyone, but I knew I'd heard something. As I got closer to the window, I saw her truck.

She was there, and I prayed it wasn't just for her things in the upstairs bathroom. I'd refused to move any of them.

I walked out on the porch, still only wearing my sweatpants.

"Hannah?" I called.

Then I heard her voice coming from near the garage. "I'm over here."

My feet creaked across the old boards and I walked to the sound of her. My first glimpse of her after not laying eyes on her for the past few days was invigorating.

I hopped the railing and it took me no time to get to her.

Seeing her wasn't enough. I needed to touch her. To hold her. To convince her that she was where she belonged.

She seemed startled by my rush, but didn't back away. Her eyes landed on my chest and then my mouth, same as always, her lips parted in my nearness.

I stopped short of her, needing to know first, if this was really what I hoped it was.

"What are you doing here?"

"I'm ready to paint that porch," she said and beamed.

Damn, how I'd missed that smile.

On one of those first nights I'd told her I'd wait until she was ready to paint it, not knowing then how much it would mean when it finally happened.

"I'm sorry, Vaughn. I was scared. I didn't know what to do." I didn't have to grab her, because she came to me. Her arms wrapped around my back so fast, so tightly. "I didn't mean those things I said. I freaked out and I was worried about my dad being alone. And you're so good, I thought I'd never be enough."

I pulled away a little so I could look into her eyes. I wanted her to know I meant every word I was about to say.

"Hannah, I want all of you. Every. Single. Part. If you're not ready to move in, fine. I'll wait."

Her mouth came up and met mine, and it felt like we hadn't kissed for years. I was hungry for her, and I deepened it as she let me in.

I lifted her in my arms and knew I'd do whatever I had to do to keep her there.

"I love you, Vaughn," she said when our kiss slowed after a few minutes. "I'm sorry I left. I won't do that again."

"It doesn't matter, if you're really back. None of that other stuff matters. I love you. We'll figure it out as we go. No more pressure."

I felt her hand come around to my chest.

"No. I need you to push me. I've been living in this town my whole life and I love it here, but it wasn't until you came that I saw who I was. Who I wanted to be."

Her hazel eyes were bright, so different from the last time I'd been that close to her, when she'd told me to leave on her dock. There was new clarity and the excitement I'd watched grow over the summer was back.

She said, her voice sure and proud, "I want to be with you—in this home. You're what makes me better. Every now and again, I might need a little shove, but there is no Hannah without you."

"This doesn't feel like home when you're not here."

"Then I'll stay."

We didn't get much of the porch done that morning. Our time was better spent in my bed making up for what lost time.

I showed her with my body how much I loved her, and she showed me with hers that she was mine completely.

I'd never spend another night without her, and I'd spend every day proving she was mine—and that was forever.

Epilogue

Hannah

"You can put them on the porch, I'll carry them upstairs in a minute. The burgers are just about done," I said to Dean and my dad.

I slept there every night. We'd stay at the cabin, or he'd stay at my dad's house, which wasn't as awkward as you'd think. It took a few months—okay, three—but it was finally official moving day, and our family and friends were there helping us.

"You'll have *Vaughn* carry them," my Dad scolded.

Sunny was on her way back with more beer, and Aaron and Vaughn were in the garage setting up my new workstation for the online tackle shop. That old shed would always feel like mine, but Dad sold more than just the shop to Dean.

As of that week, he'd sold the business and the farm to him. Dad claimed he'd rather have Dean's smaller house in town. He admitted to me he was ready to be somewhere new. Somewhere where he wasn't waiting for my mom to always walk back through the door.

Secretly, I was glad he wasn't going to be out there alone. Instead, he'd be living next door to Diana, who he'd invited over that evening to eat with us.

"Okay, where's that blond with the beer? It'll be Christmas before she finds her way back," he teased, as Sunny walked up behind him carrying ice in one hand and a case in the other.

"Oh, I don't know. The dumb heifer probably got lost," she fired back.

He cackled as he took the things from her hands and headed around back.

"I never thought you'd do this, you know?" she said to me as she climbed the porch.

"Neither did I," I admitted. Things were changing fast, and sometimes that still freaked me out, but overall I was the happiest I'd ever been.

"Those flats are cute, by the way. I might borrow them. I have a hot date next weekend." Hell had frozen over and Sunny wanted to wear my shoes. Wonders really wouldn't ever cease.

"I'll think about it," I joked, knowing I'd let her use whatever she wanted.

We walked through the house to get to the back, and Vaughn was at the sink washing up.

Sunny went ahead, but I stopped to steal a kiss and placed one on the side of his cheek.

"Everything ready, Momma?"

Yeah, you guess it, he knocked me right up. I was a stereotype, but didn't give a shit.

After I initially freaked that morning at the cabin when we found out, it didn't seem like the end of the world. We were in love and the news made Vaughn was so, so happy. It was hard be that happy, too.

For once, I wasn't afraid of change anymore.

"Stop calling me that. My name is Hannah," I argued, but secretly loved it.

"Now you protest nicknames? So unlike you," he taunted as he spun around and wrapped his arms around me, pinning me to the counter, and kissing my neck.

"You know this is how that happened, right?"

"I'm sorry. I'm just hungry." He playfully bit at my neck, and then kissed it some more.

"The food is ready. We're just waiting on Diana," I said, but what he was doing was already taking a toll on me, and I stretched my head to the side giving him more.

"Let's tell them to leave."

"I think you can wait a few more hours, Dr. Renfro."

He grunted just like I knew he would. "God, I love it when you call me *Doctor*."

"I've been a bad patient today. I crunched my way through a whole glass of ice earlier."

"Stop, you're killing me," he said, and in his discomfort, backed up. I held tighter and went on.

"And I didn't fucking floss. On purpose," I added seductively.

His eyes flared. He took dental care seriously. Then he leaned in and whispered in my ear. "You know how I feel about that. I think you need another lesson. You and your dirty mouth."

After dinner was over and everything was cleaned up, Vaughn carried all of my things up to my new half of the closet. Then, dutifully, he inspected my flossing technique and surprisingly approved, but he showed me he could deliver on his word, giving me two orgasms before I fell asleep.

A few days later, when I was unpacking my lure-making things and organizing them on the new workbench he'd built me, I heard him clear his throat behind me.

He was down on one knee with a ring in his hand.

"I've been trying to come up with a memorable way to ask you, but, I'm taking your advice and not overthinking it." He winked and smiled, melting my heart. It was perfect. "Besides, I can't wait anymore."

I climbed off my stool, getting down onto the garage floor with him, and held onto his hands as he spoke.

"Hannah, will you give me the privilege of being your husband? Let me be the one to take care of you. To love you unconditionally. To be your partner. Marry me, beautiful? Let's grow our roots here. In *our* home. Together. Forever."

It was soon, and everything was happening minute to minute, but you know what? I didn't think twice.

Yes was all I got out before he had me swept up in his arms, kissing and reminding me that was where I belonged. I'd never leave him, and I was sure of that.

Sometimes having wings and choosing *not* to fly away is the whole point, because when you have a love like ours there's no place you'd rather be.

Acknowledgements

Thank you to my incredible readers. To everyone who's bought one of my books, visited me at a signing, added one of my titles to their ever growing TBR, messaged me online, or sent me an email—thank you for allowing me to have this beautiful, crazy life.

To the incredible souls in my reader's groups, Take the Bait and the Mo Stash, you make the writing experience such a joy.

To my family and friends at home, who still don't see me even though I promised when I was writing full time I'd pay more attention to them. I'm sorry. I really thought that would work out for you. Hahaha. I miss and love you, even though I'm right here.

To my dear writer friends who motivate and challenge me, you keep me sane. Okay, you keep me as sane as you are.

To Aly, I can't. You know. You know everything.

To Erin, I can smell your arousal from Texas. You must have loved this book. Very musky.

To Meghan, thank you for generously giving me a great line to use on my cover and for begging me to read this book. It made me feel pretty damn good that you'd want to.

To my beta readers, Bianca, Megan, Natasha, and Rachel, I hope you guys never realize you could totally write your own books. I'd be up a shit creek without you. You invest so much time in my characters that I feel like they partially belong to you.

To Cassy Roop at Pink Ink Designs, thank you for this stunning cover. Although, I'm pretty sure the outside *is* the best part of this book.

To Lori, my talented and humble editor. You're so thoughtful and nurturing. You care. That's what it boils down to—you care. You've never made me feel like an inconvenience, even when I am. Also, you're really good with my words.

To Stacey Blake at Champagne Formats, you always do exactly what you say you will. You over deliver and underestimate your worth. And, you're awesome.

To Danny, I love you, lunchbox. Fifty5cents. Thanks for always believing I can do stuff. Where in the hell does that come from anyway? ARE YOU MENTAL? Sometimes I think that it's your belief in me that gets me ninety-nine percent of the way there. You never let me feel like I'll fail, and I know that even if I do, you'll still have my back. And, thanks for feeding June when I'm gone. Keep doing that.